Forced to live by blood alone ..

John smiled generously in the dim light and pulled a bill from his pocket. He waved a twenty over the ball like a magic wand, and watched his victim's resolve weaken. The boy grabbed for the ball. John held the ball firmly to the grass and reached for his knife in his belt.

"Now!" exploded as a hiss from clenched teeth.

A force caught him, knocking him off balance. He felt the weight of another body; he kicked savagely as he rolled over. He faced his opponent — a woman. She lay stunned on her back. The kid chased his ball into the street, narrowly missing a car as he screamed for help.

He angrily clenched both fists and swung for the woman's head. She blocked it. She was too fast and strong to be human. Confusion swept through him. In a fraction of a second, he was running and disappeared across the street. He looked back at a police car led by a frantic little boy. The woman had disappeared.

DISCLAIMER:

This storyline deals with vampyric blood drinking people and includes scenes where the characters drink blood, hunt for blood, kill for blood, or shed blood. It is not our desire to promote fear yet it is human nature to have an adverse reaction to blood drinking. This is why we refer to these living people as having a vampyric medical condition. They are not undead nor occultic. While violence may be present, it is never glorified. These people survive as best they can under difficult and bitter conditions. Any that survive any length of time become efficient predators.

We claim no responsibility to any perceived or adverse reaction to the content of this storyline or content derived from the discussion of the subject matter.

Silently Comes The Night

by

Douglas Robinson

Without Love
Nothing
Changes
™

SILENTLY PUBLISHING
Birmingham Alabama

SILENTLY COMES THE NIGHT

A SILENTLY SERIES NOVEL
BOOK ONE – MODERN DAY

Silently Comes The Night
Published by Silently Publishing

Copyright © 2011 Douglas Robinson
All Rights Reserved.

Cover Art © 2012 Sam Wall www.samwall.com

Library of Congress Control Number: 2012920820

ISBN 978-1-62551-002-0
ISTC A03-2012-0000B8C4-3

TRADE PAPER EDITION: June 2013

Printed in the United States of America.

10 9 8 7 6 5 4 3 2 1

This is a work of fiction. Names, characters, places, and incidents either are the product of the author's imagination or are used fictitiously, and any resemblance to actual persons, living or dead, business establishments, events, or locales is entirely coincidental. The publisher does not have any control over and does not assume any responsibility for third-party websites or their content.

Silently Publishing
PO Box 11732
Birmingham AL   35202-1732
United States

ISNI 0000 0003 7313 132X Douglas Robinson
ISNI 0000 0003 7313 1290 Silently Publishing

www.silently-publishing.com

ACKNOWLEDGMENTS

For Randy
– thank you for believing
For Carol
– thank you for careful proofreading
For Margo
– thank you listening

The SILENTLY Series Storyline

Modern Day

Silently Comes The Night
Rites of Passage
With Deadly Intent
Overkill

Eve of Delusion
Shadow-Wielders
D'mirri's Curse
Flight 7486

Sacrifices
Heaven's Gate
No Safe Haven
Beddia's Endgame

Historical

Majken's Story
Ester's Song
Scot's Lament
Lost Voyage of the St. Therese Marie

Prolog

Rain had swept across the city of Trenton without warning like a bandit in the night. A cold, silver gray twilight greeted a host of travelers and tourists on the evening Greyhound bus. Most of the passengers were gaily talking about what they were going to do or see when they arrived at their respective destinations.

The massive expressway had been cleaned by the rain and now sparkled from the lights of many streetlamps and cars. A solitary young woman viewed the city from her window, speaking to no one. Her dark, violet eyes sparkled. Majken returned a shredded paper with a hastily drawn map of the city to her coat pocket.

The bus descended to the train station in the heart of the city. With a final spiraling turn, the bus parked at its terminal. The passengers embarked to waiting family or friends in warm cars. Majken got off the bus and breathed the cold air deeply, as if testing for a scent. She wore a beige overcoat and carried a leather suitcase. Earlier in the day, a man had tried to gallantly carry it for her. He could barely pick it up. She strode gracefully through the crowds, then stopped for a moment to watch another woman greet her two children, a boy and a girl, and a man; her family.

For a moment, her eyes softened and she smiled slightly. Then she left the station, walked past rows of passenger vehicles to cross the street, and disappeared in the mist.

Nearby city streets crisscrossed at obtuse angles, awash in the copper yellow glow of streetlamps; filled with a battery of merchant shops and businesses designed to separate tourists from their money. She walked to the nearest slum district; broken streets lined with boarded buildings and abandoned factories, where drunks and derelicts soaked their brains in cheap alcohol. Here, where no sane woman would go, she went alone. Majken stood on a corner under a streetlight looking from one block to the next, as if lost. Not more than twenty yards away, men huddled around a fire burning in a soot blackened drum. One of the men, a burly looking man with a small mustache, sneered and poked the men next to him.

Majken caught his eye for a second, then disappeared from their view behind a building. The men followed her. She could easily hear their combined footsteps. She turned on a deserted street. Two thugs had broken off from the pack, running to cut off her escape. Unexpectedly, she turned into a blind alley.

They gathered around the entrance to the alley. The man with the mustache and wide sneering grin led the others, forming an arrow shape. She saw them trying to peer over the rubbish and trash, into the gloom. She waited as the dark shapes approached, highlighted from behind by the neon streetlights. Her feet straddled an oily pool on the concrete. A car whizzed past; a cat meowed from hunger in the distance. The thugs spread out in front of her. The leader gave her a what's-a-nice-girl-like-you speech.

Her throat tightened, then relaxed.

Her whole being was calm, serene, ready.

He ordered her to give him her bag. She stood, waiting. He ordered her to pull up her skirt, and tried to grab her. Majken stepped quickly out of his reach. The men behind the startled man started to hoot and jeer, "Whatsa matter, Shark, forgot'n how?" Shark shoved the nearest man, yelling nobody made a fool out of him. Majken whispered his name softly. The man charged the inky blackness; she heard the snap click opening of a butterfly knife.

Iron-like fingers closed around his wrist, and crushing pressure forced him to drop his knife. He found himself being propelled and smashed into the brick wall face first. With a sickening crunch, blood oozed out of his forehead. The quiet lady was not through. A cut appeared under his chin, out of nowhere. She bent over, putting her mouth over the cut.

Six street tough veterans listened in horror to the unmistakable sound of drinking, and ran.

Majken ripped his front jeans' pocket, stuffed the wad of money she found in her coat pocket, wiped the knife clean of prints, and left his body behind a trash can. Trash collectors could pick it up in the morning. She felt that would be quite appropriate. She strapped her suitcase over her left shoulder. With catlike grace and agility, she jumped and climbed the rough brick structure to the roof. The alley windows had long ago been broken and boarded over. On the roof, she jumped across a chasm, once, twice.

Nearly a mile away, she found a nice tenant dwelling, paid for her room in cash, and threw herself on a faded bedspread in her room. Her priorities were, in order of importance, to find permanent shelter, secure usable identities, then establish herself in public. She perused a ragged telephone book. She chose a common name, Mary Harris. Her given name, Majken, had been lost in antiquity; lost in time. There were, relatively, very few of her kind in the modern world that she knew of. Human, yet not human; forced to live by blood alone.

She repeated her new name. "Mary Harris, Mary Harris, ... "

Chapter One

Majken stroked the smooth polished surface of the cafeteria table as she waited for Thomas Kline, her boyfriend, to return from the line with his food. She could feel the walls of the brick structure hum with vibrations as human bodies moved within. About four months ago, she had arrived at Trenton seeking a new life. No matter how things changed, for her they remained much the same; at least they had for the last three hundred years or so.

A new life meant new contacts. New contacts meant security and secrecy problems. Majken considered herself fortunate. She could have done worse than choosing a small conservative college to live, and a friendly young athlete to help her meet and select the people on whom she depended for fresh blood. People in the cafeteria line chatted with neighbors and shook umbrellas and coats free of the afternoon rain. Thomas returned to the round table with a Coke and an order of grilled cheese a few minutes before his three o'clock class.

"Hi, again, Mary. I'm back. That line wasn't as long as I thought." Thomas smiled.

"I never mind waiting on you," Majken said. "If you don't hurry, you'll be late for your social psych class."

Thomas looked for the wall clock. "Dr. Brennon is

at least ten minutes late for every class. I don't see how he stays employed with that kind of record." He wolfed his food.

"I think owning part of the school helps." Majken leaned toward him. In spite of his casual manner, she knew he cared a great deal whether he was late for class. "Will you be free to go clubbing tonight?"

Thomas stopped chewing and blinked. "Seven okay?"

Majken performed a fast time calculation in her head. She had an appointment at five she dared not miss. "That's fine," she said lightly. "I'll meet you at the Student Center."

"I can pick you up at your dorm. No problem. I'll even lash a raft to my car, just in case." Thomas ate the last of his toast.

Majken laughed. "The Student Center is closer for you."

Thomas smiled broadly as he grabbed his jacket. "Got to hurry. See you later." He kissed her briefly, then disappeared into the afternoon deluge.

The moisture and warmth of his kiss lingered on her cheek. The small unassuming gesture showed how much Mary Harris was beginning to mean to Thomas Kline. She pushed a pang of regret deeper into the recesses of her subconscious mind. Deception had long ago become part of her very survival in a world full of humans. Majken's fingers, sensitive yet durable, brushed the spot on her face. *Yes, long ago*, she thought.

Majken sipped her cup of hot tea, letting it warm her. Soon two girls from her dorm stopped by, talking mostly about college men. While she tried never to lose an opportunity to be one of the crowd, their slang and jargon confused her at times. Her relationship with Thomas protected her from certain kinds of close scrutiny and provided a semblance of normalcy. Beth and Suzie, roommates, left as quickly as they had come.

She left at three-thirty. Her schedule was not so busy to prevent a few extra minutes rest in her room. She tightened her beige overcoat and pulled the hood over her eyes. Thick, late summer clouds darkened the sky. While walking, she laughed to herself over the content of her seventeenth century history course. Her depth of understanding astounded her instructor. It was a struggle at first, but now, she was adapting.

Majken rested. Her bedside clock emitted a soft hum at four. She grabbed her shoulder bag and set out.

* * *

Thomas strutted to his room after class, whistling. His roommate, Phillip Barton, looked up from a desk cluttered with legal notepads and a fat chemistry text. "Hey, buddy. How was your day?" Thomas tossed his book and jacket on his bed and rubbed his fingers through his thick ash brown hair.

"I pick up Mary at seven. We're going to Eighty Eight." Mary was a great girl, he thought. Pretty. Friendly. He remembered it all started when he had accidentally collided with her during a practice session. He helped her to her dorm. Fortunately, the new girl on campus was not hurt.

He liked her because she was easy to talk to. Their first date was to one of his games. They lost. A smile crossed his face. She liked to hang out at the numerous clubs in the city. He was starting to get the hang of it. Phillip bounced his pen off the wall. "Don't you think you're rushing it? You've only known her a short time."

Thomas collapsed across the foot of his bed.

"I've never met anyone quite like her, and I've known a lot of girls."

"Do you think it's fair to deprive all those other women?" Phillip teased.

Thomas answered with a straight face.

"No, it's not." Phillip chuckled.

"Everything's going great, but –"

"But?" Phillip asked curiously.

"Every once in a while, she's, ah, distant. She evades some personal questions like a pro. All I want to do is get to know her better." He punctuated his concern by waving his arms from side to side. They sat there, thinking.

"I wish she would open up to me a little more, that's all."

Phillip kicked his chair back. "It takes some people longer to really open up to others. That's probably it." Thomas rolled over, placing hands behind his head. He sighed.

"I wish it would be sooner than later."

Phillip replied, "Better wait and see, Thomas."

Majken stepped off the transit bus in the heart of the city. Her date, a young man named Marc, would be meeting her soon. His sullen eyes reflected the same fire and intensity of a dormant volcano about to erupt. Marc was highly susceptible to her suggestion. For pleasure, he allowed her to withdraw a few pints of precious blood.

Majken steadied herself among a group of onlookers in front of a shopping complex. This world seemed light-years from her simple homeland overseas. She stopped to change clothes in a washroom. From there, to one of the apartments she reserved to bed and bleed the eligible men she picked up. She found Marc pacing restlessly in front of this week's selected apartment. Silently closing the distance between them, she wrapped her arms sensuously around his neck and chest.

"Hello, my love," she whispered in his ear. "Are you ready for me today?" Majken pushed her hands under his shirt to caress the hair on his chest.

Marc turned and kissed her passionately. "I want you now," he growled. Majken held him back as his eyes raced over her body.

"Wait until I'm ready for you."

With that, Majken left him to stew in his own juices. It was a game she played to heighten his anticipation and give herself time. Reaching in her bag, she found a key hidden within a sewn compartment. At the apartment, she listened within, then unlocked the door. A musty odor filled the unused rooms. She left the heavy drapes closed from daylight. Her key bounced on the dresser. She undressed quickly and changed into a sheer negligee of smooth lavender silk and white lace. The black leather case resting beside her shoulder bag would be used later.

Footsteps. Marc was coming.

Majken opened the door and received him.

Later, finished, Marc lay next to Majken, resting his head on her side. She curled a lock of his light brown wavy hair as he stroked her thigh. He twisted to face her.

"I want … " he stammered.

"What do you want?"

Marc cleared his throat. "I want more than once a week. I want to see you day and night!"

Majken looked straight through him. "Marc, my love. I want you, but what you ask is impossible."

Her consolation fell on deaf ears. Marc sprang abruptly off the bed and started pacing. Majken rested on her knees in the center of crumpled bed sheets. Marc was pushing his luck, she thought. For his own good, she met him no more than once a week. She needed him healthy, not temperamental.

"What we have is special. Our arrangement must remain like this to sustain it." She hoped he would back down.

"You don't understand–I love you!" he wailed. He grabbed her roughly.

Majken turned her arms to break his hold, held his wrists in a viselike grip, and squeezed hard. Marc's fingers clawed empty air; his face was grim.

"You never touch me unless I allow it!"

Majken held him until he stopped struggling. He rubbed the circulation back to his fingers. His left wrist was limp against his stomach. Repentant, he curled up on a pillow and mumbled under his breath.

Majken stepped to the window to see if anyone had noticed the disturbance. He lay extremely still. She sat next to him and massaged the tension out of his neck. Better, she thought, to leave him peaceful for the next time. She tried to lift him gently; Marc refused to move.

"I've waited for you all my life," he panted, "and I don't think you even told me your real name."

Majken marveled at his perceptivity. Softly, she answered, "Someday, my love, you may find out more about me than you want to know." She kissed him on the bare shoulder and nudged him off the bed. "It's time for you to leave."

"Why do I have to leave so soon afterwards?" he protested.

Majken replied lightheartedly, "You take so much out of me that I need the rest."

Defeated, Marc pulled on his shirt and shuffled to the door. "Can I see you early next time? At least grant me that."

Majken smiled and smoothed his hair. "I promise to try." She escorted him out and locked the door.

Her sharp hearing traced his departure; then she lay down and closed her eyes. She felt her limbs grow numb as her body began to assimilate the blood she had consumed. Majken slipped into a deep sleep.

Majken and Thomas arrived at Eighty Eight while the festivities were in full swing. A merry bunch of men at the bar exchanged loud bawdy jokes. Majken felt Thomas' hand tighten around hers as he pulled her closer to shield her. They found a side table.

He spoke over the racket. "I got a call from my parent's today. They're all doing well. Talked with my baby sister, too."

"I thought Kim was in high school?" Majken asked.

"She graduated this year, but we all think of her as the baby. Makes her furious. I hope you get to meet her someday." Thomas paused as Majken's dark violet eyes swept the lounge. She heard a sound; felt something out of place. "Uh, I'm sorry. I didn't mean to dredge up unpleasant memories."

Majken smiled at Thomas, distracted. "You didn't," she assured him.

It was easier to have no family or living relatives, than to continuously put him off on meeting them. "What have you been doing since three?" he asked.

Majken placed her full attention back on Thomas. The strange feelings continued to needle at her mind. She felt a powerful urge to be careful.

"Very little: took a nap, went for a walk, studied."

"I heard you got on a bus and went into the city." Thomas frowned. He waited on her response.

"I did–," Majken stopped for a loud burst of laughter from the bar, "go window shopping to relax."

Thomas motioned toward the bar. "Guess they're having a good time. Mary, I wanted to ask you something."

A waitress stepped up to take their order, silencing Thomas. The waitress left with a single order. She glanced aside, then found him staring at her face. "Why are your eyes dark violet?" he asked.

She reflected. "I had an illness, a fever, as a child, so long ago I hardly remember."

Thomas touched her hand. "I'm going to a state campground ninety miles south of here. It's very pretty there. If you're interested, would you like to try to go camping with me this weekend?"

He sat back.

Majken beamed. She could hear him wringing his hands under the table. "I've never been camping before," she said, "but I think it would be fun."

"Does that mean you really want to go?"

She nodded, although she worried about things other than camping.

"Great! Why don't we leave right after tomorrow's game."

Majken was glad he was happy, but the game was early and she would need time to feed before leaving; probably at her dorm. "Thomas, I can't leave until later. Still want me to go?"

"I want you any way I can get you!" Thomas sprang up and clapped his hands enthusiastically. "I'll bring you home if you don't like it," he said, "but you'll love it!" He excused himself for a few minutes.

Majken scanned the full club. She watched to see who was sitting alone and who came in alone. She looked for signs of vulnerability in their faces. Like a cold wind, a foreboding impression swept over her that intruded deeply in her thoughts. She met the gaze of a man leaving with a shapely blonde woman. She was drawn to his dark, penetrating eyes. He had the visage of a hunter. He cradled the girl like a fragile doll. When Majken turned her attention to Thomas, returning, and the waitress bringing his food, they were gone. The feeling left with them.

"Where were we? Oh, yes, camping. I went with my parents every summer until my sixteenth birthday. Enough to hook me for life."

Thomas began a story of the first camping trip he could remember. He was halted mid-sentence by a man running to the bar.

"Oh, my God! Call a doctor!" the man panted breathlessly. "A girl in the parking lot. She's dead!"

A bartender grabbed a telephone and the man who reported the girl. A couple of college boys ran for the parking lot. The club manager tried to calm him and asked him to describe what he saw.

Majken noticed that he was hyperventilating.

"I don't know her name," he said, "the blonde girl in a black dress. She was sitting over there. Now, she's dead, she has to be dead, she's just lying there face down in blood." The man gagged and tried to leave. The manager forced him to sit and wait for the police. The man sat, slumped, on the stool. "There's blood everywhere," he said to no one.

Thomas commented, "I'm sorry this happened, Mary. Did you know her?" Majken replied no. Club patrons were drifting toward the exit, huddled and whispering nervously, or drinking. The manager opened up the bar. Free drinks.

"Thomas, I think we should go," Majken said.

"Shouldn't we wait for the police?" he asked.

Majken tugged on his arm, insistent. "There is

nothing we can do for her."

As they left the club, Majken noticed the night sky had cleared, and the city streets had been polished by the rain. She glanced at the slain girl's body as the first police car arrived. The crowd of bystanders around her moved aside, careful not to step on the spreading pool of blood.

Thomas left his girlfriend safely on the steps of her dorm. The parking lot slaying weighed heavily on his mind. This evening, he thought, had been a blend of ecstasy and tragedy. Now, it was tragedy. The wet grass glistened under the white floodlight outside his dorm. He was proud of his school. The white marbled facings and eves reflected its tradition and intimate ties to the past. He trudged to his room. Phillip was studying late for an exam. Not like him at all.

"Hello, Phillip," Thomas said. He headed directly for his bed.

"What happened to you? Did she turn you down?"

Thomas plopped in a chair instead. He crossed his arms and rested his chin on the back of the chair, then buried his face in his arms. "She's going."

"Then what's the matter with you?"

He sighed. "We saw a murder tonight. A girl was

killed in the club parking lot. I was telling Mary about my first trip to the Ozarks when this chubby guy barged in and started screaming bloody murder."

Phillip dropped the text off his bed. "How'd Mary take it?"

Thomas went to his bed, unlaced and pulled off one sneaker. "Scared," he said. "She didn't say two words all the way home." The other sneaker dropped. "Mary wanted to leave immediately."

"Can't blame her for that," Phillip said. Thomas and Phillip watched each other. Phillip broke the silence. "Hey, what else did you and Mary talk about?"

Thomas stretched out and lay facedown. "I hardly remember." He groaned. "It isn't nine o'clock and I'm already wiped out."

"What'd Mary say when you asked her to go camping?"

"She was happy to go." Thomas rolled on his side, and stared vacantly into space. "Whoever did it was especially brutal. I remember a wreck we passed on the highway when I was little. A car had gone off a steep hill. My father said it wasn't right for passersby to stop and gawk at wrecks." He hurt inwardly. "Made me sick the way those people gathered around her body. I caught a glimpse of her dress as we passed."

Thomas stared blankly at the floor. Phillip waited, listening. "They stood there doing nothing."

"Dammit, Thomas! Think about something else, or you'll make yourself sick."

Thomas gave in and drew a purifying breath. Phillip was kind to let him unload his troubles. The heaviest burden had lifted.

"Mary wants to leave late tomorrow. I'll have the car packed early anyway."

"Why late?" Phillip asked.

"I don't know." He shrugged and smiled. "Before I got my nerve up, I finally asked her about her eyes. She said she had an illness as a child that changed the color to violet."

"I've never heard of an illness that does that. What color were they before."

"She doesn't remember." Thomas sat up.

"Didn't her parents tell her?" Phillip sounded impatient.

Thomas hesitated. "Mary grew up in an orphanage; she never knew her parents or any of her family." Phillip gaped at him.

"Why didn't you tell me any of this before?"

"She asked me not to tell anyone. She was afraid students would pity her. You know she hardly talks about herself. I guess it's natural she wouldn't want me to talk about her either."

Phillip swayed easily on his bed, then stooped over to pick up his textbook. He asked quietly, "Does she know that this trip is overnight, as in spending it together?"

"She knows," Thomas replied. "Heaven knows my palms get sweaty just thinking about it."

Phillip laughed. "Have you got something extra special planned for entertainment?" A mischievous smile spread across his face.

Thomas wished he had something to throw. "I haven't asked her yet. I really like her and I don't want to blow it."

Phillip raised his eyebrows. "That's a start."

"It certainly is," Thomas said. "It certainly is a start."

Chapter Two

Majken cheered with other students as the home rugby team scored. The game was very close. The challenging team could still win in the last half hour of play. She saw Thomas, wearing the white shirt with broad orange stripes, wave in her direction. She waved. By all standards, it was a beautiful day, for humans. A partially clouded sky along with frequent trips to the sheltered area next to the concession stand was her only relief. The sun would burn her without benefit of oversized sunglasses and a specially prepared sunscreen.

The old adage of when in Rome, came to mind when she was forced to attend these daytime conventions to appear like everyone else. Nearby, two coeds oohed and ahhed approvingly as substitutions were made in the game. *Such is the life of two college coeds*, Majken thought.

The home students hissed as a play was blocked by the opposing team. Thomas had taken time when they started dating to explain the rudiments of the game. Of late, he seldom brought it up. She saw this as an indicator of their developing relationship. Majken liked the game because it was not strictly American; its overseas flavor forged a subliminal link to her past.

* * *

Far afield, a sullen young man entered the playing field. He delayed as long as he dared. He only came because his father wanted to show him off. The great Dr. Albritton was not one to make angry. The young man's blood boiled. He hated orders. Marc Albritton thought to stop at the concession stand for a cool drink but decided against it. If his father asked him where he had been, he planned to say he got stuck in traffic. Most of the time, he got away with it.

Marc walked toward the bleachers. Spectators jeered as he blocked their view. He did not care. He spotted his father's silver crown and mane. Around him sat three of the stodgiest old-timers in history. He had started toward his father and friends when he spotted another face. His heart skipped a beat; it was a face he recognized. He stumbled into a man and a woman on the front row to get a better view. She was surrounded by students, but even with dark sunglasses, he knew it was her.

Marc ran to reach her before she disappeared from his life. He pushed two students into the bleachers in his haste. Memories of her silky smooth skin, her scent, and her warm embrace played in his mind. He raced past the concession area. Few students were there in what should be the final minutes of the game. Too bad he would be late to see his father and pals. His mystery girl sat in an aisle seat with a group of college girls. He dragged her off the bleacher and pulled her sunglasses off. The girl's face registered stunned surprise; one arm was poised to strike. Hope bubbled inside him. "It's you! I knew it was you!" he shouted, as he jumped up and down.

The home team scored at that moment. Students cheered. The girl pulled him by his jacket to the rear of the stands. He screamed over the cheering. "That's why I never found you in the city. You were here, under my nose, all along." He stumbled forward as she pulled him into the relative privacy of a doorway. He smiled and pushed his body against hers.

"You're a student here, aren't you?" His lover asked him to be quiet. Marc continued talking. "You were sitting in a student section. I know you are a student." He repeated the phrase with glee.

"If you ever want to see me again," the girl said, "never come up to me on campus." Her face turned dark with anger.

"Leave immediately or you will get hurt."

"You can't do anything here," he said snidely. He twisted the front of her blouse; his intentions were clear. "I have the goods on you now. Come with me." His chest heaved when he tried to pull her by the arm.

She calmly answered, "No."

Marc propped both arms on the wall, blocking her exit. "I can make you regret you ever knew me. Everybody will find out we're lovers, and what you do for kinks."

"Lower your voice," she commanded. She kicked his instep; the shock of pain traveled up his leg. Marc howled. She pushed him aside, her exit was clear. "Marc," she cooed softly, "making trouble will not help you see me more often."

Marc leaned in the doorway and rubbed his sore leg. *The bitch*, he thought, then he remembered her strength. He swallowed before speaking. "I want to be with you today, please."

She stepped out of the doorway and glanced toward the concession stand. "I'll meet you after the game," she whispered. She pointed toward a distant building. "Meet me over there in fifteen minutes. I came here with other students. Please wait until I can get away safely." Her eyes and face softened.

Marc pulled her body close, bubbling with triumph. "I expect to see you behind Wilson Hall in fifteen minutes." Arrogantly, he pulled her by the neck and kissed her roughly. She did not resist, he noted with great pleasure. He left her feeling like he had conquered the world.

*   *   *

A slender, silver-haired older man with a distinguished beard moved clear of the concession stand.
He had followed his son and this girl, and had edged
as close as possible but was unable to hear what was
being said.

Dr. Albritton stopped a coed and described the
long-haired girl who sneaked off with his son.

The coed thought for a moment. "Her name is
Mary Harris. She's a history major," she said, then
hurried to catch up with her friends.

"Marc," Albritton said. His colleagues had to
leave, and Marc had disappointed him. Dr. Albritton
looked to the stands, where the girl had melted into
the crowd, and in the direction his son had gone. His
jaw clenched. His son had embarrassed him for the
last time.

Marc Albritton stood unevenly on the sidewalk,
glaring at the distant playing field, then paced into
the alley. "Where is she?" he muttered. He'd been
made a fool of. She had no intention of coming. He
swore. He wanted to grab her and—he remembered
what had happened the last time he tried that.

Crazy people were always stronger than normal
people, he thought. He refused to consider why she

wanted to drink his blood; she needed him and he needed her, badly. He could help her stop and live a normal life because he loved her like no one else in the world could. She had to know that.

Marc moaned. He wanted to feel the thrust of her white thighs, kiss her in that special place, and love her forever. She was meant to be his alone.

Shaking his throbbing fist, Marc checked his watch and started to leave when he heard the last person he wanted to see call his name.

"Marc! Marc, what are you doing here? I was worried when you didn't meet us at the game."

Marc looked down at his father and scowled. "Sorry about the game. I remembered something else I had to do. Maybe next time." *Cleverly avoided the ol' traffic alibi,* he thought. His father looked angry enough without it.

Albritton frowned. "I saw you chatting with a young lady behind the stands. What could have been more important that a few minutes of your time to meet my colleagues visiting today? I'm not pleased, son!"

"I'm sorry," he shouted. He looked past his father to watch two girls in shorts walk by the alley. *Oh, God,* he thought, *here comes the lecture.*

"I've never asked for much and you've been given

the best. I expect a little common decency and respect from you in return." Albritton raised his voice.

Marc cursed under his breath and turned away.

"Perhaps, I shouldn't have been so lenient!" his father snapped. Marc glared back. He saw many lines etched on his father's brow and around his piercing light blue eyes; eyes so sharp, he used to say, that they could cut glass.

"I said I was sorry. What more do you want?"

Albritton uncrossed his arms and tried to move closer to his son. "I am worried, and concerned about the way you have been behaving and sneaking in and out at all hours. Your professors tell me that your scores are dropping."

"For crying out loud! What do you want from me?"

"I want you to become all you're meant to become as a man."

Marc jerked away from his father and grimaced. "I can take care of myself!" he yelled. He pushed a path around his father and walked to the edge of the alley. He shrugged off the arm placed on his shoulder.

The icy edge in the older man's voice melted. "You're proving how little you can take care of yourself. You've needed looking after ever since your mother died."

Marc responded with stony silence. He bit his lower lip to staunch the swelling hurt. Why did his old man insist on running his life?

"What were you and that girl talking about?"

"None of your damn business!" Marc blew up. His father's jaw tightened. *Now, I've done it*, he thought.

"Son," he said evenly, "I have to ask you – are you and that girl in trouble?"

"Leave her out of this!" Marc snapped.

"Let me help you," Albritton pleaded. The older man embraced his son; Marc wanted to push him away. Finally, he released him. "There is no talking to you when you get this way. I'm going home now, if you want to talk later." He managed a slight smile.

Marc watched his father leave. Suddenly, Albritton stopped, turned to his son, and said, "But, it would look foolish indeed for you to stand here all afternoon."

Majken knew traps, and she pondered how to handle Marc as she made her way to the playing field to meet Thomas. He would not leave her alone of his own free will. Several students pushed past her. Her immediate solution was distance.

"Mary," shouted Thomas, "we won!" He pulled

himself out of a bevy of players and held her. She hugged his sweat-soaked shirt; pleased in his triumph.

He smiled broadly. "I have to take a shower."

"Thomas, can we leave right away?"

His smile faded. "Last night you wanted to wait until later. What gives?"

Majken searched the empty bleachers for unwanted company. "The more I thought about this trip, the more I couldn't wait to be with you."

Thomas kissed her. "I'm off! Never keep a lady waiting."

As Majken packed the necessities for her trip, a plan crystallized in her mind. Marc believed she was a student, but he did not know her assumed name here. Let him search the entire campus. Confused, he would be easier to handle, she hoped.

She waited for Thomas at his car that was parked in a gravel parking lot behind the men's dorm. She smiled at him cheerily as he walked up. "Let's go," she urged.

Thomas smiled. "You're fast, aren't you?"

Majken grinned. "Never keep a gentleman waiting is what I always say."

His green Honda roared as it entered highway traffic. Thomas shifted to put his arm around her.

Majken relaxed as the campus faded in the rearview mirror.

"We'll be there in a few hours. Can I get you anything?" Thomas reached and pulled a soft drink from a small cooler.

Majken kicked off her shoes and curled her feet under the seat. "I'm fine." She pulled a pillow and blanket from the backseat and packed them against her side. Sunlight poured through the windshield. She adjusted her large sunglasses and sank into the cushion.

"You look tired," Thomas said.

"I didn't get much sleep last night."

Thomas fidgeted. "If you're not well, I can take you home."

"I need sleep," she said. "I want to be refreshed when we arrive at the park." She settled deeper into the pillow. Through half-closed eyes, she watched Thomas release the steering wheel he had been gripping. The next thing Majken saw was late afternoon shadows fall across her face. She stirred slightly. They were now following a winding country road. The angle of the sun had dropped below the trees lining the road. Thomas had rolled his window down. The turbulence of the open window twisted her long chestnut hair.

Majken said hello.

Thomas glanced at her morosely. "Glad to have you back. We're nearly there."

Majken sat up. The air carried the sweet smell of wide open country. She smiled wistfully. "I've been under a strain lately. Thanks for letting me rest."

"Tell me about it," he asked.

She removed her glasses and brushed her hair out of her face. "It's a ... female problem."

"Oh," he replied.

"It's beautiful on this road. Have you been to this park before?"

Thomas answered while leaning to check the gas gauge, she knew. "Twice," he said. "I want to go swimming so bad I can taste it."

Majken's smile waned. She looked at the still too high sun as they passed under the main gateway.

"We're here!" Thomas announced.

Their primitive campsite was a rectangle patch with barely enough room to park and pitch a tent. It had a place for a fire and a rusty iron grill set on a pole. Uncut grass extended a distance of twelve feet to the undergrowth.

Majken hopped out of the car as it stopped, wrapped her arms around her waist, and waltzed to the edge of the clearing. She shielded her face with her hand, looking in all directions. "Where is everyone? I thought the park would be teeming with campers."

Thomas walked next to her and explained that during the busy season, their little spot would be crammed. He teased her. Tonight, they would have all the privacy they might want. Majken helped Thomas pull the tent off the roof and set it up. Then they moved the cooler and arranged their sleeping bags to air.

Thomas unpacked his swimsuit and towel. "C'mon, let's get into the water."

Majken stalled. "I haven't been in water for a long time." She reluctantly pulled the suit he asked her to bring and a towel from her bag. "Can't I walk around while you swim? How big is this park anyway?"

He waved his arm over the valley behind her. "As far as you can see – no deal," he replied. "We stay together."

"Before we get into the pool, will you show me around the park?" Majken looked carefully at the angle of the sun. Thomas shrugged and reached over her shoulder. As the late afternoon sun receded, Majken mapped out a hunting territory.

* * *

The new vampyric arrival in Trenton prowled the city streets at dusk. Few details escaped his notice as he searched for tonight's mark. The girl had been easy. He knew — flash a little money and they followed him everywhere. Caressing her firm body had been very pleasant. His movements were fluid and unyielding. He lurked near a convenience store where he knew less fortunate humans would come to purchase necessities.

He turned at a slight squeaking noise on the sidewalk. An elderly black man pushed a wheelchair carrying an elderly woman who was probably his wife. He smiled in contempt as the pair entered the store; his dark burning eyes reflected unquenchable hatred. He called himself John.

John followed the slow-moving couple from the store. He matched their pace from across the street and studied them. The old man had a round, pleasant face. He wore a gray sports coat, tan sweater, loafers, and a cap. His thinning white hair was crew cut. He grunted as he pushed the wheelchair. The woman in the wheelchair carried the bag in her lap. She wore a light house robe, a small quilt, and slippers. John listened as they talked. "You didn't have to go," the man said. His thin reedy voice carried well. "The doctor says you should rest."

"If I don't go out with you, I don't get out at all." The woman shifted the bag of groceries in her lap.

The man reached and straightened her bathrobe. "Ever since our kids is grown, there's no one but us left." The elderly woman reached to hug her husband. "It's been a good life. I won't want to live it with nobody else," she said warmly.

John's face remained a mask of impassivity as pedestrians passed him on his side of the street. He was just another person trying to get home safely in a crime-ridden neighborhood.

The couple reached a small, whitewashed frame house with a hedge growing wildly along the wire fence. They walked up a short wooden ramp on the side of the porch and entered the house.

John paused and examined the frame house in a row of very similar homes. The nearby buildings appeared weathered and abandoned. He stepped into the street going directly toward the house.

They would die, easily.

Thomas scanned the rippling water before diving and swimming underwater to his girlfriend. She stood in water that reached to her waist and moved slowly, as if testing the water. He did not think the water was that cold. He surfaced next to her. The moderately sized pool was shared by three kids and a middle-aged couple. The young lifeguard blew his whistle at one of the kids for jumping. Thomas took her arm, thinking how much more fun they could be having if the pool were totally private. The two other kids jumped in, splashing Majken and Thomas.

He asked if she was all right. Majken dove underwater and swam to the deep end. Thomas followed. He laughed. "I was beginning to think you couldn't swim."

She smiled. "I haven't been in the water for a hundred years. I had to adjust." They swam together another lap. Thomas met her underwater. He reached for her as they surfaced together.

Water trickled off her long hair, plastering it to her shoulders and back. Impulsively, Thomas kissed her. "I love you." She wiped the water out of her eyes and asked him what he had said.

Now self conscious, he stammered, "I love being in the water." She smiled at him. He watched her swim a lap. Thomas winced at a loud splash and wiped the water from his face. Ripples of gold, silver, and turquoise blue light swam on the surface of the pool, highlighting the beauty of her dark violet eyes. Katydids chorused in the early evening night air.

She swam to his side and surfaced next to him.

He imagined her warmth next to him, and stammered, "Uh, Mary, you pull to the left. It'll help your stroke if you keep your right shoulder level." They treaded water in the deeper part while Thomas helped her perfect her crawl stroke. In the chest deep water, he supported her while she practiced. The early evening sky gradually darkened.

Majken swam a few full laps, then stopped by the lifeguard for a rest. The kids had gone. Thomas was an excellent swimmer. She admired his graceful rhythm in and out of the water. Majken smiled at the young lifeguard and asked to borrow his towel. She noticed he had been watching her closely. The boy sat next to her on the deck.

Her legs were numb and cold. Her one-piece suit clung heavily to every curve. As she rubbed the dry towel through her hair, she talked to the boy. He was sixteen, she learned, and helped his parents, who worked here, by keeping the pool in order. It was a big responsibility.

Majken smoothed her suit, accentuating her figure, and whispered to him. The boy blushed; his mouth was agape. When Thomas completed his last lap and stepped out of the pool, she went after him to change.

* * *

John opened the peeling wooden door carefully, peering from behind a torn screen. He listened. No neighbors had seen him enter. No one would see him leave. He glanced at the bodies, one stuffed in the bedroom, the other in the bathroom. The old woman had choked to death. He had to stuff a thick cloth down her throat to stop her screaming. Her husband would not stay down. He had to push him repeatedly, until he tired of the sport and drew his knife. John smashed the light in the window and wiped his knife on the towel-curtain. He left satisfied. The little money they had seemed hardly worth the trouble, but it would make the incident look more like a robbery that went too far. In this neighborhood, who cared. The bodies probably would not be discovered for weeks, he reasoned, because the couple lived alone. John waited until a car passed the intersection a block away, then quickly walked away from the house.

John disappeared into the empty, dark-shrouded streets.

Majken made a conscious effort to relax. She needed blood soon. She watched Thomas prepare the food at the campsite. So far, she had avoided the need to eat in his presence, but now – another hurdle to jump. The night air off a nearby lake had a slight chill. A pungent smell of wild growing flowers made her nose crinkle.

He clapped his hands. "Just wait until you see the food I packed. It's a meal fit for a princess." He smacked his lips. "I'm starving."

"Thomas, I'm not hungry. I don't want any food."

She watched Thomas continue unpacking the basket. Thomas stammered. "You've got to be kidding," he said. "Neither one of us has eaten since lunch. How could you not be starving?"

Majken got up and walked toward him. "You've known me long enough to know how little I need. My stomach must be smaller than normal." She paused and looked up at sparkling stars in the night sky. "I went without many times as a little girl." Majken knelt beside him. He looked bewildered.

"A squirrel couldn't live off all the food I've seen you eat." He looked directly into her eyes; his gaze narrowed. "I thought if your stomach was small, you would eat frequent meals." Thomas stopped unpacking the basket.

"I am the way that I am," Majken pleaded. "Please accept me that way. If you cared for me, you wouldn't force me to do anything bad for my health."

Her argument must have struck home. She heard him mutter to himself as he repacked her share, "... must be anorexic." Majken rested by their small camp fire, settling on a cup of warm tea. Thomas ate ravenously. Small animals scurried in the wooded area around the tent.

"Are you sure I can't get you anything to eat? I have some freeze-dried." Thomas gulped some milk.

Majken shook her head, politely, and slipped off the cooler to sit next to him on his sleeping bag. He finished his snack and placed his arm around her. His gas lantern cast ghostly shadows on the trees. A soft breeze stirred the limbs above with the quiet scratching of leaves in the air. Majken reached across Thomas and turned the lantern off. The crisp, night air enveloped them.

Majken felt Thomas' pulse quicken.

Thomas reached around her and pulled her close. "Mary," he whispered, "I didn't mean to get angry at you a while ago. I wanted you to have a good time, and, I guess I tried to push it on you."

Majken gently nudged him in the ribs. "I've had a good time."

It is a beautiful night, Majken thought. Her eyes quickly adapted to the near total darkness. Her perceptions altered. Majken pointed toward and described for Thomas the amber reflection of starlight off the lake, the iridescent sheen of gossamer strands of a spider web in the bushes across from them, and the blue-white halo of the lights off the pool nearly a mile distant over the ridge to the south. As Thomas shifted his position slightly on the sleeping bag—grass, leaves, and twigs snapped loudly to her. Miles away, she presumed, she heard a generator or compressor turn on. The ceaseless movement of living creatures in the nearby forest felt like vibrations she could feel within her body, made distinct in the chill night air.

Thomas peered through the bushes, into the night, where she pointed. He said he could barely see the lake.   Majken smiled faintly.

He kissed her.

She tensed before she realized it. She was irritable and apologized. "I guess I'm still a little nervous outdoors."

Thomas sighed. "It takes a little getting used to. It is lovely. You don't see many sights like this near the city."   Majken felt him nudge her closer; his arm fell in its place under her arm and across her abdomen. Thomas held her tighter. "What do you think about when you see nights like this?"

Majken reminisced; her thoughts drifted far away.

"I once lived with herdsmen on a mountain range. They were a proud and robust people. We depended on their goats for food." She spoke in a whisper, smiling faintly. "We never stayed long in one place, but I'll always remember how the moonlight spilled over the peaks of snow and rock."

She bowed her head. Memories arose warm within her, and, in a few moments, she was aware that Thomas had become strangely quiet. Majken finally said, "It's late. Time to turn in."

Thomas gingerly turned up the lantern, then patted his knees and rubbed them nervously. "Uh, yeah. It might get cold tonight." He hesitated. "There's enough room in one sleeping bag for two people, if it gets too cold," he offered. He looked like he had swallowed a rock.

Majken grinned. "We'd better sleep separately. I'm not afraid of what you would try. I trust you."

She gave him a sisterly kiss on the cheek.

"Great," he said mockingly, "you *trust* me."

Majken laughed.

The atmosphere lightened between them. They prepared for bed separately, and Thomas entered the tent after Majken had curled up in her bag. She had a plan. Thomas kissed her good night and fell asleep quickly.

* * *

Dr. Albritton waited for his son to come home. He sat at the huge desk in his study, waiting. He pulled off his reading glasses and tossed them on a closed book. He regretted the times he let his anger push him and he raged at Marc; his son made him sorry for the times he yielded. *What is a father to do with his only son?* He rubbed his eyes wearily.

A wall clock chimed twice. After two in the morning. It was not safe for Marc to be out at this time of night. Albritton pondered his son's actions. He had only suspicions, which led to the eventual arguments; bitter and so unnecessary if only his son would talk to him. It had all started after his mother was killed.

Albritton picked up a desk picture of the three of them in a younger, happier time. He had no grey hairs then. He held the photograph gently, and rubbed his finger along the gold-plated frame. Teresa had a firm hold on the boy. He swore aloud. "Dammit, Marc, I miss her too."

He loved his son; Marc had to know that. But his problem was wanting to become a man without the benefit of years that forged maturity. It goaded him to see Marc not do his best, not be the best, especially at his studies. He had a family tradition to maintain. Albritton heard the front door opening. Marc was home. He rushed to stop him.

"Marc, what have you been doing until this hour?" He asked him more harshly than he intended. His son had left the front door wide open; Albritton closed it. Marc balanced unsteadily on the bottom step. His shirt was pulled out and his hair was a mess. It was painfully disheartening to see him this way.

Marc wiped the dribble off of his mouth with his shirt sleeve. He spat a monosyllable at his father. "Out."

Albritton rushed forward and shook him. "Look at yourself," he swore in dismay. "No son of mine is going to run at all hours of the night like a common tramp. What were you doing until this hour?"

Marc laughed and tried to go to his room.

His father stopped him.

Marc shouted, "Looking for a girl!"

Albritton let go. "A girl? Not a whore!" he raged.

The young man sneered, as if enjoying seeing his father suffer. "I found someone special to take me away from you. I … misplaced her today. But I will find her, I swear I will!" Marc jerked away.

Albritton stepped back while his son talked crazy nonsense. He cleared his throat. "When can I expect the privilege of meeting this special young lady?" he asked politely. A different tact was needed.

Marc teetered on a stair. "Never," Marc intoned.

"What do you know about her family," he asked, "her background?" His son responded with stony silence as he glared down at his father. Albritton returned his son's blank stare, never certain how to take his son's silence.

"Listen to me, son, please. I'm concerned about what has been happening to you. I think you're throwing your life away without a thought or care about your future."

"I don't need your help," Marc said coldly.

Albritton clenched his fists; he fought the rising anger. "I want you to be the best, and not throw your life away because of a cheap, two-bit whore." Only then, did Albritton see that his son's eyes were wet and puffy. He realized his son had been crying.

Marc pulled free of him and stomped up a few stairs. "Stay out of my life!" he screamed. He sprinted to his bedroom and slammed the door.

Thomas woke to chirping sounds and a heavy damp chill in the air. He shifted his body slowly, hoping not to wake Mary, but rolled on her sleeping bag. He whispered an apology. No sound. Fast asleep, he thought. He tugged gently at her blanket.

It slid easily.

"Mary," he whispered. He called again, "Mary?" He reached to the center of her sleeping bag. She was not there. He sat upright and groped around inside the tent to find she was not in the tent either. "There must be a logical explanation for this," he mumbled to her empty sleeping bag. He crawled outside and searched the area to his car.

Where could she be? "Maybe a bear got her," he said to relieve his uncertainty. Fear stabbed at him. He called several times, then retreated to wait for her return. Soon, he fell asleep.

Chapter Three

Early morning mist wafted about the tent. Thomas became aware of a presence next to him. Warm. Soft. Heavy. Female! His vanished girlfriend had curled up asleep in his sleeping bag. Faint morning light gave her face a soft glow. She breathed slowly as if in a deep sleep.

He could not think of how she got in his bag without him knowing it. He must have fallen asleep waiting. He was cold. She stirred. Thomas moved back to give her space. An image of a pale, delicate orchid moist with the morning dew flashed in his mind. He knew he loved her.

Majken came to life. "Oh, it's cold this morning." She rubbed her arms to generate heat.

Thomas cleared his throat. "Adhump. Good morning."

She kissed him. "Good morning."

"I hope you slept well." Thomas waited to see if she knew where she was. "I woke up last night and you were gone."

Majken searched his brown eyes. "I don't –," she started. "I got up to use the facilities. I didn't want to wake you."

"I was worried about you. What took you so long?" Thomas suddenly realized a single sleeping bag crammed with two people was no place to have a quarrel. He unfastened it and rolled out.

"I'm sorry you worried," she said gently.

She seemed so much at peace this morning, Thomas thought. "Next time, tell me when you're leaving." Thomas quickly pulled on his pants and left to cook breakfast. His breakfast. Majken flounced out of the tent in ten minutes. Thomas was eating.

He watched her stretch. Her movements were quick and energetic.

Thomas noticed her bright disposition. It was a metamorphosis from last night. Maybe it was adjusting to the country, he thought. Doubts of exactly what she did plagued him. Of course, he had to accept what little she told him. How much did he know about the woman he loved?

Majken surveyed the campgrounds with a sweeping glance as Thomas finished his breakfast. No doubt, the burning question in his mind was why she refused to eat. Her nocturnal habits would also raise eyebrows if openly revealed. She was nocturnal, by habit and necessity. Daytime meant weakness, the use of a special sunblock, and a pair of dark sunglasses. At least the sunglasses were in style. Her preferred alternative was to remain indoors during the high time of the day. When not possible, she suffered. She knew a full weekend with Thomas would be a challenge. The loud clatter of pans interrupted her thoughts.

"Everything's cleaned up here. I thought we'd try to go canoeing today. The rental is five dollars for half a day."

Majken wanted to faint. "I know it is asking a lot, but could we try hiking the forest around the lake? As we drove in, I noticed a pretty cove on the far side. I'd get sick on the water." Majken leaned against an elm tree for shade. Already the sun was higher than comfortable; seven-thirty by Thomas' watch.

"All right," Thomas said, giving in. "We can pack a lunch in my day pack and take our time." Majken helped him prepare for the trip.

The harder part in reaching the thickly shaded, cooler forest around the lake was the quarter-mile jaunt across open ground. Majken struggled and swayed uneasily. The sun blinded her, and she held on to his pack for guidance.

Thomas stopped midfield. "Mary, are you sure you know where we're going? I never saw a cove by the lake." Majken gasped, trembling, hurting. She assured him it was there. She hardly wanted to stand there and talk about it. He stared at her, then continued.

He stumbled over a piece of wood buried in the grass. "This isn't as bad as I thought."

"Thanks," Majken replied.

"You know what I mean. I wanted us to do what you wanted."

Majken sighed with relief when they reached the forest. She indicated an overgrown path winding up-hill into a thicket. "Let's follow this trail."

Thomas squinted. "What trail?"

Majken pulled on his arm. He followed hesitantly.

"For a city girl, you seem to know what you're doing."

Majken saw something on the hill. Partially hidden, untouched and unspoiled in the wild undergrowth, stood a small cabin. Simple wooden slats for walls gave it a rustic appearance. The door had been broken off its hinges and leaned against the frame. Broken glass from the windows littered the porch. The little shack was not an antique. Majken stepped by a rail, pulled the door aside, and looked in.

"Don't do that!" Thomas exclaimed.

Majken ignored him and went inside. The one-room shack was surprisingly clean in contrast to the bramble covered exterior. A used mattress lay in the center of the floor. A broken chair lay toppled by a window.

Thomas followed her in. "What kind of place is this?"

Majken retrieved a half-bottle of scotch and an empty bottle of wine. The room had been occupied recently, with obvious intent. Majken sat, pulled off her sneakers, and lay back on the mattress. It was soft in spots.

"I need a rest," she said, and sighed. She curled on the mattress and patted the spot next to her with her hand.

"I don't think we should stay here." Thomas looked out both windows.

"You're free to go," she said.

Thomas scowled. "What if we're caught trespassing?"

Majken rolled on her stomach and stretched. She moaned. "I'm sure the owner won't return until tonight."

Thomas reluctantly sat on the mattress. "This is another fine mess you've gotten me into."

Majken laughed. She helped him pull off his pack and lie on his side, then rubbed where the straps had dug in.

He stifled a yawn. "I have to admit, I'm tired after walking so far."

"Let's stay here for a while. We have all day, you

said." She idly scratched his arm with her fingernail. She watched as Thomas looked over the drab interior while trying to make up his mind. She wanted him to stay with her, but would never plead. The lines around her eyes tightened. She never wanted to be in a position to plead for the blood she needed to survive. *Never again*, she vowed.

She pulled him gently to face her. "If I roam in the daytime any longer, I'll become deathly sick."

He held her respectfully. "I knew something was wrong." Her body pressed against his. "You're fair skinned, for sure. I never heard of getting sick in the daytime, or not eating for days."

He shook his head sadly. "I care for you a great deal, but I'm afraid I'll never understand you."

Majken felt a mood change. "Thomas, I've been in this condition for many years. All whom it touches, suffer. Believe me when I say this and don't ask me to explain everything." Majken caressed his face; her touch was soft and light, like a gentle mist of sea spray.

Thomas kissed her. "We'll stay for a while. And I'm hungry. I'll fix my lunch outside."

Majken grinned and urged him ahead. It was time for his midday meal.

She was used to the heavy, clammy feeling of

alienation. It was like everyone was invited to a grand party – except her. All she was allowed to do was stand outside a darkly stained window and peer within, where there was joy and peace and love; things that made a person's existence bearable. They were inside; she was outside. It drove some like her to madness.

"Those dark windows go both ways," she whispered to herself. Thomas glanced her way.

To pass the time, Majken told Thomas of her years in her orphanage, and later her high school. She borrowed experiences from real, living humans. Some were Lisa's, her roommate. She believed the important thing was to believe it herself. And be consistent. Consistency was difficult with Thomas because he listened and remembered practically every detail.

It was her game and she usually liked to play.

The latter part of their afternoon was filled with gentle caresses and kissing, holding and being together. She liked the fact that Thomas was not grabby, like a certain other young man she knew. She pushed him out of her mind. Now was a time to feel almost like a human. After all, she had to practice being human if she was going to live among them. *Practice makes perfect*, she thought, as she kissed him again.

They arrived back at their campsite at near dusk. She felt relaxed and calm over the experiences of the day, but worried that her need for blood would increase steadily with the night. She had fed well on the lifeguard, Davey, but to do so two nights in a row on a boy his size would seriously endanger his life.

Majken grimaced. Marc would not listen to reason. She vowed to let him die if that was his wish. Tonight, she had to find a different donor.

Thomas' blue day pack bobbed in front of her as they hiked the last incline to the campsite. Majken listened ahead and heard the scuffling sound of running. Reddened evening clouds shielded the sun so she could begin to see. Thomas stepped over the rise.

"What do you say we go for a swim after that long hike?" he asked jovially.

"I swam enough yesterday," Majken answered. Her eyes darted to the bushes as she heard movement.

Thomas unslung his pack and began rattling the contents. She wished he would unpack more quietly. "I don't blame you for sitting this one out," he began. "You looked pretty tired last time." Thomas knelt over a woodpile and began preparing a fire. "Is it okay with you if we both relax around camp tonight?"

Majken heard another sound.

"I'd like to—," Thomas started. They looked up in time to see a boy running hurriedly away. The lifeguard. Thomas frowned and stared at Majken. "Wonder what that kid's doing here?" Majken shrugged. Their evening passed lazily with the incident quickly forgotten.

Majken tried to separate from Thomas long enough to hunt, but he refused to let her leave his sight. She decided she would have to drink his blood, but not before her need forced her.

Late at night, she again doused all lanterns and sat beside him, facing the lake. Her dark-adapted eyes easily made out details invisible to human eyes. Soon, Thomas said he could make out part of the rippling surface and surrounding trees. This pleased her.

She trembled and shoved clenched fists between her knees. Thomas held her tighter, against the cooler night air. *Probably thinks I'm having my period*, she thought, sulking. They got ready for bed at eleven. She changed in the tent while he changed in the car. Modesty seemed hardly worth the effort. They were alone in case he screamed. She waited to render him unconscious by a simple, but dangerous, maneuver of firm rapid pressure against the carotid arteries.

The simplest method to get blood involved using a sharp knife to cut a superficial vein in the arm or leg. The most sterile technique was to use a hypodermic needle in the vein or artery; that was a safer method of withdrawal for the donor. If she was desperate and forced to kill, she could use her adequately sharp teeth. She also had a hollow, pointed stabbing weapon that could be pushed into the heart or neck to kill, or the leg to incapacitate her victim.

The moment came too quickly. She held the two-inch blade over his arm and made a penetrating, slantwise cut. The vein bulged and she controlled the bleeding with a pressure point. Her acute senses focused on the first trickle. She lapped the flowing nourishment and closed her eyes, allowing a tingling sensation to spread through her. She could no longer hear anything outside the tent.

Majken finished quickly. The bleeding stopped. A purplish-blue clot formed under his skin. Cradling his arm in her lap, she swabbed it with alcohol and wrapped it snugly with white gauze from her bag. Wounds healed faster when allowed to breathe. She positioned herself alongside him, supporting his arm outside his sleeping bag to give it a chance to heal before he regained consciousness.

Cold night air licked her face. She gazed into the

darkness inside the tent to the darkness without. Majken checked his breathing rate. It was impossible to monitor a donor's heart and lungs while engrossed in feeding. Going too far was a constant possibility.

Numbness spread gradually through her entire body. She had to wake and remove the gauze before morning. Majken kissed Thomas lightly on his cheek as she succumbed to a deep sleep.

Thomas woke with a start at the cough of a passing motor home. Groggy, he wiped the sleep from his eyes and adjusted to the full morning light diffused red and blue by the tent. He found Mary, his love, asleep in her own sleeping bag, curling disappointingly in the opposite direction. She was beautiful. He could easily get used to a life with her. He arched his back like he had seen her do, and felt the vertebrae stretch and compress. He rolled his head and felt a pop, then nudged his girlfriend and whispered softly, "Mary, you asleep?"

Majken wiggled slightly, pulling the cover tighter around her.

Thomas tried to sit up, but fell. He twisted weakly on his side and felt a twinge below his elbow. He gingerly touched the swollen area. It hurt now that he was fully awake. He groped for his watch at the head of his sleeping bag. It was late.

Majken stirred.

When Thomas called her, she sat up slowly. Her expression was blank and a dull glaze seemed to be over her eyes. She rubbed her face with both hands. Then she smiled at him.

"Good morning," she said, "did you sleep well?"

Thomas rested on his haunches. "What are you doing way over there?" He unzipped one side of his bag for her. If they were on campus, the gesture would have been too bold. It was peaceful here. Majken crawled over and lay next to him.

He held his arm up to examine it in the light. It looked like a typical, everyday bruise, except for the red streak running to his wrist and the paleness next to it. "How in the hell did I do this?" He rubbed his finger the length of his forearm, and started to squeeze the purplish swollen area.

"No!" Majken exclaimed. "You'll make it bleed." She brushed his hand away and examined it closely. "Does it hurt?"

He pulled his arm out of her grasp. "Yes," he said. How it happened, when he might have bumped it, was a complete mystery to him. He circled the area with his finger.

Majken inched her body closer to him and reached around his waist. She kissed him and suggested that he not worry about it.

He tried to put his arm around her. "Ow!"

His girlfriend sprang up and began feeling under his bag along the edge of the tent. "Here," she said. She pulled a modest-sized rock from under his sleeping bag. It was the rock he had used to hold the tent flap in place. "One of us must have dragged this in by mistake. You must have fallen asleep with this under your arm, and that caused the bruise."

Thomas marveled at her deductive prowess, especially so early in the morning. He had little choice but to believe her. What else could have done it? He embraced her loosely this time, kissed her, and left to change and prepare his breakfast.

While he ate breakfast, he watched Mary sit on the cooler and look at the scenery. She seemed distant this morning. The trip was worth it, but how strange she acted, he thought. Thomas told her about his plans for the day.

He loved being out of the city, away from his studies, and wanted to postpone returning until the last minute. He wanted a leisurely drive home. After breakfast, Majken helped him clear their campsite, and especially roll the tent and lash it securely to the car.

They said goodbye to their campsite. It was fully morning with a slightly overcast sky. He noticed she already wore her sunglasses. The young lifeguard waved him over at the check-out gate. *Can't shake this kid,* Thomas thought morosely.

The boy leaned out of the booth, apparently to get a better look at both of them. "Enjoy your stay?" he asked politely.

Thomas gave him the perfunctory reply. A strip of shriveled gauze circled his upper arm. It had not been there at the pool, Thomas remembered. Majken was resting on her pillow. The young lifeguard winked at Thomas.

"Tell her I missed her at the pool last night."

What was that all about? he wondered, as he left the campground. He checked his mirror and saw the boy waving. When he looked to see what his girlfriend would say, he found her asleep.

Daniel Albritton mulled over a cup of over-brewed coffee. It was the only way his ex-Army compatriot and longtime friend, Campus Chief Vincent Baggetta, knew how to make it. Pristine curtains fluttered in the stiff afternoon breeze, threatening to topple the assorted knickknacks on the sill. He glanced over the polished white counter to face his friend.

Baggetta's home was squarely in the center of the campus, to most effectively manage the five man, one woman security force. His sworn duty was to protect campus students, faculty, and property. They knew each other from their younger days when Albritton was a brash new officer, and they had parted after the service. Albritton had brought his beloved wife and son to this school partially because Baggetta worked here. Baggetta was also a widower. Many years had passed.

"Marc's behavior has deteriorated for the last two or three months. Teresa knew how to handle him, but I'm at a loss." Albritton held his cup stiffly. He paused, knowing Baggetta's deceased wife, Marlene, was still very real to her husband; all the way to the tea cups he gave her on their last anniversary.

"Marc and I both had a time of it after his mother died. He's going off the deep end, Vincent, and I don't know how to reach him."

Baggetta eased his massive frame in a chair and balanced a china cup in his palm. "Unless he breaks campus rules, there aren't many ways I can step in. If I had a son, I might know better how to help you. Kids today are not as responsible as we were expected to be."

Albritton pounded his fist on the table. "He's

whoring his life away! He's lost control. I want him to tell me what is wrong and he refuses."

Baggetta finished a long sip, still listening.

"He comes in late and slips away early before I can talk to him. I hoped if I eased off after our confrontation last week, he might come to his senses." Albritton eased his empty saucer on the table. He commented bitterly, "I haven't seen him for two days."

"You are rich, Daniel, to even have a son. Give him time. Let him come to you his own way." Baggetta placed their cups and saucers in the sink. "Remember what you were like at his age."

Albritton chuckled, then clasped Baggetta's hand. He waited by the door. "I'll let you know," he said, as he walked out.

Majken knew they were close to the city. The air was thick with the smell of asphalt and packed earth. She listened and heard sounds of heavier traffic from a nearby interstate. The sun hid behind thick cumulus clouds, making it darker than it should have been. The weather should be changing.

She saw Thomas driving with an arm balanced on top of the steering wheel and the other propped outside his window. He looked tired after driving over half of the day without companionship. So far, she had kept him at arm's length. This weekend changed their relationship. Now, he had questions. She examined the swollen area just below his left elbow out of the corner of her eye.

Thomas glanced at her.

Majken eased in her seat while rhythmically flexing her spine. "Hello, handsome."

"Did you have another good nap?" he asked. Majken felt the icy tone in his voice, and she could not blame him.

"I feel much better," she said softly. Thomas continued to drive with an expressionless stare at the highway. Majken shifted in her seat. "Thanks for letting me come with you."

Thomas nodded. "Glad you had fun."

Silence again. "I owe you an apology, Thomas."

"Why?" he snapped. He laughed nervously. "I'm sure you have a terrific explanation for why you've been acting like this. I can't wait to hear it."

Majken drew a deep, cleansing breath.

"What bothers you the most?"

He glared at her. "Where did you go the first night?"

"When I wake up at night, even if I've only slept ten minutes, it's hard for me to go back to sleep. I wandered that night for a few hours, until I was tired enough to fall back asleep immediately without disturbing you."

"You sleep all day! It's driving me crazy." He hesitated. "When we left the park, that kid from the pool wanted to know why you didn't come to the pool last night. Why do you think that was?"

Majken replied evenly, "I went for another swim." Thomas made a sarcastic comment and asked how she got in. "Climbed the fence," she said. Nothing less than the truth would have the ring of credibility she needed.

"I took off my clothes and slipped into the water, but I'm afraid I wasn't alone. He watched a pretty good show." She omitted the messy, unimportant details.

An embarrassed grin spread across Thomas' face. "That explains what that little pervert was doing in our camp." Thomas laughed.

"I'm sorry. You're still mad at me?"

Thomas propped his other arm on the steering wheel and glanced at her to the road, probably deciding. Then he smiled a little. "Next time you go skinny-dipping, promise to invite me." The muscles in his jaw visibly relaxed. The crisis was over.

He turned on the radio. Soon, the obnoxious music stopped for a news report.

Majken homed in on the phrase, "bloody carnage of an elderly Negro man and woman." The police were quoted as admitting witnesses were nonexistent, but they fully expected to have several suspects in for questioning within the next few days.

Thomas whistled softly under his breath after the report. "What do you think of that, another murder." The tone of his statement was rhetorical so Majken did not respond.

A special, reserved part of her mind was busily filing this reference to a brutal murder, as well as disappearances (especially of children) and other inexplicable events. This incident fell too neatly in place behind the young woman's demise at the lounge. Perhaps a coincidence, she thought. Thousands, maybe millions, died daily in traffic accidents, violent crimes, and self-abuse. Criminal or preternatural? Majken grimaced at the possibility.

"Does bad news frighten you?" Thomas jolted her out of her chain of thought.

"Millions die every day," she answered abstractly.

Thomas placed his arm around her. "We can't let anything happen to you. I wanted you to come on this trip to give you a chance to know how I feel about you."

Majken slid her hand silently along her thigh,

clenched, then relaxed. It was becoming too easy to play the role of lover to this young man, she thought. For the remainder of the trip, she took care to talk with him. They arrived home soon.

Thomas stalled before letting her leave. "I've got a full day tomorrow, but I really want to see you. Can we meet at the Student Lounge at seven?"

"Seven would be fine. Too bad we're both going to be busy studying for exams." Majken tiptoed around his car door and kissed him playfully on the cheek. "I'll be thinking about you between every chapter."

She picked out her baggage, dropped it on the ground, then leaned against the car. Birds scratched in the branches of a tree overhead. Few students could be seen from behind the dorms.

Thomas sat next to her and took her hand.

The air was cool on her skin. She spoke softly, "I'm glad we had this time together."

"Did you really enjoy it, or are you just saying that?" He rubbed his finger absently on the chrome.

"You've seen things that are different about me. I worried that you wouldn't want to see me anymore."

Thomas squeezed her hand. "Look here, I like you very much. All you have to do is tell me what you're thinking and planning to do. So I don't have to find out the hard way." He winked at her. "Okay?"

Majken smiled, kissed him good night, and stepped away from his car.

"Did I tell you how beautiful you are?" he called.

Majken waved and watched him drive away, then walked purposely to her sanctuary. Her roommate, Lisa Simmons, was leaving as she entered her dorm.

"Well, well, look who's back. Did you and Tommy have a good time?"

Majken smiled at her. "We had a good time. He wore himself out trying to make things go smoothly." She dropped her bag on the carpet and checked the message board next to the telephone.

Lisa grinned. "I wish I could find a guy to wear himself out over me." She sighed and shifted her tennis racket to her left hand and practiced a backhand swing. Her black hair was tied and she wore white. "What did you and he do together all weekend?"

Majken hesitated a second to figure out how she meant her question. "Mostly, we swam, hiked, and toured the countryside."

"And –"

Majken motioned her closer and whispered, "I'll tell you tonight."

Lisa squealed and twirled her racket once. "Gotta

be going or my teacher will think I'm not coming."

"What do you need a teacher for? You've played for years."

Lisa laughed. "Yeah, but he doesn't know that." She started to leave, then, "Oh, before I go, I ought to warn you about this guy who has been lurking around the dorm. He came in here and said he was looking for a girl he saw at Friday's game. His description favored you, the poor snook. We kinda shooed him out the door, but I heard he's still around."

"Thanks, Lisa," Majken replied. She watched her roommate prance down four concrete steps and run out of sight, to the tennis courts.

Turning to leave, she noticed a young man with light brown hair hiding behind a group of trees. Angry eyes met hers, then he ran. Majken cursed softly under her breath. Marc would have to be dealt with quickly. She decided to stay in her dorm.

Majken prowled the deserted second floor hallway well past midnight to return to her room after feeding. So far, she had found six girls who slept soundly enough to have blood withdrawn by venipuncture. Only one girl had woke up during the delicate procedure; the disturbance had roused the girl's roommate as well. Majken escaped and was forced to seek nourishment outside the dorm until the clamor died.

The upper hallway was very dark. A faint glow from downstairs was the only light source. She padded lightly on the carpet, her robe swishing softly. She brushed her fingers on the wooden trim that ran the length of the hall at waist level, and upwards over the floral design wallpaper. Her hand stopped within a rectangular patch. She felt the rough contour and knew a picture had been removed.

Dark-adapted eyes scanned the row of closed doors in front of her. She often attributed her ability to navigate in near total darkness to her acute sense of touch, as well as sight. She stopped by the washroom to briefly check for traces of blood on her face or hands. Confident, she headed for her room.

Her problem with Marc caused her to realize how much she liked living in a campus environment. A continuous influx of young, healthy potential donors and access to the newest information was a wonderful advantage. Her plans to search for a colorless, topical anesthetic of sufficient strength to dull a puncture site and still not pollute the blood would have to wait. Her security was threatened.

Majken mentally rehearsed a list of excuses to use in case her roommate found her wandering in the middle of the night. Lisa was an early riser, and let her sleep in. She hardly ever saw Lisa in the mornings.

Comfortable and safe in her bed and with hours to go until morning, Majken allowed herself to gradually slip away. Her final thoughts were on how to persuade Marc to leave her alone permanently.

Majken slept blissfully until she felt her bed tilt with the combined weight of her roommate and several other girls. Out of a fog, she heard, "Are you awake yet?" directed at her. Lisa shook the bed for good measure. Majken stirred and buried her head under her pillow.

"What's the matter?" Majken sat up to find a roomful of girls. *So much for being a light sleeper,* she thought.

Lisa snapped a piece of paper in her face. She unfolded the note. Most everyone tried to read it as she read it.

I know your secret. Come to where we first met at six – or else!

Her assumed name was scrawled on the other side in Marc's handwriting.

"What are you going to do?" Lisa asked.

She was immediately bombarded by girls asking what the note meant, if she knew who wrote it, and comments that it must be a joke, and she should call the police. Majken folded the blackmail note and dropped it on her bedside table.

Majken crossed her arms defensively. "It must be a joke," she said uncertainly. A blonde girl at the foot of her bed persisted.

"I'll find out," she replied, "whatever it is, but promise me you won't tell a soul until I find out where it came from." They all promised reluctantly. The entire school would know by lunch. Majken decided to speak to Thomas first, to lessen the shock.

She found him in late afternoon practice. He smiled broadly at seeing her unexpectedly and joined her at the fence. Shouts and jeers from his teammates drifted overhead. Their conversation went smoothly, she thought, until she told him she would be occupied this evening and why. "I have to see a blackmailer," she said so casually she knew he would think she was joking.

Thomas' eyes went hard for a second; his coach was calling him back.

His eyes then softened and he reached for her.

Majken kissed Thomas longer than she had to, and left. The transit bus took her to the heart of the city by five-thirty. From there, Majken walked to a pickup bar on the east side where she knew Marc would be waiting.

* * *

Marc Albritton grew restless waiting in the small booth. He nursed the same beer for an hour. The bar was thick with smoke and the sounds of billiards. The entrance appeared as a shaft of light through a haze. He disliked this dreary bar. Its sole saving grace was that this was the place where he had met that fox that fateful night.

Her long brown hair had been braided on one side, she wore a skirt slit up to her hip, and looked very much in need of male companionship. Overwhelmed, he remembered walking up to her. She seemed to see straight through him. The best conversation he could muster was babbling about the latest football scores. She was patient and understanding of his nervousness. She said she was recently divorced and nervous, too. This was her first night of freedom. She was so pretty, all he could remember thinking was how to get her into bed with him. He asked her out.

She led him to an apartment. He found himself alone the next morning with a simple letter of instruction. The same woman would be coming to him soon, he thought. Marc fantasized often about their life together. She loved him and needed him. He pulled a black velvet box from his pocket, tapped it on the table, and put it away when he remembered where he was. This ring would prove how much he loved her.

Marc squeezed his eyes closed. In a wild woodland, he imagined her running toward him, shedding her dress. He ordered her to strip and kneel. He ordered her to spread out on a cushion of fallen leaves. He ordered – a feminine voice shocked him back to reality.

"Marc, why did you leave this note at my dorm?"

Marc looked up. His love was towering over him. She was draped in a shawl and wearing amber-tinted lenses. She removed the note from her pocket, tore his note in little pieces, and sat in the booth.

"I'm sorry about the note and how I acted at the game." His hand trembled as he opened the velvet box for her. "I wanted you to have this ... token of m-my ... love for you." Marc chewed his lip. She removed her glasses; her gaze tore through him. She made no move to touch the exposed jewelry.

Marc pushed the trinket toward her. "Take it," he commanded in a subdued voice.

Majken closed the black box with a snap, using the palm of her hand, he noticed. She arose and leaned over the table. "I never want to hear from you again."

Wounded, he placed the gift in his pocket. "You

don't want it?" he stammered. He cradled his head and cursed the pounding in his head and the noise in the bar. His chest felt tight. He felt smothered. "I'm trying to apologize," he said. He tried to caress her hair, her face. Majken leaned out of his reach.

"I've warned you enough. My life and yours depends on my ability to live on campus peacefully. Our relationship is finished, and if I see you again, on campus or anywhere else, we'd better be strangers."

He followed her icy gaze to the doorway. A comfortable twilight had spread over the city. When she started to leave, Marc grabbed her shawl.

"Wait," he shouted. "I have no life without you. At least let me hold you one last time; give me another chance," he pleaded. She stopped and slowly peeled his fingers off her shawl, then motioned for him to follow.

Outside, she asked him where his car was. He followed her across a boulevard and down a street to a condemned building. She pushed open the door; it left a trail of broken glass. Marc hesitated before entering with her.

She entered a small, rank-smelling room. The entire building was a trash dump. Broken plaster littered the floor. A broken pipe in the wall leaked oily slime. She pulled him to the center of the room and calmly ordered him to undress. She pulled his jacket off, tore open his shirt, wrapping it around his arms. She pushed him face down, and, with her knee in his back, removed his boots, trousers, and underwear.

Marc screamed when he saw the reflection of a streetlamp in the scoring knife she carried. *She was never this strong before!* he thought wildly.

He screamed when she stretched his abdomen taut and punctured the soles of his feet. He felt something wet trickle down his ankles, something he knew was blood. She whispered, "I love you, Marc," before she started to lap his blood. He stopped screaming when she told him it attracted rats. She tossed a roll of gauze and antiseptic next to him, and left him sobbing and writhing violently on the floor.

Night shrouded the stranger standing before the city park. The white glare of lamps mounted overhead gave the man's pale features a ghostly appearance that contrasted with the rough-hewn pillars at the entrance. People milled around him; a shrill man somewhere ahead shouted for passersby to purchase his wares. Next to him, a baby carried on his father's shoulder sneezed.

John moved purposely, noiselessly, striving to show a bored expression while keeping tabs on two adolescent girls in front of him.

The first girl had hair the color of honey and a short upturned nose. Her lips were wide and full with the onset of maturity and open with a ready, friendly smile. Her name, John overheard, was Marcia. The second girl had closely trimmed mousy hair and talked much less. She was stocky, like a child. He had trailed them from a laundromat a half mile away. He had watched as Marcia waved goodbye to her mother and pulled her playmate out with her on this adventure.

John matched the girl's stride. They stopped. The light-haired girl pointed down one path while the other protested her choice. He seized a discarded newspaper and sat down on a bench while they argued. He heard bits, but lost the conversation upon hearing the stiff, polished gait of a policeman or guard moving in his direction. A dog on his chain leash sniffed and emitted a low growl.

John ignored the dog and tipped his hat forward and hunched smaller in the threadbare charcoal grey coat he had taken from a derelict snooping too close to his temporary home. The policeman tugged on the animal's collar, called it a stupid mutt, and walked out of sight. John swore vehemently; his quarry had disappeared down a narrow walkway branching to the left. He followed them, searching.

The girls had vanished. He headed toward the largest collection of humans standing in front of the man-made lake. The thick triangular blade of his knife rested comfortably and invisibly in the small of his back. The thrill of chase stimulated him. It was nearing the time when he would move to more comfortable quarters. The money he had taken from a drug-pushing pimp would go nicely to that end, he thought.

John halted on a fine pebbly path. He liked the artificial nature around him. Once he learned the area thoroughly, he could add it to his places to hunt. Before him lay the watery grave of several future victims. Wonderment filled him in modern man's ability to create lamps that burned without oil, a vehicle powered by a combustion engine, or a lake where nature had not seen fit to place one. Suddenly, his pulse quickened upon seeing the light-haired girl pass a bend in the trail.

The centuries had taught him that humans never change; they remain weak and stupid. The prey stopped. The smaller girl pulled against the larger, and both were oblivious to being stalked. Ignoring the rabble, John concentrated solely on his victims, and started to circle in front of them when the girls split up, with the smaller girl leaving to join a group of strangers at the lake. The light-haired girl, Marcia, slipped into the bushy cove. The still, stagnant air carried the sounds of two humans within as John blocked the exit. A tall elm hid his approach. Pausing in silent fascination, he watched the girl and a boy of the same age try to smoke cigarettes.

What passed for blood rifled through his arteries as the time came to attack. A red blur momentarily fogged his vision; his knife was poised and his right fist had closed. The short, stocky boy's skull collapsed with the first blow; a red slash pulsed on the girl's face and chest. John smacked the girl as trembling lips formed a silent scream. He drained the boy's body quickly, but found the girl had crawled out of sight in the bushes. Uttering several oaths, he wrapped the body in the stained coat and searched for a place to hide it. His needs were sated for tonight.

Chapter Four

"Nobody likes to hear about murder while they're eating breakfast," Suzanne said, "it's not natural."

Thomas put down the morning newspaper long enough to take a long sip of orange juice and scowl disapprovingly at his classmate. "This is serious." He studied the attractive figure across his table to the sawing rhythm of a fingernail file. Suzanne was all right to study with, he thought, but the high point of her day had to be deciding which color of nail polish to use. He guiltily squelched the accusation and smiled slightly.

"The police found this unfortunate kid's body in a tree. Doesn't that strike you as highly unusual?"

The pretty brunette acquiesced. "Go ahead and read it then, if that's all you have on your mind."

Thomas summarized the remaining article: "It happened in the new city recreational complex. A girl was found injured and in shock hiding in the shrubbery. An unidentified boy was found entangled in tree limbs fifty feet off the ground. Police were stunned by the viciousness of the assault."

The seriousness of the crime apparently penetrated Suzanne's consciousness, and she stopped filing her nails.

"Do you know the section that talks about motives for murder?" he asked. Thomas found the page in a latter chapter and showed it to her.

"That chapter isn't even on the syllabus."

"The article didn't say it, but I think these fatal attacks are done by the same person or group of persons. This is current events, and Dr. Brennon might change the schedule to talk about it."

"He probably will." Suzanne was quiet for a minute.

Thomas tossed the newspaper on an adjacent table. The cafeteria was filling steadily. A woman with an apron moved from table to table sweeping up paper and plastic debris into a garbage bag.

"Thomas?" Suzanne got his attention. "Are you going to the award banquet next week?"

"I haven't had time to think about it. It's a good thing it's next Friday, and not this week." Thomas glanced at the wall clock and a batch of newcomers ordering breakfast. He noticed a hopeful gleam in Suzanne's eyes. "I planned to go," he said.

"Have a date?" she asked. Thomas looked past her. Majken entered the cafeteria and was standing out of Suzanne's line of sight. Suzanne mumbled, "Speak of the devil," when Majken stepped up to the table.

Thomas pulled out a third chair. "Good morning, Mary. You're out early today."

Majken took the proffered seat. "I haven't seen you in days." She looked at Suzanne and smiled. "I wondered what you've been up to." Thomas' glance shifted subtly, from Majken to Suzanne, Suzanne to Majken.

He grinned, and said, "Studying, what else?"

"I hope I'm not disturbing anything," Majken said to Suzanne.

Suzanne closed her notebook. "We were only discussing the rise of societal pressures to conform and their relationship to latent aggressive tendencies and marked antisocial behaviors." As an afterthought, she added, "Advanced theories of social psychology."

"In other words," Thomas injected, "why people commit murder." He showed her the newspaper article.

She scanned it faster than Thomas had, then her gaze drifted slowly downward and left. He watched her eyes dull for a moment. Her expression was unfathomable.

"Must have gone over her head," Suzanne butted in.

Thomas ignored her and asked his girlfriend what was wrong. "I worry about you when you get that faraway look on your face. What are you thinking?"

Majken blinked, then looked at him. "This is the same man that killed the girl at the lounge."

Suzanne let out a small gasp. "This is too much for me!" she exclaimed. Thomas ignored her. Then a triumphant smile spread across her face. "Tell me, Mary, is it true that someone left a blackmail note at your dorm yesterday?"

Thomas leaned forward. "I hope you took it to the police."

Suzanne's smile shrank a bit. "She told you already?"

Another presence limped to a table across the aisle. The young man's face was flush with anger. He sipped a large Coke and slowly tore open a candy wrapper. Thomas noticed, he seemed to be staring at them, then dismissed it.

Suzanne gathered her books and stuffed her ballpoint in the midsection of a notepad. "I think I'll be running along." She smiled generously at Thomas. "See you in class."

Thomas watched her swaying behind disappear from view, then returned to his girlfriend. "I deserve a better explanation than that," Thomas said in a low voice.

"I agree, but not in here."

They left the cafeteria solemnly. He touched her

arm lightly once, but followed at a distance. Early morning birds chirped and trilled in the slight breeze. He followed her to a thickly shaded spot with a bench; her favorite spot, he remembered. As they strolled, Thomas was reminded of their camping trip. He had told Phillip it was "eventful" without being more specific. He wondered how many more surprises she had to spring on him.

Majken sat smoothly at one end of the bench and picked a different topic.

"I heard you were going to the award banquet. Still want me?" Thomas' heart flip-flopped.

"I'm worried about right now. A note like that is serious, even if you think it's a prank. I'd have taken it to campus security in any case." He gripped the black wrought iron railing on her side of the bench.

Majken brushed her slender fingers through her hair and pulled it off her neck, then rolled her head in a circle to relieve tension. "It was a joke," she explained.

Thomas shook his head. "Who sent it?"

"What do you want?" she asked.

He gestured furtively in the air. "I don't know." He planted his hands accusingly on his hips. "You're hiding something, and I'm damned if I know what it is, or why."

Majken kept her hands folded in her lap. Thomas knelt beside her and sought out her eyes.

She removed her sunglasses and returned his gaze. Her saddened expression touched something that seemed to understand. He communed freely with her in the flicker of an eyelash, then the impression faded, leaving him helpless and frustrated.

"Talk to me," he implored.

She looked away.

"Do what you want," he said bitterly, "I'll never know you at this rate!" He left abruptly.

A deep chill coursed through Majken's body as she felt her relationship with Thomas dissolving, ironically because he really cared what happened to her. She smiled bitterly, and listened to her heartbeat. It gradually slowed. This had ceased to be a game, and she knew in her heart that Thomas would make a poor donor risk because his feelings for her would get in the way. Drained, she closed her eyes and tried to revitalize herself. She held a slender hope that salvage might be possible after things cooled off.

Dark, violet eyes scanned the desolate grounds between scattered buildings; most students were in midmorning classes. Thomas was gone, but an intruder had followed her at a distance, she noticed. Majken returned to her dorm, and finally, in the relative safety of her room, tried to find a longer lasting solution. Marc was dangerously persistent. When she decided, she packed a few extra items in her bag for a trip to Trenton. On leaving, she checked the campus directory and swore silently on finding a listing for Dr. Daniel Albritton. This matter, she thought, would be difficult to resolve.

Pain slowed Marc Albritton's entry to his father's colonial home to a crawl. He limped across the doorsill. He was bearing the scars of an unusual love affair. He could hear his father now: the outburst, the lecture, the warning, and an apology to top it all off. What Dr. Albritton expected of his students, he expected all the more of his only son.

Marc called his father. His plea sounded hollow and pitiful in an empty house. His father was busy educating the heathen, he thought sarcastically, at the time he needed him the most. The school admired his dedication. The army admired his service. His mother, Teresa, had missed him. Dr. Albritton expected perfection.

Climbing the stairs to his room required effort. He laid out fresh clothes and prepared a bath. His feet were tender and swollen, dried blood stuck like grains of sand to the gauze. Even in that filthy place, she had used sterile procedures and allowed him to wrap his injuries to prevent infection. Marc let the water swirl around his waist, soaking away the pain. She hurt him; was that love? His insides were plastered to his chest; he choked on humiliation. He finally cried. Tears of loss drained away with the pink-stained bath water.

Physically rejuvenated, Marc dressed and pulled on a pair of shoes with thick foam padding to cushion his steps. Walking was much easier. He fixed himself a sandwich, then entered his father's sanctuary with awed respect. He could not count the number of reprimands his father had given him in this study. A strong, irresistible force drew him. He hated and loved this room; so like his feelings for his father.

Marc went to the plush, leather-bound chair, its thick padding conformed to body contours. His father often dozed off in this chair when working on a paper or a special presentation kept him up late. The huge desk in the study was beautiful with its fancy scrolling on the top surface. The right side displayed a faint scratch from a penknife Marc used when barely a teenager. His mother was alive then.

He remembered waiting the whole day for his

father to come home and deliver severe punishment. Marc met him at the door and confessed as he trembled very hard. His father took the knife and brought Marc to the study. The scratch was ugly and long. His father closed the knife, returned it, then embraced his son asking him not to do it again. He swallowed a lump. His old man was not all bad.

To love, and have it rejected, possibly hurt him more than anything else could. Marc recognized how dangerous she was. The keys from the bottom desk drawer jingled in his fingers. He arose and unlocked a cabinet on the wall, then smoothly removed a single working handgun and a box of ammunition. His mother had disapproved of guns. He loaded each round with deliberation. She would be reasonable, he thought, and he would not have to use the weapon.

Marc rubbed the blue metal finish of the gun as if it were living. He grabbed a pencil and pad of paper and spoke out loud as he started to write. Dear Father; he stuck a sharp pencil point in his mouth to find the words, then: You may think I'm crazy, but here goes. He wrote in silence, stopping occasionally to remember. When he had finished, he hid the note in his father's memo folder. Marc idly traced the outline of the gun with his finger. Her time had come.

* * *

Majken tried to relax on the bus. Her senses automatically trained on colors, sounds, scents, and movements. She sat on the side opposite the piercing sunlight. A man carried a bouquet of flowers which filled the bus with their aroma. Another played a radio loudly. The bus stopped periodically to load and unload passengers. It was impossible to relax. The dividing line between suburbia and the inner city was acute. Once Majken was shaken by an odd feeling, but the bus continued and the impression subsided. Her first stop was at a wholesale jeweler.

Mr. Stein was a pudgy and effusive man who claimed to be an authority on eighteenth century jewelry. She had left one of her favorite pieces with him to be appraised, a pendant given to her as a gift. Majken entered the ornate shop. Mr. Stein was busy examining a man's watch under a magnifier and commenting on its quality. She waited while they politely discussed the price. The customer walked out with his watch in his pocket. Majken greeted the balding proprietor and was compelled to assure him that mademoiselle had had a pleasant journey. It was beyond her what prompted her to let this man touch her favorite possession.

At least a third of her accumulated wealth was in the form of fine jewelry, much she could never sell, but it was useful to know its current value. Majken joyfully collected her pendant and the card of a purchaser she would contact herself. She paid a fee and left. Her next destination was to a respectable, midcity bank. She maintained a savings account under her assumed name. She knew money could be invested in treasury notes, bonds, stocks, collectable jewelry, artwork, real estate, gold, and other commodities. As a rule, major holdings were maintained in out-of-city or out-of-state institutions. She felt safer with a low profile in her home city.

Majken entered her bank, signed a release, and waited while it changed hands from teller to cashier to manager; the sum was five thousand dollars. She thumbed through a magazine while waiting. She rarely moved funds in excess of ten thousand. The manager suggested a cashier's check. Majken insisted on cash. Eventually, he brought her money to his office. She thanked him, tucked the money safely away, and left. Majken burned the receipt outside. It was past noon.

Shadows from tall office buildings overlapped the busy streets. Majken blended in the mass of pedestrians moving toward an office complex two blocks away. Below the office complex, a hidden cache was located in the lowest level of the basement parking deck.

She entered from the main street entrance with a group of workers returning from lunch. Careful to remain unobserved, she disappeared to the lowest level.

Majken pried a slab of concrete loose from a supporting joist. The grating sound was barely audible over distant traffic sounds. She retrieved a small metal box, then placed her pendant and two thousand dollars inside. Once mailed, it would be securely stored at her private address until requested. She pushed the slab in place and brushed away traces of splintered concrete. She left by a side entrance.

Her business affairs concluded, she felt free and unencumbered to deal with Marc Albritton.

Thomas came out of his afternoon class flipping through seven pages of instructions on an assignment due at the end of the semester. Most of his free time had been devoted to Mary and team practice, which left little time for cerebral activity. It was hard to sit in class. The communication gap between him and Mary widened by the day. A good relationship was due to go up in smoke if something was not done. Phillip caught up to Thomas in the hallway.

"What are you doing over this way?" Thomas asked.

Phillip looked tense as he asked, "Have you seen Mary?"

Thomas drew him aside. "This morning, but I hope to see her later."

"I heard a few things you ought to know. People are laughing behind your back." Phillip stalled. "I don't know if I should tell you."

"It was important enough for you to chase me down, so spit it out." He was puzzled. "Does this have anything to do with Mary?"

"She … she's been sleeping with different men, and –"

Thomas collapsed against the wall. "How could she do something like that?" He winced painfully. "When was this?"

"It could be jealousy. I mean, you've had her pretty much to yourself, and she is a class act." Phillip stared at the floor and rested his arm on his friend's sagging shoulder. "I know how much you like her."

Thomas straightened up. "I'll be okay."

"Yeah, I believe that. Did you and she have an understanding?"

He shook his head. "Not in so many words. How do you know it was her? Tell me who you heard it from?"

Phillip waved Thomas off. "You can't stop talk

by slugging it out with them. Let it die a natural death."

Thomas stared at Phillip hard. "Them?"

Phillip nervously looked at his watch, the wall, the girls.

Thomas bowed his head, tapped Phillip lightly on the arm. "Thanks for telling me."

"What are you going to do?"

"It's her life," Thomas said. "Talk to her, and maybe find out what's going on."

The incessant hum of air-conditioning units drowned out sounds. Majken crouched, ready to strike. Her tormentor, Marc, had been waiting at the campus bus stop. Only spotting him before he saw her allowed her to bait her trap and detour him to the abandoned library delivery docks. The brick enclosure and aluminum canopy protected her from curious onlookers and direct sunlight. It was the perfect place for their discussion.

Marc stepped on the dock, holding the steel door open with one hand. He was panting and out of breath from running. "I know you're here," he called uncertainly. "I just want to talk."

She studied him. He wore the same type blue jeans and T-shirt from their game encounter. He carried his tan jacket in a bundle under his arm. Majken reached Marc fast and clamped a hand over his mouth. His jacket dropped with a clump; his escape route closed with a satisfying click. She pressed him to the brick wall.

"I don't want any trouble." His speech was spastic; a sign of certain fear.

Majken eased off and presented herself. "I will not ask you again to leave me alone."

"I know," he said, wheezing. He held out his arm, wrist up. "But I have something you want. I thought we could strike a bargain." Released from her grasp, he tried to wiggle out of arm's reach. He rubbed his throat.

"Marc," she said gently, "do you really understand what I am?"

He relaxed on hearing the softness of her voice. "You need blood, I know that," he said. "You don't have to stop seeing me because I know who you are. We can still help each other out."

Majken looked deeply into his eyes. Most of the fury was out of sight and bubbling beneath the surface. She had raised a demon to match hers. "I stopped seeing you because you're unstable, and I don't trust you." Majken felt his pulse quicken.

"I can still help you. I think I love you."

"How can you love someone like me?" she taunted.

"I do," he protested. "I'll do anything to get you
back!"

Majken wanted to laugh, but repressed it. His
obsession drove him as strongly as her blood needs
drove her. "If we continued dating, I could easily
lose control and let you bleed to death before I knew
what I had done. I change partners often. Listen to
reason, Marc. Do you want to die?"

"I'll die without you," he said earnestly.

His infatuation threatened them both. Majken
considered giving in to him until he prodded her in
anger. "When I think about it, all you have is me.
Your boyfriend should be getting an earful by now."

"What are you talking about?" she said in a hard
voice.

Marc's voice turned equally cold. "I know how to
hurt you, bad. I can see to it that you're locked away
for the rest of your life as a freak."

Majken remained calm. "In this country, Marc
dear, person's like me are a myth. The odds of any
sane person believing you is highly remote."

He started cursing and tried to shake her roughly.

Majken slapped him, leaving a crimson streak
across his face and jerking his head sharply. He fell

against the brick and next to an open cardboard box. He was alive, she knew, but unconscious. She wished he had said more about how he might hurt her.

Suddenly, she turned to face the high-pitched bark of a poodle. Now what? she thought. She heard giggling beyond the enclosure; the sounds a couple makes when looking for a private place, and a feminine voice calling the dog. Her situation with Marc was compromising at best. Majken pulled him flat, crossed his legs, locked his fingers over his chest, and pressed a discarded notebook over his face.

The students froze at the corner. Majken stomped indignantly away and gestured angrily in Marc's direction. "If that stupid jerk would rather sleep than talk to me, he can find himself another girl!"

The couple exchanged glances. His hand was still under her blouse. Majken did not look back.

Order restored for a moment, Majken made her way to her dorm. She looked forward to a hot shower, but found a message from Thomas on the message board. The message taker had recorded the men's dorm number and wrote the word *upset* on the note. She ripped the note off the board and started to dial, but waited for three lingering girls to clear the hallway.

Her timing was perfect. He had just returned from his workout.

"Thomas, you don't usually call me. Is anything wrong?"

"I need to talk to you. Your roommate said you had gone for the day. Where?" His voice sounded husky over the phone.

"I had a few errands. I hurried so I could see you tonight."

"Great," Thomas said. "What kind of errands?"

Majken absorbed his suspicious remark. She checked to see if the way was clear. "I picked up an heirloom appraised at thirteen thousand from my jeweler, transferred five thousand dollars out of my savings, and was pursued by a deranged maniac across campus. How was your day?" she added.

The telephone was silent, then, "How soon can you meet me at the Student Lounge; that's halfway between dorms, if I remember?"

"I'll come as soon as I can get away. About thirty minutes." She thought she saw Marc, but decided it was her imagination. "I really missed you today."

"Did you, Mary?" he asked.

His goodbye sounded ominous to her. She waited until he hung up, then cradled the phone without a sound. She took a fast shower, changed into a fresh blouse and skirt, and brushed her hair. When she felt respectable, she hurried out of her dorm by the rear exit.

Dusk was approaching. A bitter cry startled her. Marc stepped beside her without warning. She faced a gun pointed at her midsection. "You think you're smart leaving me like that. You're not bulletproof," he sneered. "I have a few things to get off my chest." He prodded her to a remote clearing that was well hidden in the woods behind the campus. He made her kneel, then backed to the opposite side of the clearing. The gun was pointed at her head.

Majken surveyed the area. Marc stood way out of striking range. She might be able to take a hit, kill him, and possibly survive, but that would raise more serious allegations than his ranting about her drinking his blood. His gun hand trembled.

"It is your fault for making this harder than it had to be. I wanted you to return what I was giving you. All you had to do was change. Why didn't you? We could have had a perfect life together away from here. You're the most important person in my life, and you slap my face!

"Since I met you, I knew you were the one for me. My … my problems at home, or my rich and powerful father, didn't bother you. You made me feel whole and complete for the first time in my life. Like a real man. All my father wants me to do is follow in his footsteps, and I can't!"

Marc stood in the center of the clearing, playing the most important role of his life. "I want you to know, and suffer, like I've suffered all these years," he ranted.

Majken spoke his name softly. His gun hand wavered.

"You're a creature from hell!" he shouted.

She called his name again, sensuously. She had to regain control or die. She felt his humiliation, his rage, his lust. Majken moistened her lips with her tongue and held her arms toward him. "Do you still want me?" she whispered in the wind.

Marc wiped his face with his free arm, then placed both hands on the gun. The hammer clicked. "I have to kill you," he intoned. "I'm sorry."

"If you loved me, you would still want me." Majken unbuttoned the top of her blouse. "Make love to me, Marc." She urged him to look deeply in her eyes. "Love me, Marc," she chanted softly as she finished undoing the buttons. She tugged her blouse open and off her shoulders, baring them.

Marc's hands remained locked on the gun. He let her rise to her feet.

Her blouse dropped to the ground. "You want me more than anything else in the world," she coaxed.

Very slowly, Majken unfastened her bra, hooking her thumbs under the straps, and lifting it off. Her firm breasts jiggled; his gun arm lowered slightly. Not enough. She began swaying her hips, in rhythm, as she unfastened her skirt. She moaned softly, "Yes, yes. I want you." Her skirt slid past her white hips. Marc took a faltering step in her direction. Majken kicked free of her skirt and reached for him. The gun remained pointed at her chest. *Yes*, she urged mentally, *you want my body pressed against yours*. Marc took another faltering step.

Majken charged, pushing the gun downwards. It fired, then dropped from his hand into a pile of leaves. Blood spread over his left side. He collapsed to his knees, in shock. Tears trickled down his cheeks.

"Don't blam—" he gasped.

Majken lowered his body gently to the ground. His heartbeat was erratic. She knew his injuries were fatal. His skin and lips were cold and clammy, his eyes glazed. She tested the air; the shot would have been heard. Majken cradled his upper body and caressed his face. His eyes were squeezed shut.

She whispered in his ear, "You brought this on yourself. Goodbye, my love." Majken kissed his forehead gently for the last time. She retrieved her clothes and left nature to take its course.

* * *

Majken found Thomas at the Student Lounge propped over a staircase railing, watching students pass underneath. She was late. His face became rigid when she spoke his name.

"I apologize for being late," she said timidly. He refused to look up. Something was smothering him. "I finished those errands I told you about." Majken paused awkwardly. "Can things go back to normal?" she asked softly.

Thomas stared at her, she felt, as if for the first time. "Mary, if I ask you something, will you promise me to tell me the truth?" He jabbed at a flaw in the banister with his thumb.

"What I can," she promised.

"Are you sleeping with other men?" Thomas shifted on the rail to look at her, to see her squarely in the face. Majken saw betrayal pour from an open wound. This was Marc's goodbye present. Her grip on the rail tightened. She looked away from him.

"Tell me the truth," he begged. "Rumors ... about you are all over campus."

She told him part of the truth. "Yes."

He stared at her in shocked disbelief. Finally, he stammered, "I don't understand this. We meant something to each other, I thought."

Majken clasped her hands and leaned far over the rail. "I knew you would be hurt."

"Hurt!" he shouted. Other students were watching. "How did you think I'd feel when I hear you've screwed the entire campus? I don't know how things between two people work from wherever you're from; where I come from, the first thing is honesty. What really hurts – what really hurts is being led on like a stray puppy!" Thomas backed off to let some voyeurs pass by. "What you do with your life is your business," he continued, "but I wish you would have let me in on your game."

Majken hesitated, then replied softly, "My life simply is."

"Is that all you have to say?" he stammered. "We might have had at least a decent friendship, a chance if you had confided in me first. I'm sorry, Mary." Thomas bowed his head and walked away.

Majken watched him leave, unable to stop him, even with the truth.

Sirens screamed as a police car rushed Dr. Albritton to the Mercer Hospital Trauma Unit; they told him his son was seriously injured, and now was fighting for his life. The ride was fifteen minutes by ordinary car, five minutes by siren. He was perched on the edge of the backseat. He begged them to hurry. His son was dying! No, he swore, not Marc!

Albritton clawed at the handle before the police car screeched to a halt. He flew through the lobby to the intensive care unit on the fourth floor. A receptionist, the stupid woman, chased him because visiting hours were over. She gave way when the police arrived and a doctor received him. It had to be a mistake; this would be someone else's unfortunate son.

The doctor gently guided him to a glass enclosure. He saw a nurse attending to the supine figure. He noticed bottles sending vital fluids to the body, and the monitors and instrumentation. He forced himself to look at the face. The features of the young man blurred, but he knew it was Marc. The nurse made a final adjustment to a respirator, then left for the next cubicle. His son did not belong in this alien place. He touched his son's pale chest, mesmerized by its slow rise and fall.

Words that barely registered before started to focus: internal injuries and hemorrhaging; too weak to operate, but Marc was holding his own; gunshot wound into the upper left quadrant. Albritton gripped the bed frame.

"Marc, son, can you hear me?" he croaked. The figure lay cold and still. He brushed Marc's forehead and spoke in his ear. "Marc, I'm here. You're going to be all right."

Albritton cursed the lump forming in his throat. He had to be strong for Marc. The nurse returned. Someone wanted to speak to him. Albritton clenched the hospital bed and leaned over Marc. "Hold on, son," he pleaded.

A policeman was waiting for him outside intensive care. He wanted to ask questions. Albritton answered in a daze. He had last seen Marc at lunch, yesterday, in good spirits. He said he had a date. He had been a bit moody the past month, he admitted, but Marc was a good boy. The officer scribbled notes on a memo pad.

Albritton asked what had happened to his son.

"Students heard what they thought was a gunshot, they searched and found him in a thicket. We have the gun. It's registered to you."

Albritton was speechless.

"Can you tell me if Marc was especially upset or disturbed? Anything specific?" the officer asked.

"He was seeing a girl. Her name is Mary Harris, and I saw them together at a game. Marc refused to tell me much about her." He reflected. "You're not saying that my son shot himself!"

The policeman denied comment.

Unexpectedly, the white light over Marc's enclosure flashed; monitors buzzed frantically. A team of doctors and specialists were unable to save him. Albritton leaned heavily on a nurse and the hospital chaplain. Marc was gone. Slowly, the first tears pooled at the bottom of his wire-rimmed reading glasses.

Majken strolled alone, very late, through a secluded open field toward her dorm. Conflicts tore at her mind. She regretted the incident with Marc. He took his own life by forcing her, and nothing could be done about him tonight. Eventually, he might have forced her to find a permanent solution. The outcome would have been the same. She pushed him from her mind as a problem potentially worse than Marc dominated her thoughts.

People were being killed, terrorized in a manner that strongly suggested another vampyr might be in the city. The spreading fear was already making it difficult to secure new donors. She suspected the stranger she remembered from the lounge. Vampyr, or not, he was destroying her territory, and her.

Tomorrow, while human students struggled with midterm exams and worried about who to party with that night, she would find out about Marc, and use every instinct to guide her to the slasher. She knew a very deep part of her would miss seeing Thomas.

Chapter Five

Majken brushed her long hair carefully, using even uplifting strokes, brushing outward and letting it fall toward her waist. She studied her reflection in the vanity mirror. Slight creases at the corner of her eyes spoke of her troubled night. The brushing eased a light headache and the tightness at the base of her neck. The tightness had spread from her neck to engulf her chest; deep breathing produced a flutter, a sensation of falling. Perhaps she was.

The person she saw in the mirror was becoming someone she hardly recognized. She was unable to pinpoint the source of her anxiety. Brushing her hair helped her sort priorities. Her thoughts at once drifted to Thomas; that interlude was over. All those of her kind had to accept starting over. Majken continued to brush, using gentler strokes closer to the ends. Her roommate entered.

"Good morning, finally," Lisa said.

Majken perked up. "Hi, Lisa. Come back to get your books?" She pointed to a stack of books on the desk. Lisa grinned and tumbled on her bed.

"I need to take a break." She sighed. She punched her pillow and stuffed it behind her. "Did you hear the terrible news? A student shot himself yesterday. He died last night. Everybody's talking about it."

"No, I haven't heard. Who was it?" She knew he

would die; the remorse she genuinely felt was for her lack of foresight. She listened as Lisa told her the public story.

"I hope they find whatever was responsible," Lisa said.

Majken changed the subject. "Are you still having trouble with blackouts?" Lisa settled into her pillow and shifted her position for comfort.

"The doctor couldn't figure it out. He suggested I was studying too hard. Now really, me, study too hard?" She paused. "He told me to take a couple of aspirin, a month off, and call him in the morning." The girls laughed.

Lisa rubbed the row of bruises on her arm. "The doctor couldn't explain these either. He suggested maybe I blacked out and fell, and didn't remember." She smiled wryly. "Sorta reaffirms my faith in modern medicine."

It was so like her to end on a lighter side, Majken thought, as she sat next to Lisa on her bed. She gingerly touched the bruised arm, secretly taking her roommate's pulse. "Rest now," Majken suggested gently. She prompted Lisa to lie down, and adjusted the pillow under her head. Fully reclined, she kicked off her shoes and relaxed. Time to leave her alone, Majken thought.

Lisa bolted upright. "I'm scared! A lot of girls are going home because of the murders in town. And now this. I'll be a nervous wreck before I graduate!"

Her face was ashen. Majken gently prodded Lisa to lie down and regain her strength.

"From what you told me," she said softly, "this poor student's death has nothing to do with the slayings in Trenton. It's just an unfortunate coincidence."

"My parents worked too hard for me to run away," Lisa said. She rolled on her side and watched Majken remove an opaque jar from her bag. "Besides," she smiled, "my boyfriends wouldn't let me go anywhere alone." A glow returned to her face.

Majken spread a thick white cream over her skin.

Lisa crossed her legs. "What's that?" she asked.

"A moisturizer," she replied, "a sunscreen I use to protect my skin."

"Your skin's good, but what you really need is to lay out with me and work on your tan. I think you'd look great! It's not bad for checking out the guys either."

Majken laughed. Her roommate was returning to normal. "You're incorrigible, Lisa. I'll pass this time."

Majken stood between the beds and stretched

from side to side, languishing in the sensual movement. Marc's untimely death was promoting panic across campus. The task of finding and stopping the murderer the press dubbed the "slasher" was going to take considerable effort. Majken bent forward, silently reviewing her store of knowledge on the killer. Lisa started talking, but Majken relentlessly focused on the problem at hand.

The police currently believed the assailant was male, a transient that recently moved to the city. Majken agreed. The longer he stayed, the greater fear would spread in the streets, and the more free movement would be restricted. She could easily see her blood supply from potential donors in the city dry up.

Lisa rambled, "When he came out of the water, I slipped – Mary," she said, "are you listening?"

Majken frowned slightly. "I'm sorry, Lisa. I guess I was distracted."

"How are you and Tommy getting along?"

Majken slowly reached for her shoulder bag. "It's time I was going," she said absently. Even Lisa could see it, she thought. "Not very well," she said stiffly.

"Things may work out," Lisa offered hopefully.

"They may," she said quietly as she stood by the door.

Majken smiled as her roommate snuggled in for a brief nap. She assured herself that Lisa would recover with extra peace and quiet, and left the dorm.

A hot, early morning sun greeted Thomas lying awake face up on his bed. He had slept fitfully. He repeated to himself for the millionth time, that a relationship had to be built on mutual trust and communication. So far, her only communication had been her disastrous admission of guilt. He did the right thing, he assured himself, by demanding that she explain.

It was hard not to think about her. So much of her previously filled his life.

Thomas flung the bed covers off; the motion released the mounting tension in his shoulders and back. It felt good to move. He knew he could not stay in bed all day, especially on exam day. Phillip had given up on him and was long gone. Thomas pulled out of bed and stumbled to the showers to get his circulation going, he hoped.

He wished he knew where he had gone wrong. He found himself wishing that she would call, or maybe try to see him. Only a fool would try to reconcile a gap as big as the Grand Canyon. Then let him be a fool. Remorse stabbed very deeply as their hopelessly deadlocked situation came into focus. She was in trouble, he realized. He turned the water as hot as it would go.

Two freshmen stood in Thomas' way to his room. One of them called him.

"Hey, Kline. Don't you have anything better to do than sleep late?"

Thomas watched him coolly. "Yeah, like what?"

"Let's leave grouchy alone," the other student chimed in. "I hear he's got enough to worry about." He giggled.

Thomas resisted the urge to punch that silly smirk down his throat. When he pushed past the freshmen, the second boy pulled on his arm.

"Kline," he said lowly, "I heard your lady likes to spread it around." The other made obscene gestures. "Think you can set us up with a date?" Both laughed. Thomas jerked free and ignored their taunts. They called after him in unison, "Got laid yet, Kline?"

Thomas slammed the door to his room; his ears were burning with their laughter. He hit the wall, wishing it were two feet thick, and spun away. "What do they know?" he swore bitterly.

Thomas imagined it was going to be a long day. *Hell*, he thought, *it's going to be a long year!*

* * *

Dr. Albritton rubbed gritty eyes as he rested against one of the many trees lining the path to a familiar white brick building marked Campus Security. He smoothed his rumpled suit. He sought the support of his friend, Chief Baggetta. He entered the headquarters silently. The lovely dispatcher glanced up from her console, then nudged Baggetta.

"Daniel, what are you doing here?" Baggetta dropped the report he was studying and guided his friend's arm.

"Vincent, I need to talk. Can we go into your office?" The two older men entered a compact, usually cluttered office. Physically, Baggetta towered over Albritton. His own hair had turned white instead of silver gray. He was always clean shaven.

"My son is gone," Albritton said flatly, before Baggetta could sit down. "I had a long unproductive discussion with the Trenton police. The doctors are saying that Marc's ... body was riddled with needle marks and cuts. They think," he paused to wipe his face with a damp handkerchief, "they're suggesting he was a drug addict, although nothing showed up in his blood work, and had the gall to say his murder was suicide!"

"We are all very sorry to hear about Marc's death," Baggetta said calmly.

"God, Vincent, the police have already made up their minds," he wailed. "I knew my son. I have to know what happened to Marc; will you help me please?"

Albritton met his friend's square, direct gaze.

"What are the police doing?"

"They are planning to talk to Marc's friends and classmates. Marc was also very evasive about a girl. I think I know who she is because I saw them sneaking off from last week's game. Her name is Mary Harris, a history major. I know my son could not commit suicide."

Baggetta copied the name on a memo pad and studied it. "She doesn't stand out in my mind. Forgive me, Daniel, but what makes you think this girl was involved?"

"I have no proof," he admitted, "but she is the only clue I have to Marc's behavior recently. All I ask you to do, is make your own inquiry. At least, then I can be at peace with my son." Albritton crumpled with grief. Baggetta placed a massive arm around his friend.

Albritton spoke very low. "One more thing, Vincent. I can't go home."

"Say no more, Daniel, say no more."

* * *

Majken smiled at the reaction of her history instructor when she asked to take today's scheduled exam early. As soon as possible, she begged, to be free for an interview for a part-time job. Working students were near and dear to any teacher's heart. He agreed to let her take the exam in his office in an hour, giving him time to run off copies. Fifty minutes to kill.

As she entered the library, two uniformed policemen approached her and identified themselves. She stepped to a secluded corner. They gathered general background information first, the type that could be easily verified by the registrar. She sensed a setup, and wondered how these men knew her by sight. The library clerk smiled at her. *Of course*, she thought, *the library staff pointed me out.*

"How long have you known Marc Albritton?" one of them asked.

A light turned on for her. "I think I saw him a few times on campus," she replied hesitantly.

The policemen pressed her for specific details, such as the last time she spoke to him, how well she knew Marc, whether they dated, and why not. Majken explained that she had a boyfriend and Marc was too arrogant for her taste. They concluded the interrogation, saying it was a routine procedure, and thanked her for her time. Majken was decidedly relieved to see them go.

Majken vowed to alter her daytime routine more as she passed the main desk. She felt safe, for now. But that the police spoke to her at all meant someone had seen her in Marc's company. The unsettling fact refused to go away. Majken descended a seldom used set of stairs to the archive section in the basement. This section of the library was a frequent point of refuge during the high time of the day. Her time in the library completed her student illusion; it was also private. The librarian let her research undisturbed and very few people came down there.

She let her mind and body wander free through the aisles. It was impossible to maintain intense levels of concentration and worry. Here, she floated from shelf to shelf. Majken removed an old volume carefully and set it on a small table. The thick book was dusty with cracked bindings and yellowed, weathered pages. But it survived, and while she held it she felt more whole.

Her exam took her nearly an hour to finish. The next to last set of questions dealt with the extremes of wealth and poverty in pre-industrial England. Her mind was seeking the proper conclusions that would unlock the killer's pattern. His actions appeared random, young or old, male or female, city or park. He would try to cover his trail and make sure his actions were unpredictable.

It struck her suddenly – he was using a "switch" pattern, a means of alternating victims and locations. She had him. Majken turned in her paper without a moment to lose. The last reported slaying was in the park. He would strike in the city with possibly a much younger or much older victim. An old Negro couple had been killed. Younger children in the city? she thought.

Majken ran. Would he rotate counterclockwise or clockwise from the city park? A wrong guess would place her on the opposite side of Trenton. She chose clockwise. She remembered to bring extra cash and change of clothes. Between her dorm and the bus, she realized she had forgotten to complete her exam. She reached the early afternoon city-bound shuttle barely in time.

Thomas was filled with apprehension as he inched closer to the class where his ex-girlfriend would be taking her history midterm. He chided himself for coming, still, he wanted to at least see her. The class was full; his stomach sank between his knees when he saw her chair on the second row was empty.

Where could she be?

Several students were staring at him, so he turned away from the door. He glanced inside again. A student turned in his paper and started to leave. Thomas wanted answers. "Hold up," Thomas called.

The student stopped and faced him. Thomas pointed through the glass pane. "Do you know the girl that usually sits on the second row, right there?"

He stared blankly at the empty seat.

"Her?" the student repeated. "I know her. Why?"

"I wanted to speak to her. Do you know where she is?"

"Funny you should ask about her," the young man said. "It's the weirdest thing. I saw her running across campus as fast as she could go."

"When?" Thomas sputtered.

"Right before class." The student examined Thomas. "Do you know her? Where was she going in such a hurry?"

Thomas frowned. "I thought I knew her. I don't see how she could afford to miss her exam, though?"

"She took it early, I guess. Our instructor came into class, all smiles as usual, and asked if we were ready. He added, we should be ready because one student took the test early. Had to be her."

The student went his way. Instead of answers,

he had found questions. He was more confused, and still worried. He did learn one important fact. His decision to see her made him happier than he had been all day. Thomas decided he had to look on her face once more.

Dusk. Majken wearily crossed a street, like the myriad of identical streets crossed that afternoon. City blocks and houses began to run together. She sensed he would wait until dusk. He liked to kill at twilight.

He was in the area; she felt him. To prepare, she had spent much of her afternoon, the remaining daylight hours, scouring the city by transit, seeking places a vampyr on the run might hide or be seeking temporary shelter. It was too much to hope that the slasher would politely decide to leave. Several potential locations refreshed themselves in her memory. She even rested. The bus windows were adequately tinted, comfortable, and close to her sunlight tolerance.

Majken searched three adjacent neighborhoods hoping the vague impression she briefly had at the lounge would return. It was an extremely long shot to tune into his vibrations, like an identical tuning fork. If he turned out to be human, a mentally deranged human, she planned to gut him with his own weapon. The police would find another slasher victim, and that would be that. The paranoia would die in less than a month.

If he was of her kind, she planned to convince him to leave politely, if possible. His actions showed a blatant disregard for life, human or vampyric. She assumed he was dangerous. As a weapon of last resort, she planned to use an extremely fast and subtle form of hypnotism. Females of her kind could temporarily influence males, seeming to work through the eyes, but penetrating much deeper. The duration of control varied depending on the will, physical condition, and environment of the subject. An older, more experienced vampyr could kill her, she thought.

Majken examined her surroundings: an occasional car; an old man watched her from his porch; very few people were on the street after dark. The streetlamp overhead buzzed. She heard the scratching sounds of a woman walking her dog. In many ways adapting to the twentieth century restricted her life in more ways than in her day. She had much to overcome, like driving an automobile. The engines frightened her. It was an unconscious fear, and even the powerful diesel engine on the bus made her tense at times. She carefully watched how Thomas drove. He made it look so effortless.

From several blocks away came the faint sounds of merriment and the cheering of tiny voices; children were playing in the street. The woman with the dog entered her home. Majken started toward the children. She ignored the foreboding impression that the slasher may have already struck in a different part of the city. The sounds of play became more distinct, and she could distinguish a bouncing ball. Car headlights and streetlights had been on for twenty minutes. It was now fully night. Majken hurried, crossing the street in the middle of the block.

A patrol car pulled behind her. "Hey," a man's voice called. Majken wheeled about. A policeman stepped out of his car. "We've been watching you for the last fifteen minutes. It isn't safe for a woman to wander the streets at night. Would you like an escort home?" The man asked politely.

Majken smiled and replied, "No, thank you. I came to visit a friend and had a little trouble finding his place, but I know which way to go now."

The officer glanced at his partner behind the wheel. "You should not be on the streets alone," he repeated more forcefully. He closed his car door, then shone a flashlight in Majken's face.

She recoiled involuntarily.

* * *

The game was ending as boys became tired and went home. Parents gathered them by twos and threes to take them to nourishing meals and warm, safe beds. Night advanced. John melted invisibly into the deep shadows between neighboring houses, observing, waiting for opportunity, for no witnesses. Three boys remained. The boy closest to him had short sandy hair and large brown eyes. He played recklessly in and out of the street, while straining to outplay a larger, chubby kid throwing the ball from the corner of the block. A third kid watched. The chubby kid bounced the ball hard, making it fly into a hedge running from a house to the sidewalk.

John moved. The boy screamed at his playmates that it was his ball. The boy's sneakers squeaked on the pavement as he jumped. His shirt was ripped on the sleeve. John noticed an old ragged tear. He obviously did not have a conscientious mother to sew his shirt. John swiftly retrieved the ball and bent low. The boy came to the hedge, pulling it apart with his small hands. He gasped in surprise.

"Is this your ball?" John spoke low and held the ball up. He remained crouched, ready. The boy's friends jeered at him from a distance.

"Throw it here," the boy asked. "It's mine." His face turned pink to red.

John spun the ball beneath his hand on the grass. "I never had a ball to play with. I'll buy it from you." The boy pleaded for his ball. "I don't see a name on it," he taunted. He twirled the ball temptingly close, then smashed it under his hand. "What is your name?"

The boy looked hurriedly over the hedge that was as tall as he was. His friends were leaving. John smiled as the boy stepped forward bravely, but remained several yards away from this strange man.

John asked him again, kindly, what his name was.

"My friends call me Sandy. Will you let me have it now?" He stomped a foot closer.

"How much will you take for it?" John said. "Your parents could buy you a dozen with what I give you."

Sandy hesitated. "I'm not supposed to talk to strangers," he said. "I want my ball, mister!"

John smiled generously in the dim light and pulled a bill from his pocket. He waved a twenty over the ball like a magic wand, and watched his victim's resolve weaken. The boy grabbed for the ball. John held the ball firmly to the grass and reached for his knife in his belt.

"Now!" exploded as a hiss from clenched teeth.

A force caught him, knocking him off balance. He felt the weight of another body; he kicked savagely as he rolled over. He faced his opponent – a woman. She lay stunned on her back. The kid chased his ball into the street, narrowly missing a car as he screamed for help.

He angrily clenched both fists and swung for the woman's head. She blocked it. She was too fast and strong to be human. Confusion swept through him. In a fraction of a second, he was running and disappeared across the street. He looked back at a police car led by a frantic little boy. The woman had disappeared.

Majken huddled in a cramped dark space that smelled of oil and rubber. Survival had taken precedence over following the killer, and she had lost him. He was a vampyr and the man she suspected from the lounge. Her exit had to be immediate. Sprinting behind the nearest moving car, she dug her fingers between metal and snapped the trunk lock with a heave, then curled safely inside. She pulled the trunk closed while leaving enough space to see the red and blue flashing lights.

Good thing it was a Cadillac.

As best as she could tell, the car was heading to-

ward the central expressway. Majken sprang lightly out of the trunk when the car stopped at a light.
The driver gawked in his mirror as she slammed
the trunk. She waved at the poor man, and walked
briskly away.

Her evening went badly. From now on, the slasher would be on guard. He got a good look at her, too.
Finding him a second time would be difficult, and
the first time had not been easy. The persistent policeman gave up when she insisted she was only a
few blocks from her destination. His partner told
him they had more important things to do. The man
let her off with a warning to be off the streets by
the time they circled back. She was surprised they
did not check her ID. Maybe they only had orders to
seize and harass strange men.

She ran across the grass lawn, and changing tactics, climbed from wooden privacy fence to rooftop
for an overview of the street. The boy had taken too
long to recover his ball. She had arrived on the scene
barely in time.

Majken took stock of her condition. Her personal
need for nourishment rose higher. She called for a
cab to take her to the largest city hospital where she
planned to call on a few patients. The hospital was
across town. Majken noticed her skirt had a thick oil

stain over her hip. Her evening was looking up. At least she had held on to her supplies and change of clothes, securely strapped around her body.

She entered through the visitor's entrance, and stopping to splash her face with water in the washroom, successfully passed the attendant in the lobby for the intensive care waiting room. When unobserved, she entered the employee locker room and changed into blue scrubs, secured her ID and white nurse's cap from her bag. Ten rooms later, she had collected a pocketful of Vacutainer tubes filled with precious blood. She went up to the fifth floor. A key admitted her to a private office. She locked the door and turned on the desk lamp. The tubes clattered in her bag when she placed it on the desk. It paid, she thought sarcastically, to break down and cry in a doctor's office.

Majken settled down to enjoy her meal in privacy.

John loathed humans, for their weaknesses and their freedom, but found them useful when faced with special circumstances. He knew most humans craved money. He sought the indigent population – men of the back alleys and predators of their own kind – and knew he could count on them to do his bidding.

His anger increased with each step. The presence of another vampyr threatened him and forced him to move before he wanted. Perhaps, he thought, she could be manipulated and used to serve his needs. Otherwise, she must be destroyed. John knew how to destroy his own kind; she would not sway him.

Four men lounged recklessly outside a plaster-torn building. A stiff breeze carried the sweltering temperature and only hardened or unfeeling souls would wander the city on such a night. John instructed them briefly, speaking to them no longer than absolutely necessary. He explained simply, some of them were as children, and paid them half in advance.

A short, puny man with long skinny arms clamored for his attention. Large and protruding yellow teeth and squinting eyes contorted his features. He was bolder than the rest and eager to serve his new master. John rewarded his enthusiasm with an extra fifty as an example to the others and appointed him the important task of reporting in person when the task was done. Any vampyr's home territory was their greatest strength or weakness. He instructed the men on where to wait, and departed.

With the unpleasant task done, John prepared for his next move. His need to consume his nightly ration surged; that the female had delayed his feed-ing angered him greatly. He promptly found a store with the supplies he desired, and barely managed to prop his foot in the door before the owner switched the sign and locked up for the night. A few custom-ers remained in the store. John assured the owner that he would finish quickly.

The merchant, balding, prematurely gray, and bent from years of stooping to the lowest shelves wore half-spectacles and coveralls to complete his down-home country image. The man extended his hand and introduced himself as Mr. Goodson. John shook his hand without undue pressure, and charged inside. The merchant flipped the sign and locked the door, then waited on a customer ready to leave.

John took his time as he picked over the entire store waiting on the remaining customer to leave. He suspected the merchant was the last employee to remain at the end of the day. The man soon hobbled after John and asked how long he intended to shop. The man's incessant banter about camping and sports, obviously an endearing quality to his regular customers, irritated John as he collected his supplies: tent stakes, rope, kerosene and butane lighters, a thick ground cloth, and other oddities. Mr. Goodson nervously eyed the clock at eleven past eight and continued to rattle off a list of the best fishin' spots. John picked up a medium backpack to store his supplies in and threw the items on the counter.

The owner tallied his purchase, probably wishing a police car would suddenly appear outside his store. The man licked his dry lips and hurried. John perused a display of cutlery. The array of razor-sharp steel attracted his interest. He knew he could rip a body open with his bare hands, but blades were more efficient. His right arm trembled with a familiar reflex; he could see rich dark blood spurting from a cut. Mr. Goodson asked him if there would be anything else. John faced him with a dark penetrating stare, silencing the buffoon. He was missing an important item, but found it in a bin next to camping stoves.

He needed a machete, and picked up a black burnished blade and hefted it. Its handle was a cheap plastic, an imitation ivory. This he would use. It was a cruel weapon. Centuries taught cruelty. For an instant, he was again stretched, helpless on the rolling deck, receiving stinging lashes for the minor infraction of stealing a piece of bread. The foredeck was stained crimson, and rightly feared. The sea that was his birthplace was now far, far away.

John purchased the machete with the rest of his

supplies. The merchant took his money with trembling hands and locked the door firmly behind him. He smiled at the merchant through the window, who would remember the fear for a very long time. His victim tonight must serve a dual purpose, being in a place close to his former retreat.

His victim tonight would be the bait.

Majken left the borrowed office well before five in the morning with no trace of her visit. Plush carpet in the vestibule cushioned her steps. She had rested and felt refreshed in her spare clean dress, a satiny rose-colored floral. Searching Trenton all night would have been useless without a clue to the other vampyr's hideout, his home territory. Majken entered the deserted hallway silently and took the nearest elevator to the ground floor, to go to the morgue.

Police procedures varied from city to city, but when a body was found in suspect circumstances, as had the slasher victims, it would be taken to the medical examiner's office. A grapevine stretched from ambulance drivers to the chief of police. She hoped to obtain the valuable information she wanted without making a formal request to the police. The elevator opened and a weary nurse passed dolefully by with a medicine cart. She paused to read the floor plan mounted in a glass frame on the pastel wall, especially the exits. She waited until the nurse entered a room, then headed for her destination.

She remembered the shock on the slasher's face when he realized she was one of his kind and in his territory. And in shock, he might make an error in judgment, and choose his next victims poorly. His kill pattern was broken, she thought morosely. Otherwise, an anonymous tip on a suspicious man would cover him with police. Capturing or killing him would require many lives, thus placing the responsibility squarely on her shoulders.

A security guard nodded politely as she passed his station. No one tried to stop her, yet.

Majken turned a final corner, and was there. She steadied herself before entering the restricted area. The staff would be a minimum, she fervently hoped, and went inside. Her heels made muted clicks on the tile, the long high-intensity fluorescent fixtures contrasted with the dimmer hospital hallways. A silent approach was impossible. The attendant looked up from reading his paper.

"Can I help you?" a young man asked.

"I don't know," Majken replied, uncertainty in her voice. "Where am I?" She swayed past his desk and managed to glimpse the work area in the next room before sitting on the edge of the desk. Silky fabric clung to her thigh.

"You're in pathology, the morgue. It's a restricted area."

"I'm sorry, I didn't mean to intrude." Majken let her body relax and slip on the desk. "It must get pretty creepy staying down here alone with dead people all night."

"This time of night, no one comes down here, even by accident. I've worked here for over a year and they still keep me on the graveyard shift." He examined Majken closely and offered his hand. "My name is Michael."

"My name is Marianne. What sort of work is done here?" she asked.

Michael stood up and moved between her and the swinging steel doors. "I'm not supposed to allow visitors down here." He stepped aside and gestured to the work area. "This is where patients are brought so doctors can figure out exactly why they died. I hope to be a pathologist someday."

"Is it hard to be a pathologist?"

"It sure is." He beamed with pride. "It takes seven years, including internship and studying in your area of specialization."

Majken smiled in return. "One of my uncles at home is a pathologist, or was. He worked for the police for a long time. They'd bring him bodies, decayed or torn apart, and expect him to determine how and when they died." She crossed her arms tightly and shivered. "I could never do a job like that."

"It's not easy, but it has to be done." He hesitated a moment. "Do you live in the city?"

Majken tensed the muscles of her face. "I came to visit my girlfriend. No sooner do I get here when this man assaults her. He tried to cut her with a knife. She's shook up pretty bad." Majken pursed her lips sorrowfully, then bowed her head. "Trouble follows me wherever I go. I came for a visit, and look where she ends up." She sensed the attendant feeling sorry for her, and starting to open up. She confronted Michael, calling his name and looking deeply into his eyes, then softly asked, "How often does this kind of thing happen in the city?"

The young attendant stammered, "I, uh," Michael composed himself.

"We have a decent city. This weird stuff started about three weeks ago. Now, it's all we can do to figure out what's going on." He restlessly paced around Majken and propped himself against the wall. "Our department has several specialists on loan to the police until they manage to round up the slasher. The newspapers call him that. We've gotten bodies coming and going; he must kill a dozen people a week!"

Majken led the distraught young man to his chair, whispering reassurances that the culprit would surely make a fatal mistake soon. She pressed him for information about where the latest victims had been found. He told her the city parks and a district west of downtown. Majken reasoned: The parks, with its several acres of bordered woodland would make it easy to strike and slip away unnoticed; the other place was a rundown neighborhood with many abandoned houses, closed factories, and numerous warehouses along the rim for shelter.

Michael expressed sympathy for her injured friend and asked if she would be in town a while longer. She exchanged a fictitious address and telephone number with him. He lived within a block of the hospital, she noted. She thanked him for talking to her and excused herself, but left the door open to all manner of possibilities. He could spend the greater part of his shift thinking about them.

Chapter Six

Majken waited patiently on a curb as the pale blue skies turned purple; the invading darkness that shortened human perceptions heightened hers. She idly watched black smoke escape from a chimney across the street. Her ride, a taxi she had hired to tour the west side most of the day, was past due. Her driver was a husky black veteran in his late thirties, owner of Rawls Taxi Service, Clifton Burnum Rawls himself. She had paid him well for two full days, in advance. He claimed to know the central west side and abandoned factories like the back of his hand.

She guessed C.B. was a curious man. He waited and pumped a set of hand weights while she spoke to several homeowners and a number of men that worked the warehouses. She decided to concentrate here because the parks were filled with police decoys. This area was a blight; the kind of place he would very likely come.

The neighborhood rule was nobody sees nothing. She used the pretext of searching for her wandering husband; a man that had deserted her and the baby, and gave the other vampyr's description. At midday, a lone Hispanic worker broke the thick silence to tell her he saw a man as she described in a loft of a certain warehouse high above, but refused to take her there because the man had given him the evil eye.

He clutched a bag of white powder strung around his neck with a cord and shook it ceremoniously.

C.B. was probably dying to know what she was doing. He kept his mouth shut, having lived in this neighborhood a long time.

They drove and searched until late afternoon. She knew it was time for a break when he complained about not eating all day. Majken released him to go home and have an early supper with his family. She used the time to wire an out-of-town bank for extra funds. He should have been back by now, she thought. On cue, a custom black taxi sped around the block and screeched to a halt inches from the curb.

C.B. opened the door for her. "How are you this evening, miss?" he said with a southern drawl. Majken greeted him and slid into a brown vinyl upholstered interior. He closed her door, ran around the front and bounced on a formerly-white fur that padded his backside, then twisted over the front seat to face her. "I've been listening all day like you asked me to. Never heard a call for the coroner or a ten-eighty-nine. I'd be in a lot of trouble if the police found out I have this thing rigged under my dash. You promised not to tell, right?"

Majken reassured him and stuffed her shoulder

bag in the floorboard, out of sight.

Her driver started the car. "I can't figure out why you want to ride all over west side. Surely, you ain't thinking about living there; your skin's too white. Now, you're wantin' to go back to the worst place in the city after dark." C.B. squinted when he looked over the seat for confirmation. "Sure I can't talk you outta this fool idea?"

"Mr. Rawls," Majken said politely, "I have to go there tonight." She heard him mutter under his breath that she was the strangest detective he knew, but she never pretended to be connected with the police. She idly examined the homes they passed for signs of life and enjoyed the spreading twilight. At dusk, the other vampyr would strike somewhere in the city. She planned to find his hideout and be waiting on his return. Immediately after feeding, he should be easier to manage. She probed her own need; she could wait for hours yet.

When they arrived at the warehouse, several workers were still at a dock unloading a late truck. Majken considered the long brick structure. Dirty windows, almost opaque, circled the top half of the building.

She asked C.B. to douse the lights and drive to the rear of the building. She rolled down her window to test for a scent and look for traces of blood in the grass. She stopped him when she saw a crease in the rear metal door, like someone had recently forced it open. She got out and told C.B. to drive to the front and wait. It was becoming fully dark now and he protested. She pulled the red metal door; the door gave easily, like the internal lock bolt had been sheared.

Majken ducked inside and immediately touched a metal ladder ascending to a platform overhead. She started to climb cautiously.

She reached the loft and noiselessly pulled herself over the edge. The inner sanctuary was pitch-black. She knelt and scanned the platform. A squeaking roof fan rattled somewhere in the distance. The loft was filthy with shredded debris and grime, except for an area the length of a man's body in the center. It took minutes to search the entire platform. She found only pieces of wax where candles had been burned. The air smelled of death. She climbed down and decided to watch from the front of the warehouse. Huge stacked crates lined her passage. She listened. Everything had become silent.

C.B. knew something was wrong when the men at the truck dropped what they were carrying and disappeared inside. He groaned and fidgeted with the ignition keys. There was going to be trouble, deep trouble. Every street sense told him to stay out of it. He had a wife, a boy wanting to go to college, and three more kids at home. He was not about to stick his nose in someone else's business. But, she paid him well – for taxi service, he told himself. He could lose it all just to help an unarmed woman fight seven or eight thugs alone in a warehouse at night, smack in the middle of a crime-ridden neighborhood. He laughed nervously, weakly, as he flicked on his radio and tuned it to the emergency channel. He tapped the mike and clicked it, waiting for the unit to warm up. He held it close to his mouth, to whisper, fearing they might hear him call the police. *Don't get involved*, screamed from his innards. Abruptly, the truck pulled away and the dock workers closed the loading bay. C.B. dropped the mike and gunned his engine. The police would never arrive in time.

A man of short stature, hidden partially in the shadows, smiled wolfishly upon seeing the woman described by his new employer enter the warehouse alone. He had predicted she would come, eventually, and they were instructed to prepare and wait. She was a looker, too. He manned a position of authority, next to the switches. Men awaited his command; he felt a thrill, a rush of power. The stranger had recognized his potential, and made it clear he rewarded a person who pleased him. His parents cursed him by letting him be born dwarfish and naming him Edgar. Tonight, all will change, he vowed.

Edgar cackled gleefully. His stubby fingers sweated on the all important levers. The men in his charge moved into positions overhead, waiting on top of stacks. There was no way for them to miss; he had followed his employer's instructions to the letter. He also warned them that she was extremely dangerous, and was adamant about no man trying to attack her directly. The men had scoffed at the idea that this broad was capable of killing them all. They moved at his unspoken command. Edgar smiled. He would move high in the stranger's organization.

Majken tensed on hearing the massive garage-type door close. Her instincts warned her of a menace and she knew she could not exit the way she had come in. A glimmer of light filtered through a dirty window at the front of the building so she could see the entrance. She ran through the dark bewildering labyrinth, then entered a large rectangular clearing. A shoe scuffed the concrete floor in front of her.

Suddenly, all overhead lights flared on. Majken froze and crouched in the clearing. A disembodied voice yelled *run*, and she heard a steel cable whip the air. A massive crate fell. She dove with her arm over her face for the nearest passage and felt a splintering crash at her heels. A man wielding a heavy oak board swung madly for her head. She dodged; the weapon grazed her shoulder. She reached his throat before he regained his balance, squeezed, and smashed his head into a crate. Her next assailant looked stunned to see her miraculous escape, and tried to grapple her barehanded. She met him, sidestepped, and shoved him into the smashed crate. He fell, unconscious.

C.B. knew he had done it now by stumbling into a private war. He did not like the odds. Men were screaming and cursing ahead. He had shouted on impulse when he had seen the crate dropping, but he doubted that she lived. A searing pain ripped through his right biceps. A man struck him with a board with nails driven through the end. He screamed, spun around, and jerked on the thug's arm. The weapon splattered on the floor when C.B. kicked him solidly in the groin. Dizzy from the exertion, he eased himself to the floor. Shadows were jumping off high stacks and running. He was a goner, he thought, as surely as the woman he had risked his life for lay crushed under a heavy crate.

Majken ran the winding corridors. The bulk of a body lay before her. She sprinted and jumped. The body groaned and rolled over. Her driver? She dragged him to his car, climbed in the front seat with him, and turned his key in the ignition. His right arm collapsed limply on the fur; his wounds reopened. Majken shook him awake and prompted him to drive. She placed the car in gear. C.B. grimaced as they pulled over a curb into the street, but drove as she directed him, finally stopping in an empty parking lot to recover.

Majken rested her head on the dash and cradled the torn fabric of her dress in her lap. "I think we've done enough for one day," she said. Her exposed shoulder was badly blistered. The strain of battle brought twinges of her blood need to the surface.

The man next to her started to laugh, then roared. He told her nothing was worth what she put him through. When she turned and looked at him, the fresh blood she needed was pouring between his fingers. She pulled on his injured arm. He cried in pain as blood flowed from torn skin. She drank while he struggled, and finally slumped on the steering wheel. His eyes were half-closed when he mumbled, "Why?"

Majken stopped drinking to feel her tissues absorb the nourishment. She propped the man that had helped save her life in his seat; his skin was cool, but his pulse was regular. He was strong and would survive.

She retrieved her bag and placed a dressing on his arm, reinforcing it with white gauze. The bleeding slowed. Majken thanked him for helping her and gave him their current address. His home was nearby and she asked if he could drive the remainder alone. He nodded. Majken started to get out of his taxi. Her dress was ruined. She needed a cover-up. C.B. told her he kept a blanket in the trunk for cold December mornings.

She borrowed it, wrapping it around her as a shawl. She reached through the driver's window and started his car. The day had been eventful. She told him his services would not be needed for the second day. Before he pulled away, Majken leaned through the window, kissed his forehead in thanks, and told him, "Maybe I'm a vampyr." He looked ready to believe her.

Majken stood in the parking lot until he disappeared from sight. Normally, her situation would be desperate. Not this time, she mused. She crossed the street and entered a familiar complex. It was her reserve city apartment last used when she was here with Marc. The manager and a few other people gaped at her entrance. She ignored them. A key fit the lock. She crawled to bed, and slipped from consciousness.

The weasely man ran to his dilapidated Plymouth, rubbing his calloused hands, and chuckling in relief. Though the men had failed and the woman survived, all was not lost. He dreaded facing the stranger empty handed. He had tailed them here, and followed the woman to those apartments. That the cabbie was gone was unimportant. It was the woman his employer wanted.

Edgar wiped his hands on his greasy pants, started his car, and wondered if he should stay or go. A knot of fear made it hard for him to catch his breath. The man had a stare that put a chill straight through him. But all was not lost. Surely, his employer would give him a little reward for finding where she lived.

Majken awoke in a few hours after her comatose condition had passed, then showered and settled in for a normal rest. Before sunrise, she paid Michael another visit and learned no new victims had been found. She retreated when he asked her why she wanted to know so much about the killer. She returned to the apartment for the last time. Marc's ghost permeated the bed, the floor, the entire place. She thought it best to close it and choose a different residence later.

Returning to campus raised feelings of peace. The other's game of cat and mouse limited her scope of alternatives. She realized if it came to a duel, it must be at a place away from the city. When blessed night finally came, she set out to stroll familiar paths; the coolness was refreshing compared to the steamy city streets. Since their first encounter, the impressions she had absorbed had come into sharper focus. Beyond his contempt for the living lay fertile, untouched soil. If she failed again, he would try to kill her.

Students dotted the landscape, but stayed near buildings and artificial illumination. A palpable presence of fear, unseen in superficial appearances, was everywhere. Majken could take it no longer. She had to be alone, and was. A slight breeze stirred the trees and followed her to a remote bench, well hidden by foliage and a near building. It was a place for lovers.

She lay flat on the bench to watch swaying leaves of a large oak tree and let the stress drain from her body, like great drops of blood, until her sharp hearing picked up a suspicious sound. Seeing nothing, she lay back down. The rustling branches were trying to tell her something, to warn her. She sat up again at the sound of crunching gravel. Someone was coming. Thomas!

"This is nice. I found you." His approach was friendly.

Majken gasped, "How did you know where to find me?"

"You like it here." He made no attempt to sit next to her. The jacket he wore made him look imposing. Her arms were bare. "I missed you," he said weakly. "I hardly gave you a chance, and I'm sorry."

"I'm the one that should apologize. I never gave you the credit that you might understand my condition." Majken made a place for him to sit, if he chose to. "I missed you, too."

Thomas sat apart from her. "I'm willing to give us another chance if you tell me what's wrong. I honestly care about you, or I wouldn't have come back."

Majken moved closer, wanting him. She abruptly leaned forward when he placed his arm over her injured shoulder. He drew back. She hastily told him about her shoulder and let him lift the neck of her blouse to see. Even in dim light, the red welt was visible. He put his arm around her waist. Naturally, he wanted to know how it happened.

She hesitated, deciding that if she told him even part of the warehouse incident, he would think she was lying. Caught again. She eventually explained that a board from a scaffolding fell and hit her. She refused to give details. Thomas was dumbfounded, then absently slipped his jacket over her, gently. "Is that all you have to say?" he asked.

Majken slid next to him. "No," she answered. She kissed him deeply, passionately. Part of her life seemed to fall back into place, as if it had always belonged there. "I've been quite alone without your company." He asked her what kind of trouble she was in. She cuddled closer. "Nothing a few hundred kilometers wouldn't cure."

As she smiled, she became aware of a sensation of warmth in her cheeks. Thomas looked puzzled. She kissed him again to take his mind off what she had said and because she wanted to.

Thomas came up for air, returned her embrace, then took a moment to gaze at her. "You know, Mary," he said, "I do love you."

Majken gasped because it had been staring her in

the face all the time. Her eyes burned with an inner, secret flame. He drew something from the depths of her soul with that kiss. Something deep had come to the surface. She caressed his face, leaving much unsaid.

As Majken held him tightly, she felt dangerous undercurrents of conflicting needs. In her arms, she saw them embracing; she saw herself holding him from behind, cutting the carotid artery in his neck, and drinking. It must not happen! she swore. No! She tried to push him away, but found she could not.

Soon, she let him escort her to her dorm. He told her how happy he was that they had a new beginning. They walked arm in arm from the idyllic spot, promising to meet in the morning. She was eager to feed.

Nearby, overhead, the other vampyr clung to the side of the building, watching his enemy. He had followed her from the city. The fool had given him the apartment address, and for doing that much right he had died quickly. John knew the apartment was too small and exclusive to meet a vampyr's blood needs. She would have to die for her interference. First, she would pay. With an easy grace, John jumped to the ground. The sound made a soft thud on the grass. She was gone.

* * *

Majken thrilled to the thought that Thomas still wanted her. It was important that they have a chance. She lingered on the dorm steps, tuned to the sparkling night. Thomas confessed some of his trials he had endured on her behalf during their walk. This bothered her, but there was more. The trees swayed with the wind high above the sleeping campus; an unseen impression ripped her apart, matching her incessant need for fresh blood. She paused on the dorm steps, then hurried inside for a nocturnal visit to a friend's room.

John prowled the expansive campus grounds, hoping to soon find a human foolish enough to be out late, alone. He saw and heard a man approaching through the darkness. With panther-like strength, he jumped into the low branches of a tree and hid as the man came closer. The human wore the tan uniform of some kind of patrol. That the man was short and fat prevented John from killing him and taking his uniform. A radio crackled with static as the patrol passed underneath. He would give them a merry chase another night. A man was not the right victim; he wanted a young woman. He jumped down and ran in the direction the security man had come.

He was soon rewarded when a car entered a student parking lot with the headlights off, as if trying to sneak in. Like sharks that learned to follow the sounds of great cannon blasts in sea battles, he had learned to follow the sounds of a solitary car. That sound usually meant food. He lurked in the shadows about a hundred yards away. He saw a boy and a girl. The car parked and the silhouettes embraced. The girl got out and sauntered to the driver's side.

John heard faint strains of music as her boyfriend rolled down his window. The girl was well-dressed in a pale green gown that highlighted her auburn tresses. He appreciated the voluptuous curves beneath her gown, and the driver that brought her home late. Even better, she insisted she would be able to make it to her residence unattended. Her boyfriend drove away, leaving her defenseless and alone.

He slipped his knife out of its sheath and into his belt for quick access. The girl hurried down the sidewalk, careful to stay well in the light. He could charge across the grass, but not before being seen. John edged closer to his intended victim and estimated her destination to be the fifth building on the path at the farthermost end. He remembered the sounds and scents of a collection of human females when he passed earlier.

He circled silently in front of his prey and waited. John chided himself for not following that she-bitch sooner, but she would have easily heard him on a quiet campus. Only the multitudes in the city and an obvious state of distraction prevented her from detecting him earlier. He listened in hiding and urged his victim closer, then swore as he heard the heavier footsteps of a man join the girl's light clicking footsteps. He peered out and swore an oath, knowing he should have killed the patrolman when he had the opportunity.

"Rebecca, what are you doing out at this hour?"

The startled girl threw back her auburn hair. "Mr. Charles? I'm a little late getting back from my date. Please don't report me. I'm in enough trouble as it is for missing curfew." Her mouth twisted in a pout.

The patrolman spoke sternly, at first. "You know the rules as well as any student. I think," he paused, "we could let it pass this time. Don't worry your pretty head about it." He ended with a broad smile and chuckled.

The girl looked relieved. The man pulled a pipe from his pocket and began to stuff it with tobacco. He searched the gloom. John pulled closer to the wall.

"Mustn't have been much of a fella to let you walk to your dorm alone at this hour," he snorted.

The coed pulled her pale green wrap defensively. "He had to leave. I'm old enough to take care of myself."

"Let me see you to your dorm," Mr. Charles said.

Rebecca consented and let him take her arm. "No wonder you're such a favorite with all the girls," she said as she flirted. She gave him a light peck on the cheek. They walked together to the dorm steps. As the guard lit his pipe; he turned his back to John.

John sprang from his hiding place and covered the distance to the concrete steps in a heartbeat, then felled the man with a smashing blow to the skull. He collapsed like a rag doll. The girl ran up the steps, screaming, and managed to pound on the door once before the strong vampyr clamped his hand over her face and dragged her away. Her face was livid and contorted with fear.

John pulled the struggling girl over the slain patrolman's body, away from the buildings. He stifled a scream, then pinned her left arm under his knee, jerked her head downward by her hair, and sliced the knife across her back and shoulder. Not the front; he wanted this victim to last.

"Please," caught in her throat, and was barely a

whisper. The girl trembled in shock as he lapped her fresh blood.

Her attacker impatiently ripped her gown off to fondle her bared breasts, his fingers clamped over her mouth to stifle another scream. Tears rolled down her face in a torrent as he jerked her head sharply to increase the blood flow, feeding at his leisure while lazily pinching her nipples, abdomen, and inner thighs with his free hand.

Rebecca lapsed into merciful unconsciousness.

John took a last draught, for now, then clawed the remainder of his victim's clothes off. As he spread her exposed body to take his pleasure of her, a small gurgle escaped from her lips. He wrapped his hand around her throat, ready to squeeze if she awoke.

Majken crept out of her room with a towel and her robe over her shoulder and a small puncture set tucked safely under her arm, thankful that Lisa had finally decided to go to sleep. Her roommate was still recovering. Majken had started to change into her robe when Lisa saw her injured shoulder. She kept her blouse on and gave her roommate a watered-down version of what she told Thomas—that she had simply fallen. Lisa commented on her improved countenance. Majken admitted she was happier.

The carpeted hallway was dark and still. Lights out was at eleven. Just before entering a room, she heard a heavy clumping sound and a muffled scream from outside.

She knew the sounds of attack.

Majken let her robe and towel fall in a heap and stuffed the puncture set in her pocket, then hurriedly dropped from a second-story window. She moved forward cautiously.

She found a campus security patrolman crumpled on the steps, not breathing. She avoided touching his body; his skull had been crushed with incredible force. Majken took in the details of the entire area with a glance. A torn, pale green shawl lay strewn over a bush, flapping desolately in the breeze. Immediately, she sensed this was not the work of an ordinary mugger; the other vampyr must have followed her to campus. She crouched and stopped breathing to listen.

The wind carried a faint tearing sound. She ran in the direction of the sound, hoping she was not too late.

Majken found him over a body, and moving as a blur, smashed into him as hard as she could with the full weight of her body. She pinned him, face-to-face against a tree, her eyes locked on his. She fought to wrench his will out of him as he lay momentarily stunned. She felt a struggle, but ... was losing ... his will in ... an endless sea of violet. He succumbed, and was in her power at last!

She held him at arm's length; her soul felt the inferno raging beneath his dark eyes. She held him by a slender thread. He would follow her, the easy part, but his self-preservation would overrule any command against his life instincts.

Majken grimaced. She had to get him off campus before an alarm was raised.

Feeling blindly behind her, his victim, Rebecca, was motionless, but alive. A viscous pool of blood spread on the grass; the sight nearly broke her concentration because she had not fed.

Rebecca needed medical attention. She could not risk leaving the other vampyr to help her, or call attention to herself by calling the police or hospital by telephone. For a fleeting instant, she considered Thomas. No, she warned herself.

Majken pulled the other vampyr by his arms to kneel next to Rebecca's prone body.

"Carry her," she ordered. He picked her up easily. Majken's eyes never wavered from his as they moved, step by step, to a place where she would be found.

Then she led him into the surrounding darkness, away from innocent people, and eventually off campus into the surrounding woods to the north.

Uncertainty gnawed in her as she struggled with where to take him and how to avoid the certain aftermath of his brutal attack in her home territory. A sensation like nausea ebbed within; a constant reminder that she must get blood soon herself.

The two vampyrs walked away from the campus, avoiding the nearby residents. They stepped from the woods as bright moonlight poured between the accumulating clouds. She sensed a herd of deer ahead. The other vampyr's indomitable blood lust cried for more. She clumsily killed an animal with his knife. *I'm out of practice*, she thought. She watched him bury his face into a slashed pelt and drink, then killed a second animal quickly.

Majken allowed him to glut, effectively putting him out of action.

Only when he collapsed did she trust herself to let loose and drink the warm blood herself.

Majken sat on the hard earth next to the other vampyr; her needs were finally satisfied. She managed to get him up and moving, stumbling under his dead weight. A stinging, raw shoulder helped keep her from slipping into unconsciousness.

She deposited him in an abandoned shed on the outskirts of a deserted roadway. He would safely sleep until he heard her voice again. Relieved of her burden, she pushed her leaden body for home. She could not disappear under suspicious circumstances and expect to remain there.

Chapter Seven

The first grey streak of dawn floated over the horizon as Majken passed the edge of the campus. She stumbled on a curb, following the path she left by and definitely feeling the effects of consuming animal blood. Her mouth and throat were dry, the world blurred, and her eyes refused to focus and penetrate the fading darkness.

In a haze, she saw Thomas standing before her, glowing like the sun. She started toward him, questioning. He made an ancient gesture, condemning her to death. Instantly, two glowing executioners wearing black hoods appeared to take her away. She broke free, but everywhere she ran Thomas waited in front of her. Condemned, condemned, condemned. She fell at his feet, and only then realized she had been hallucinating.

She lay motionless, straining to pull air into her parched lungs. Her eyes literally burned and shed the first stinging tears in many years. Majken waited until her breathing slowed to a hoarse rasp. Death would come with the morning sun. In her weakened and unprotected condition, her body could not absorb that much radiant energy. She heaved, trembling. She could almost hear the puzzled medical examiner trying to explain this one to a deputy. She wondered how Thomas would take it. Thomas.

She propped herself on her elbows, then summoned the strength to roll to a sitting position.

Majken bowed her head, her long hair lay dirty and limp on the grass. A throbbing pain below the left side of her rib cage was overpowered by a deep void that threatened to engulf her. The same ache followed her. Her injured shoulder throbbed wildly. Gradually, her sense of the world returned. She propped on her knees, drew a cleansing breath, and looked around. Colors were beginning to replace the multiple shades of gray as the dawn spread. Majken struggled to her feet and forced herself to move.

As her cloak of darkness faded rapidly, she made her way to her dorm. She dared not approach by the well-lit front, and she doubted she had the strength to use her second-floor exit. Majken sneaked to the back door; the screen door creaked loudly. The door was locked, as she knew it would be. Some nights, nothing goes right, she thought sarcastically.

"Stop! Who are you and what are you doing here?"

The young man's voice startled her. Majken cursed under her breath as she faced an inquisitive campus patrolman. She raised her hands and stepped away from the door. "I'm a student and I live in the dorm," she said hastily. She paused, reading uncertainty in his face. He was young, she noticed. "I couldn't sleep so I came out here for some fresh air. I thought I'd take a little walk, but I seem to have locked myself out, uh, accidentally. Will you let me in?"

"Let's see some ID," he ordered.

"I don't have my ID with me. I have a problem with insomnia, and coming outside is the only thing that helps. It relaxes me." Majken tried to be soothing, hoping he would accept her impromptu story.

He came closer. "Outside is no place for a girl, especially after last night." He studied her. "What is your name?" he asked.

"Mary Harris," she answered. Majken read his silver-plated name tag, Pete Gilbroski, and tried her best repentant look. "I'm sorry if I did something wrong." Her haggard appearance from her long night added to the effect. She imagined she looked like a mess. Gilbroski was trying to decide what to do when the walkie-talkie on his belt crackled to life.

Majken tensed.

"Base to four."

Gilbroski jerked the microphone off his shoulder and answered.

"Wanted to remind you of the meeting with the police at seven sharp. You have forty-five minutes. Out."

The radio went dead. Gilbroski stared at it. "I should have reported you," he finally said. "I'm going to let you off this time with a warning, but, Mary, promise me you won't do this again."

Majken nodded, and reminded him she was locked out. He thumbed through the keys on his belt. "I would," he said, "but I don't seem to have a key for this door." He kept looking.

Majken pleaded silently as the first rays of sunlight appeared on the horizon. She feared she would have to try to break the lock or risk climbing to her window. She could do neither in his presence.

Gilbroski held up a key. "C'mon," he said.

The trail to the front was well-worn. Majken glanced at her window as she passed, retracing each step she had taken in darkness the night before. She passed the corner uneasily. The spot where the man had laid was vacant. A second bloodstain on the concrete marked were Rebecca had been. The young patrolman opened the front door without commenting on the stains. Majken thanked him and retreated. Enclosed in darkness, she staggered sideways, catching the wall. Dizziness was a side effect. The golden light of sunrise brightened the vestibule. It had been too close. She sighed. She greatly preferred a wider margin of safety.

Weak and exhausted, she removed her shoes and staggered deliberately to her sanctuary.

She picked up her robe and towel dropped in the dark hallway. She felt instinctively for her puncture set; it had been lost somewhere. Majken almost laughed. An early-riser coming out of her room stared at her as she went to the showers. Majken stumbled to her room, listening for sounds of movement, then entered quietly. Her eyes took a minute to adjust to the near complete darkness. Soft breathing came from the first bed. Lisa was asleep. Majken felt relieved as she pulled down the bed covers and began to peel out of her clothes. The menace was safely tucked away. *Score one for my side*, she thought. Unclothed, she slumped on her bed and slid between cool sheets, deserving of a good day's sleep.

Lisa broke her silence. "I covered your tail last night. Where were you?"

Majken turned facedown in her pillow. "I went for a walk," came up muffled.

"I don't want to alarm you, but security found a patrolman with his head bashed in out front late last night. Mrs. DeGauthier heard heavy knocking and nearly died of shock when she opened the front door."

Lisa sounded angry.

Majken groaned softly, then rolled over.

"You remember that nice Mr. Charles?" Lisa continued. "The police barged through about midnight and questioned just about everybody. I stuck a couple of pillows in your bed and told them you took a sleeping pill."

Majken sighed. "I owe you one."

"They found someone else, too," Lisa said.

"How was Rebecca?" Majken asked softly.

"How did you know about her?" Lisa said in an incredulous voice. "Everyone thought she was dead. When the paramedics revived her, she started screaming bloody murder. They took her to the hospital."

Numbness spread throughout Majken's body; her speech slurred.

Lisa climbed out of bed and snapped on the light. When she looked at Majken, she exclaimed, "Oh, Mary, Mother of Christ! What happened to you?" Lisa felt of her forehead. "You're as pale as this sheet, and burning up."

Majken reached for Lisa's hand, scarcely whispering. "Too many questions. Must rest. Keep them away."

Lisa tucked the covers around her sick roommate. She continued to murmur inaudibly.

A heavy sleep claimed her.

* * *

Chief Vincent Baggetta paced in a small circle around a podium, simultaneously watching the clock, his security team, and half of the Trenton police force assemble in the auditorium. One and a half minutes until seven. He rubbed his hands wearily, having received the phone call early this morning. He had just succeeded in calming his old friend down. A police foul up had delayed the release of Marc's body, delaying the funeral. A telephone call ruined everything. He had to leave Albritton then, to attend to a campus emergency. Only when he arrived at the scene, did he learn the full extent of the crisis. He clenched his fist on remembering his unhappy task of telling Mrs. Charles that she was a widow. One minute.

Forensic specialists gathered on his right. They spoke incomprehensible medical jargon: angular projection of the point of impact; coagulation assay to determine the approximate time of death. The autopsy had been completed in record time. The fatal blow was inflicted with a blunt object swung with incredible force. The indentation did not match most clubs, hammers, or wrenches commonly used. No particles of metal or flakes of paint were found in the scalp. The experts were in the dark. The only thing they seemed to agree on, was that he never saw his attacker and the incident occurred between eleven and eleven-fifty. Half a minute to go.

A goodly number of Trenton's policemen, detectives, plainclothesmen and brass waited in compact independent clusters, completely avoiding his Campus Security. The blue uniforms reminded Baggetta of overripe grapes. He would be expected to turn control of the investigation over to the Trenton police chief, who would, naturally, plow his investigation through the campus with all the grace of a bull in a china shop. He did not have to worry about the board of directors. The murder was plainly connected to the assault of the coed found next to his body. He wanted the person or persons responsible. It appeared that the police were holding back.

His own security team, small in comparison, huddled together for support. Baggetta was proud of his remaining four man, one woman force. He assured them he would do whatever it took to protect them and find the killer. The Trenton police refused to confirm the rumor that the slasher may have been involved, as they tried to avoid panic. He had followed the news accounts of the slasher and learned enough from personal sources to recognize his *modus operandi*. He guessed this was who the police thought was responsible by the sheer number of specialists and a total lack of media coverage. It was time to begin. He took a final sweeping glance of the assembly and his group, then rapped on the podium. The meeting began.

Thomas lounged in the cafeteria for over an hour, staring at the wall clock every few minutes. Mary was no-show again. They had come to a reconciliation, he thought, or was it his imagination? Thomas unshelved his leg from a chair and tossed his notebook on the table. "I still have some pride," he said to the empty chair. "Let her come to me, for once."

It was almost time for his morning class. He gathered his notebook and emptied his fourth glass of orange juice. His eyes locked on the telephone across the cafeteria when he stood up. Undecided, he propped on the table and battled the urge to call. The suspense was killing him, but he wanted to find out where she was without appearing to pry. Then Mary's roommate came in with a midmorning group. Thomas was at her side instantly.

"Do you know where Mary is this morning?" he asked Lisa.

"Thomas, you're just the person I wanted to talk to," she declared, stepping out of the cafeteria line and pulling him to a deserted corner. Lisa backed nervously against the wall. "Before I get into this, I want you to know that I hope you and Mary can work things out." Her tone was apologetic.

Thomas thanked her, growing exceedingly worried. Something must have happened. "What did she do?" he asked, expecting the worst.

Lisa plunged in. "Mary disappeared last night and didn't come in until this morning. She's in bed now, asleep."

His eyes grew wider, but that was not as bad as he thought. "She gets in these moods. When we went camping, she disappeared in the middle of the night. I woke up the next morning and found her ... uh, as chipper as usual."

"She didn't look great this morning. She had a fever."

Thomas became very concerned.

"That isn't the worst of it." Lisa visibly cringed and lowered her voice. "Last night, a man was found murdered outside our dorm." She pulled on his arm to get him closer; strain deep in her voice. "They also found ... a girl next to him, cut up and raped, I think."

Thomas caught his breath.

In tears, Lisa added, "Oh, she'll live, probably.

Don't spread this around. The police and campus security want it kept quiet."

Thomas stared blankly at the floor trying to adjust to the terrible news. "What does this have to do with Mary?" he asked. Lisa squeezed tighter into the corner. He could practically read Lisa's mind. "You can't account for her at the time of the murder?"

She nodded slowly. He refused to believe what he had just said.

Lisa brushed her hand over a tear. "I don't know where she went or what she did or–" She choked and swallowed hard. "I'm afraid, now, to be in the same room with her alone," she confessed.

Hurt and fear was plainly written on Lisa's face. Thomas shielded her from the other students and supported her and himself by leaning heavily against the wall. His heart pounded. This he could not let slip by, even if he loved her. Especially since he loved her. He then noticed a row of pale bruises on Lisa's arm. He gently pulled her arm by the wrist. "How did you get these?"

"I, uh, got them a few weeks ago. I let myself get run-down. The doctor thought I had a vitamin deficiency, or something. That's why I bruised easily."

Thomas solemnly pulled up the sleeve of his jersey past his elbow, and held his arm next to hers.

The marks were not identical, but they were frighteningly similar. Lisa and Thomas were speechless. She asked him what happened to him. He could only give her a general vague answer; he had found them on the morning of his camping trip.

"With Mary," Lisa added.

Remembering where they were, Thomas stepped away from Lisa and checked the wall clock. It was now eight minutes past the hour. This was more important than meeting a class, he decided.

"Lisa, thanks for telling me all this. I guess it wasn't easy."

"Not easy for me!" she said. "I can only imagine what it's like for you."

He looked past her, through her; a strange question was on the tip of his mind. Thomas suggested they sit. He hesitated. The cafeteria noise increased as the room filled up. "Think hard," he said lowly. "Have you ever seen Mary actually eat anything?"

Thomas sighed heavily, realizing his question bordered on madness, or a worse terror.

Lisa frowned and blinked several times, then shook her head. "I've seen her get a sack lunch with a soft drink and a sandwich out of our refrigerator, and, uh, carry it with her." She shuddered nervously. "I don't see what you're driving at—she has to eat something."

"That's true," Thomas admitted. Things were already out of hand; he had to see her, alone and fast. "Any chance on me sneaking up to your room unnoticed? I have to see her," he asked Lisa.

"Yeah," Lisa said, laughing, "restrictions aren't what they used to be." Her eyes saddened. "Poor Mrs. DeGauthier was so shook up from last night that she had a few too many and is sleeping it off. I can't say that I blame her though."

She became very quiet. "What do you think, Thomas? When I started having my spells, she was so concerned for me. It's hard to see her doing harm to anyone." She added, "Deliberately."

Thomas snapped angrily. "I'm fed up with her evasions. Whether she likes it or not, I'm going to get answers." He turned quickly.

Lisa grabbed his arm, his other arm. "Wait a minute," she pleaded. "Mary came in half-dead. What she needs now is sleep."

He stopped.

"Please," she whispered.

Thomas slowly nodded his head, consenting to wait a while. He gave Lisa a small kiss, then left to think.

* * *

Albritton studied the drained expression on Baggetta's face as he sipped bitter coffee that had been brewing all morning. He knew Baggetta was a sensitive and honest man under his heavy exterior, and the loss of a patrolman must have struck a nerve as deep as the loss of his son. The silence in the tiny kitchen was deafening as each man endured his own respective torment. Baggetta finally raised from his mirky reflection.

"We found where the coed was assaulted," he said without emotion. "The police are convinced it's the same crazy who is loose in the city. My impression is that Charles got in the way when the killer was going after the girl. She's still in shock and unable to tell us what she saw."

Albritton wanted to be supportive; Baggetta had been there in his hour of need. It was past the lunch hour and neither man had eaten. "What steps are you taking?"

"We're enforcing an early curfew, and have distributed a generalized warning to all students. The police will have a few decoys, but I think the slasher has come and gone, and I told them so. We briefed most of the faculty and some of the support staff on the true nature of the crisis. We've asked them to keep their eyes open and be extremely careful."

Albritton nodded in satisfaction. Many of the touches he assumed were Baggetta's doing. "I have no doubt that they will," he replied. "My son; what did the police say about finding Marc's murderer?"

Baggetta hesitated. "They see Marc as an apparent suicide."

"They don't see–" Albritton sprang up, shaking in defiance. "The stupid cretins! If it were one of their son's, they would be moving heaven and earth to find the culprit!" Anger subsided quickly, yielding to sorrow. Trembling, he leaned on his chair for support. Baggetta helped him sit down.

"I am sorry for that display," he said. "My temper gets the best of me at times. I only wish—I want to know why my son is dead." He wiped his tear drenched eyes.

"Daniel," Baggetta said reassuringly, "I'm doing everything in my power to find out what happened to Marc, and why."

"Fools," Albritton swore.

The air in the polished kitchen became still. Albritton replayed his son's behavior the final weeks of his life. The only variable of any significance was the mysterious girl Marc was seeing; the same girl he saw with his son at the game. Chief Baggetta called it a pet theory, but shared the idea with the police. It seemed less than proper to bring up the matter when Baggetta was in such turmoil. Albritton probed the topic carefully. "Can you talk to Ms. Harris this week?"

"The girl?" Baggetta sighed. "I've already asked the registrar to send a copy of her file. I had planned to talk with her this morning." He pointed a finger to emphasize a point. "Remember, this will be an unofficial inquiry, until I find something to take to the police."

Albritton was pleased. Faster than lightning would have been too slow as far as Marc was concerned. Mary Harris was hiding something, and he intended to find out what it was.

Thomas reclined on Lisa's bed opposite his love, waiting. Her room was tranquil with a soft glow of light coming from under the door. Occasionally, he heard and saw the soft padding of bare feet on the carpet outside. Lisa had spread the word to girls in the rooms nearby to stay clear. For all intent purposes, they were completely alone. He observed how deeply she slept; her face was buried in her pillow and her long hair cascaded around her injured shoulder. While she slept, he gently lifted the corner of her bedspread to see—the red welt had become somewhat more diffused and pink. She breathed very slowly, deeply. As he watched her, he searched his heart for the right words to say that would unlock her heart toward him. He waited for her to wake up on her own.

As he searched his mind, he had been here before. Any minute, he expected to find her in his sleeping bag, warm and ready to kiss him good morning. Yesterday, and a million years ago. How things change!

He wondered what he had done wrong, what he should have done differently. Mary—sometimes—was so different. He had done everything he knew to do. He told her he loved her and asked her to trust him and let him help. She asked him in turn to trust her and wait. She was still a closed book! He loved her still, but wondered if that would be nearly enough.

A lump formed in his throat when she stirred. Her hand reached out, fingers spread. It was not everyday she awoke with a strange man in her bedroom (he hoped). Thomas knelt on the carpet and lightly pushed strands of hair out of her face. He cupped her hand in his and whispered her name. Her eyes opened, staring ahead blankly. Then her eyes seemed to focus and the corners of her mouth flickered into a smile.

"I couldn't wait to see how you were. Lisa told me you came in sick this morning. How are you?"

Her voice was scratchy when she uttered a single word. "Fine." Her eyes narrowed, as if trying to focus. "How did you get in here?" she asked.

"Sneaked in, because I was worried. I care about you, lady, if you didn't already know."

She extended both arms out of the bedcovers, and stretched upward. She must have felt better, he hoped. Her eyes were shiny and dark. She smiled ruefully. "I told my trusted roommate I would get well." She closed her eyes for a moment, as some unseen sensation gripped her body, still weak. She tightened her lips and tensed with invisible pain.

Thomas studied her. He waited until she relaxed visibly.

"Where were you last night?" She looked as if she was trying to remember. *Oh, God*! he thought, *amnesia*! Her lips moved but she made no sound. Sadness was in her voice when audible sound came.

"... wanted to stay. He ruined everything."

"What are you talking about?" he asked frantically. "He, who?" Her eyes seemed to lose their luster and he could see that a fierce inner battle was taking place; his side was obviously losing.

She raised herself partially on her elbows and

seemed to gather strength. Her answer came in a tone of voice he had learned to dread. "It is better if you don't know." She tried to reach for him, to embrace him.

Thomas pushed her roughly down and swore.

She collapsed and held her hands over her face, the bedcovers slipping aside. Her nakedness emphasized her vulnerability. *What have I done?* Thomas smote himself. She lay very still. "Mary, I'm sorry, say something." He pulled a sheet to her neck, but the stinging words could never be taken away.

Majken opened her eyes. "You want me to *prove* my feelings for you? That shouldn't be necessary. If I thought you could help me, or even understand, I would have told you all at the first." Her eyes sparkled.

Thomas waited on her to say more. He thought, the pain of rejection had blinded him; he was indeed looking for proof of her love—not her love. He stumbled back to the other bed. His words were choked as he said, "You're special to me ... and I'll never find another like you, but blind faith can't hold our relationship together much longer." Thomas straightened his spine and went to the door. His hand lingered on the knob a few seconds, waiting, and his conviction unmistakable.

He quietly opened the door and slipped away.

* * *

Pete Gilbroski was startled when Chief Baggetta summoned him to his office. He closed the door.

"I want you to track down a student for me and bring her in for a talk," Baggetta said as he shuffled a thick stack of papers on his desk and pushed them into a deceptively thin folder.

Gilbroski's throat constricted on "her". His supervisor gave him the name he feared. His goose was cooked. "Mary Harris, sir?" he repeated. He examined the polish on his shoes, and asked, "How did you find out?"

"Find out what?" Baggetta swiveled and pointed his fingers into a steeple.

"Oh," Pete stammered, then coughed. "That I found her outside her dorm early this morning." He watched Chief Baggetta rock his chair gently, deceptively gently.

"I don't remember seeing a report."

Gilbroski snapped to attention; Baggetta's deep voice resonated with military crispness. "It was a minor incident, sir." He fixed his eyes on the window behind Baggetta's head. His boss continued to sway in silence.

"Why did you want to see her?" he finally asked.

"Tell her to please come by today."

Baggetta dismissed the patrolman with a wave, appearing locked in thought. Gilbroski gladly marched out of his office.

Majken slipped on a robe and sat on the edge of her bed, gently probing her abdomen and left side with sensitive fingertips. No swelling. She looked around the empty room. Deceiving Thomas further would be impossible. Her humming bedside clock seemed loud. She picked up the device with throbbing fingers. She had to leave anyway until things cooled down, until she had conditioned the other vampyr, John, to leave her territory.

A girl she recognized from down the hall called her through the door. She turned on the light and opened the door, holding to the frame for balance, and found a very anxious security patrolman standing behind the girl. The coed pointed her out and left, commenting on what she did to get into trouble.

Majken wrapped her robe tighter. "Hello, again."

Gilbroski frowned. "Thanks to your little stunt, we're both in hot water. Chief Baggetta wants you to come in for a talk."

"I'm sorry if I got you into trouble. When does he want to see me?" The tilt of her head could have been interpreted as coy or demure. She hoped demure. She was still very weak.

"Today," Gilbroski answered sharply.

Majken leaned against the frame. "I'll take whatever disciplinary action he sees fit. I'll be there as
soon as I get dressed. In about thirty minutes?" She
raked her fingers through her long, dirty hair, won-
dering if she looked like she felt.

Gilbroski appeared relieved and actually sorry to
have to call her in. "Have you been sick?" he asked.

"Not really, just had a very bad night."

He partially saluted. "I'll tell Chief Baggetta to
expect you, say, five o'clock."

She nodded in agreement. That would make it
time for her to leave, nearly dusk. Gilbroski left.

While Majken prepared for a leisurely shower,
the problem pressing on her mind was not her up-
coming meeting with the campus chief, but where to
take John. It had to be secure during the day, and
hopefully, far away from the city. She had wandered
around in her first few months at Trenton, and had
found a deserted place by accident. She had even left
a cache there.

Warm water soothed the various aches in her
body. She would have preferred resting in the dorm
until time to leave and feeding before she was forced
to trade her human supply for an animal supply.

Her summons would be the second to last thing she would do on campus. As she dressed, she also packed many of her clothes and carefully checked her room for identifying or incriminating evidence. If necessary, she need never return. The final thing she wanted to do was see Thomas.

She started to leave the dorm, but stopped when she overheard a telephone conversation downstairs. Another girl was pleading with her professor, claiming to have a bad case of nerves after last night's attack and requiring time off from her studies. Majken smiled; a handy excuse to leave had practically fallen in her lap. She called her instructor and made the same request. She guessed many girls were actually leaving. He said he was sorry to lose such a good student, even for a little while, and her exam grade would have been perfect if she had finished the test. He referred her to the school psychiatric center for help. Another time, maybe, she thought.

Majken reached campus security headquarters on the hour. It reminded her of a lonely cavalry outpost on a tribal frontier. The structure stood apart from other buildings. It was an imperfect blend of chrome and faded brick; a union of past and present. Its most conspicuous feature was a triple set of antennae mounted on separate towers. She had felt and heard the distinct power hum from two buildings away. She reached the cold, peeling, blue metal door and opened it. The interior fared better. She strolled past a fading yellow plant and entered the only private office marked Chief Campus Security. He was waiting.

Baggetta greeted her cordially and invited her to be seated. He seemed to look her over with great care. He remained standing. "I was curious about a few things in your file I thought we might clear up."

Majken took note of how casually he came to the business at hand. She knew he was studying her and watching for any revealing behaviors. Like many public officials, she assumed he was an expert judge of character. She relaxed and folded her hands lightly in her lap. She leaned forward, marginally concerned, like any student. "I believe my application and records are complete."

He sat in a swivel chair. "You were raised in an orphanage, actual parentage unknown. You attended different schools and colleges, then traveled a few years before coming here. Is that right?"

Majken nodded. He was a shrewd man to begin on a topic other than the reason she suspected she was here. He cleared his throat.

"Your previous school is Austin University. It's a

great school, isn't it?" Baggetta swiveled to face the other direction.

"It was," Majken replied.

Baggetta glanced from a page on his desk to her. He was testing her. "Did you know the student that was killed a week ago, Ms. Harris?"

She resisted the impulse to say his name. "The school paper said it was a suicide. It's really tragic."

"How well did you know Marc Albritton?" He pressed his hands to form a steeple.

Majken shook her head vaguely.

"When did you last talk to him?" Baggetta asked.

Majken paused, like she was trying to remember. She felt some concern for where this conversation was heading, and wondered who was stirring things up. The police had questioned her about Marc. Someone must have seen them together at the game. Rumors about her were spreading across campus. "I believe I ran into him between classes a few weeks ago."

Baggetta casually turned her file on the desk. "It is my understanding that he was in love with you, and may have been killed because of you."

Majken stammered believably. "I ... have a steady boyfriend, and it isn't Marc Albritton."

"You were seen talking to him behind the stands

at our last game."

"He was there," Majken admitted. "I made sure he went his way and I went mine."

Baggetta asked her to explain.

She crossed her arms, as if cold, and leaned back in her chair. She sighed heavily, and paused to begin her tale. "He grabbed me from behind at the game. I didn't want Thomas to see him, or make a scene, so we went behind the stands. I thought he was infatuated with me so I told him to leave me alone, and that was all." Baggetta could verify that much, she thought.

"Do you know if he had any other girlfriends?"

"If you ask every girl on campus, you might find someone eventually." Her sarcasm was dangerous, but she could not resist. The campus chief stood and leaned over his desk. Majken met his gaze squarely.

"There is another detail. You were found wandering outside your dorm in the wee hours of this morning. Restrain yourself in the future. If it happens again, we will recommend suspension."

Baggetta dismissed her. Majken answered humbly, and left the cramped building.

The brief interrogation had gone surprisingly well. She felt her cover was still intact. There would be no way to trace her at the alleged orphanage and a serious fire at Austin University had destroyed much of the records department several years ago. She never attended Austin; any check would return void. There would be no way to prove or disprove without records.

A shrill, tenored cry shattered her serenity. She wheeled around as a slight, silver-haired man bore down on her.

"Mary Harris, my name is Daniel Albritton, Marc's father, and I want to talk to you."

Majken waited in the thick shade of oak trees lining the path and peered from behind her sunglasses. "I heard about your tragedy," she said. "I'm very sorry."

He scowled at her. "I want to know why you killed my son."

"Why ask me?" Majken steeled herself.

"I loved my son, Ms. Harris. Marc was sometimes difficult, but I knew him. My son would never have committed suicide." Albritton stared at her icily. "He refused to talk about you at all, except that night. I believe you are responsible for his death."

Majken removed her glasses for an instant and saw the same volatile eyes she had seen in Marc; a grieving and obsessed father was a dangerous adversary. She wondered why everything was directed at her. She wished everyone would leave her alone!

"You're mistaken, Dr. Albritton, I did not know your son."

Albritton exploded. "How long did you and he whore together?"

The sudden coldness of his accusation pierced her. Majken shook his hand off. "Professor Albritton, what you're saying is called slander. I've just finished talking to Chief Baggetta. Leave me alone or I'll see that charges are filed." She quickly moved away from Marc's stricken father.

"I will find out what you are hiding, for my son's sake!" he called behind her.

Majken continued to walk away. Long ago, she had learned the peril of strong emotions, like anger, jealousy, or love. Her anger seethed as she tried to subdue it. She stopped moving and floated her body against the nearest tree trunk. As the massive roots drank nourishment from the earth, little by little, her mind and body relaxed, her teeth unclenched. She might have lain there if other students were not happening by. She forced herself to move. She wanted to see Thomas.

Majken went to his dorm, his class, the playing field, and finally the cafeteria. She found him waiting at his favorite table. He had not seen her yet.

She could still leave, but an invisible hand pushed her across the room. She considered telling him the truth; her secret. *Which truth?* she wondered. It was far easier to propose blood drinking as part of sex games with a virtual stranger; easier to pay a donor money; easier to find an unconscious or sleeping mark than to expose herself to him. He would reject her, she feared, not as a human, but as a loathsome creature.

Thomas still looked the other way. She approached cautiously. Being seen with him in a public place would help stop pending gossip about her involvement with Albritton's son. The pit of her stomach dropped to the floor when he faced her. *That's it,* she coaxed. *Smile sweetly, harlot. Use him one more time.*

"Thomas, don't feel bad about this afternoon. I really want to work things out between us." She took an empty seat.

"Hello, Mary," he said casually. Thomas leaned over to look at her full figure. "Are you feeling better?"

She dismissed his worry with a wave of her hand. Residual dizziness would work itself out in a few days. She did not plan on an extended diet.

"I'll be fine," she assured him. He continued to stare. "Really."

"Are you seeing a doctor yet?"

"Oh, no!" she exclaimed. "I'll be all right."

Thomas spoke gravely. "I've given this a lot of thought, and I want you to know that I'll support you in whatever decision you make."

Majken smiled quizzically. "Thank you."

Matter-of-factly, he asked, "What are you going to do?"

She seized the opportunity. "Thomas, I'll be going away for a few days. It has nothing to do with us or this afternoon." She instinctively waited for his reaction. He did not have one. It was as if her leaving was perfectly natural. *What's wrong with him*? she thought.

"When you come back, will we still see each other?"

Majken leaned and kissed him, lightly, playfully, the way she used to. "I wouldn't have anyone else." He looked more wounded. She wanted to tear her hair out. "Thomas," she pleaded, "I'm okay, really!" She had to get to the bottom of this.

He watched her more intently. "I didn't know what to do after I left your room, then I figured everything out. I want you to know I'll do what I can."

Majken was afraid to ask what. Had she twisted his emotions so badly that he would lay there and take whatever she threw at him? His strange new behavior disturbed her; she missed the old Thomas. She looked into his brown eyes for clues, believing she would always be centuries distant from him.

Then, out of the blue, he said, "If you want me to, I'll help you keep it."

She stared at him as his last four words registered and she scrambled to fit pieces of this puzzle into place. She grinned, embarrassed, as she reached a conclusion. *He thinks I'm pregnant*! Majken laughed and Thomas sat there with his mouth open. She assured him that she just thought of something funny, and it was not what he had said. His look of disgust gradually gave way to a more pleasant expression.

Majken knew her time was short. She asked Thomas to escort her to her dorm. They walked arms entwined. Outside, she confessed that she was not pregnant, then pressed him for urgent help. "I need a ride off campus."

"Now?" He hesitated, and looked at his watch.

She pressed against him and urged, "Please?" Late twilight deepened the sky. "There is something I have to take care of, before it gets late."

He hung his head, then stared in the direction of his car. He smiled slightly, bravely. "Looks like I'm going to get into trouble for missing curfew." Majken gave him a quick hug and ran to her dorm to retrieve her belongings. Within five minutes, they were heading northeast, away from the campus.

Majken rested under Thomas' arm. She planned to stop him approximately four miles from campus, then hike to the place where she had left the other vampyr. Thomas gestured toward the nothingness.

"What's out here?"

"A few scattered homes, mostly," she said. She scanned a weed-covered fence from the moving car. It was private property. When she asked him to stop, he pulled over reluctantly. Majken hopped out of his car and retrieved her suitcase and bag from the trunk.

Thomas jumped out of his car, ran to her side, and pushed her suitcase to the ground. He glared at her defiantly. "What do you expect to do out here in the middle of nowhere at night?"

Majken was sure he had been humoring her, until now. She knew he could only see blackness and the silvery promise of moonrise, and had second thoughts about the wisdom of asking him to drive her or telling him she was not pregnant like he assumed. A simple goodbye kiss at the dorm would have been so much easier.

"I must go, Thomas. It's for a good reason, believe

me." This was not the time to tell him. *Maybe when he becomes my lover,* she thought, *but definitely not now.* He looked tired.

Thomas grimaced and paced in a tight circle, then uttered a single expletive and bowed his head in submission. "At least tell me where you're going. In case of an emergency."

Majken embraced him. "When I come back, I'll take you there," she promised. He held his arms limp at his sides. She could hear his heart pounding.

"Am I—," he choked.

"Ever going to see you again?" Majken finished. She looked down at her suitcase, swept the darkened hillside, then up to his eyes. She nodded yes. *Yes,* she thought, *whatever happens, you'll see me again.* "I'll be back," she told him, "in a week at the most."

Thomas held her hard, then let her go.

After many seconds, Majken kissed him, then broke away and climbed the grassy ridge past the fence to a slender animal trail disappearing into the bush. She looked back. He stood as she had left him. A truck rushed by. The road was again desolate. She waved, but he could not see her. "I'll come back," she whispered, as she crossed the ridge and lost sight of him.

Majken picked her way carefully through thick

brush, loose rocks, and fallen limbs. She used her shoulder bag to push aside thorns in her path, then stepped clear to face a beautiful waxing moon. Hiking across the new field was difficult in places, forcing her to backtrack twice to resume the correct course.

She searched for landmarks she remembered from the night before. A distinct smell of earth and images of the roadway lingered in her mind. She knew she had to find the shed before the other vampyr's blood lust broke her tenuous hold. She knelt where she was and listened to a low moaning carried by the wind. This was the place; she found the shed as she had left it.

She twisted the wooden latch, felt for movements, listened for sounds, then opened the door a crack. Nothing. If he had awakened, he would not be under her influence. A still form rested on the burlap. She opened the door wide, cautiously, and stepped inside. Immediately, he stirred. Her influence held. Being inactive would dampen his blood needs. She led him out and began to seek the first animal sacrifice.

Hours later, she arranged for a truck to transport them far north of the city; she looked for a small white church building next to the road as her marker. Signaling the truck driver, the vehicle slowed – Majken and John jumped easily off the truck to the side of the road.

Majken and the other vampyr followed a winding road, then a fire passage and reached their temporary dwelling by the time the moon reached its zenith. A ghostly light spilled over the abandoned, weathered mansion before them. Small by present standards, it resembled a marble tombstone with unbroken symmetry, save a large gnarled tree next to the front entrance. She wished she had seen it in its grandeur. It exuded a forlorn song.

She had found it her second month and used it as a temporary, emergency home. Only two rooms were remotely usable, the upper story bedroom and a sitting room; she had reconditioned them with a new mattress, spare linen, a canopy for the bed, and extra thick curtains for daytime protection. There were lamps and a supply of oil stored in a trunk under the main staircase. She had also brought a couch and a low table purchased at auction for the library.

She turned sourly to the other vampyr in disgust. He stood, satisfied with the animals she killed for him and herself, awaiting her command. Tomorrow, at dusk, she could begin conditioning him to leave her territory permanently. She deposited him in the cellar, and taking no chances, she hammered the cellar shut with three wedges from her bag.

Branches tangled in the wrought iron work scraped a gabled window. She paused at the entrance to examine the finely tooled brass fittings and the heavily sculpted frame. She entered the mansion. The lower hallway ran the width of the mansion from the vestibule to the servant's quarters. Right of the stairwell was the once usable dining room; left was her study. Seeing clearly by available moonlight, she pulled the trunk from under the staircase and trimmed a lamp.

The upper level hallway ran perpendicular to its companion, intersecting five bedrooms. It all but one, the floors from above were rotted through. Majken entered her bedroom and prepared her canopy bed for her rest. From the window, she could see the winding road that led eventually to the highway. She sealed the window with the curtains, then settled on the freshly made bed.

Majken reminisced as she brushed her hair; her past, spanning centuries, had become her bitter enemy by taking things away. This bedroom reminded her of her dorm, and the people. The hardest lesson to learn, she thought, is that you can never go back.

She extinguished the lamp; her extremities felt numb. Going under by degrees, she heard a little girl cry inside. There was no reply; only branches scraping the tile.

Lost love filled her thoughts.

A hollow voice reverberated in the room. "Reality is a dream; a dream is reality."

Blackness.

Majken stood apart from herself. The apparition watched herself sleep. It was not the true sleep of humans. The figure hovered for a moment.

It was Majken. A separate consciousness.

A child far away ... called. It had been a long time since ....

Majken floated toward the billowing curtains and was drawn through the window.

She found herself in a mist. Walking on hard ground.

A barren place.

The decaying remains of bodies tied to huge wooden stakes lined her passage. She looked neither right nor left.

The mist returned. Centuries passed.

Majken stood beside a little girl playing in a field. It was night. She watched her run a dirt-smudged hand across her face, leaving a streak. A small upturned nose wrinkled in determination; her chestnut hair glistened by starlight. An orange-yellow glow from a whitewashed home shone on the dark hillside far afield.

Suddenly, a huge night bird swooped from the trees and frightened the little girl badly. She cried and ran for her home in the distance.

Herself, a long time ago.

It was daytime. Unseen and unfelt, Majken watched the girl, now years older, walk hand in hand with a neighbor's son. His name was Nicholas and he had been her playmate and companion for years. She remembered the strange new feelings the girl, becoming a woman, felt when near him.

Majken's heart pounded harder when two men ambushed the innocent pair, shoving them into rough canvas bags. A ruffian clubbed the boy and dragged them away.

At night, Majken again found the girl and Nicholas. He lay unconscious; his wrists were tied in a simple knot. The young girl was strapped to a slab, exposed and helpless. A man, a stranger who had come in a black coach and wore the respected garb of Chancellor, approached with a chalice and a two-sided dagger. He laid the pearl handle inches from the girl's neck.

Majken trembled, powerless, as the man raped her again. The young girl's screams were smothered. Nicholas emerged from the shadows and stabbed the stranger with his own knife. The girl screamed;

she was covered with his blood. Nicholas slashed her free and pulled her from under the man's body. Majken watched them flee.

The rural dirt road was deserted. Shutters were pulled tight. No one heard a boy and a girl run for their lives while, behind them, a horse-drawn coach pursued. The horse's hooves sounded like thunder. A chain clanked against metal; a single lantern swayed in the night. With nowhere to run, Majken and the young girl watched as Nicholas was trampled under the sharp hooves and heavy carriage. Dear sweet Nicholas.

Townspeople found the bloodstained girl lying over his crushed body the next morning. The young girl was banished in disgrace from her home by her father. Majken's chest and throat hurt, again, as she watched the sobbing girl ride away in a cart, looking back at her home.

Darkness claimed Majken.

Chapter Eight

Thomas watched a glowing red sun expand and sink below the horizon from a vantage point on the top of the sciences building overlooking the campus: students were inches high and the sprawling campus lay before him. The distance gave him breathing room and helped him to think. He felt very much a fool for leaving Mary on that deserted road. The burden of waiting became unreal when she did not return for her Monday class. Everything, the school, his classes and fellow students, was unreal. A coed stopped him between classes at midday and asked him casually if he knew where Mary was.

Common sense told him to call it quits, find someone else, but a feeling deeper and stronger than simple curiosity begged him to see their relationship through. He remembered telling her he loved her, but now, he really did not know. Thomas remembered holding her that night. She pressed herself close to him, wanting him, and at the same time somehow afraid of him.

He knew she'd had a hard life, somewhere. She put on a good front. When the mask slipped and he saw the woman underneath, he knew she was not the carefree girl she pretended to be. He traced his memory. From that terrible night the girl was killed at the lounge, she started disappearing at odd hours, more than usual, then the rumors had started. She had even admitted the rumors were true; she had a strange way of showing her love for him.

She wanted freedom, so he let her go on that dark hillside. If letting her go was what she truly needed, he hoped it would be enough to change her before it was too late. As twilight deepened, the pall of separation spread over him with the darkening sky. Thomas hoped she would return before it was too late.

Baggetta stared incredulously at the report handed to him by his junior officer. He had asked Gilbroski to gather information on Mary Harris discretely. Daniel continued to insist she was in some way responsible for Marc's demise. She had been gone now for several days. Peripherally, he was aware that Gilbroski had stepped back, and Daniel had leaned forward as he absorbed the report. He dropped the paper on his desk. "Gilbroski, are you sure about this?"

Gilbroski cleared his throat. "I wrote down only what I was told, sir." He hesitated. "This sort of inquiry isn't one of my strong points. I did my best." He clasped his hands formally behind him and held his stance.

With a nod, Baggetta acknowledged the effort

and realized the awkward position in which he had placed him.

Albritton hovered over the paper and pointed to it in triumph. "See, those days, she was unaccounted for. She could have been with Marc, I'm certain of it."

Baggetta warned his officer with a strong glance to keep his peace.

"This is hearsay evidence, at best. Many coeds, I'm sorry to say, keep flexible hours and social schedules." He fought to restore calm. "Aside from questionable rumors, I see nothing to directly implicate Mary Harris with Marc's death."

Albritton raged, "The proof is there, if you choose to see it!"

The compact office seemed to shrink. Baggetta asked Gilbroski how certain he was of the rumors and their authenticity. "No one could say where the rumors started. My best estimate is that they started sometime after our last school game. Most of it is locker-room gossip."

"She's hiding something," Albritton injected forcefully.

Baggetta asked him to keep quiet.

"No one actually admitted to being with her." Gilbroski paused thoughtfully. "When we asked her to come in, she was very decent about it. She looked very tired and worn, and not what I would've expected if half of what these students said was true."

"Yes," Albritton directed to Baggetta, "and what did you find when you tried to check her background?" He sat in the wooden chair serenely, as if he had won a major battle.

Baggetta locked his arms and examined the list of phantom accusations with great care. He thanked Gilbroski for a job well done and asked him to leave, then turned to his friend.

"She admitted to knowing Marc, but said he was pursuing her. She said she discouraged him, which we've verified, and left with her boyfriend that weekend." Albritton's face was drawn. Baggetta spoke lowly, gently. "Many other girls have scattered to parts unknown after the murder. We were afraid that the director was going to close the school."

Neither man spoke as Baggetta placed the report in a drawer.

"Find out what you can from the boyfriend, Vincent," Albritton implored.

Baggetta nodded, slowly at first. "Under one condition, Daniel. I won't have a repeat of what you pulled with Ms. Harris. She was within her rights to scream harassment. Promise me you will let me handle it."

Albritton nodded silently.

Baggetta's thoughts turned away from the investigation into Mary Harris' personal life to tomorrow. Albritton had been holding up well. Tomorrow would prove the ultimate test. He had tried to be supportive and handle as much of the planning and responsibility as Daniel would let him. Earlier, he even stopped by the cathedral to make last minute preparations, without his guest's knowledge. He stood next to his friend. "Daniel," he said quietly, "I want you to know I'll be there for you tomorrow."

His friend wept bitterly.

"The days pass quickly when you put your mind to it," Thomas asserted aloud in his room. He glanced at the new calendar on his desk and the row of red Xs across the week, and tomorrow, Friday, would make it exactly one week since Mary had left. With mild regret, he remembered the award's banquet was Saturday night. He hefted the nearest textbook; its texture was dry and unfeeling, and he considered throwing it against the wall just to hear the sound it would make. He tossed it on his bed. This week, his popularity with his dorm-mates was low.

The only good side to all of this, he thought, was that he finally caught up on his studies. Practice had been cancelled due to rain; the next game was over two weeks away. The rain made him feel pent up and restless. Last night he had donned his sweats and jogged up and down the halls. Moving felt good regardless of what his neighbors thought. Time passed bearably.

Thomas tossed a rain jacket over his arm, gathered his book and pen, and set out. The weather should be clearing. He was determined to make it a good day. As he stepped into the hall, he heard an offhand comment, "What have you done, Thomas?" Before he could ask, the student disappeared. He found the reason for the remark posted prominently on the message board downstairs. He was expected at campus security headquarters, signed by the campus chief himself. Had to be a joke, he hoped instantly, but it was too official looking.

Another student strolled past Thomas wagging his head; a laughing smile on his face. Thomas tore at the yellow note. The tack bounced on the hardwood floor and came to rest point up. He stuffed the note in his book. It would wait until after class. He knew in his heart this summons had something to do with Mary. The shiny tack caught his eye. Thomas left the dorm smiling. Let it stay there for the next person that had something to say about Mary.

Afternoon class took forever.

Thomas approached the campus security building with mixed feelings of dread and innocence. The modified brick structure stood apart, physically and aesthetically, from other buildings on the campus. He listened to the distinct hum of a transformer. Thomas checked the yellow memo again to make sure it was really for him. He had done nothing wrong, except abandon a coed who had now been missing for a week on a deserted roadside in the middle of the night. *What could I say?* he lamented. *She talked me into it.* Thomas entered and decided not to talk about Mary if he could help it.

He found himself in a cubicle, bordered by an array of desks and filing cabinets along one side. In front of him, a female officer was busily operating a radio console. A man called him. Thomas gave the officer the note. The man stepped to a closed door and tapped on the frosted glass. His upper torso disappeared. The reply sounded deep and commanding. Thomas sat.

The patrolman told him it would be a few minutes, then dropped the memo in a tray on his desk and returned to whatever he was doing. Thomas fidgeted more and forced his legs to be still. The dark green creased plastic seats were very uncomfortable; the building suddenly seemed cooler. Little sounds below the normal range of perception became louder. Thomas jumped when the office door opened and a man called him.

Thomas rose automatically. His shirt stuck to the chair. He crossed the threshold like he remembered once entering a doctor's office as a child. A large hand grasped his. Chief Baggetta was bigger in person, and older than he expected with curling locks of white hair. Baggetta asked him to be seated.

"You're Thomas Kline?" he confirmed. "My name is Chief Baggetta. I'm concerned about Mary Harris and I'm told you are close friends."

"We're friends." Thomas stiffened slightly, expecting the blow. He watched Baggetta pick up a piece of paper and scan it briefly.

"Is she in trouble?" he asked.

Of course, she's in trouble, he thought glumly.

Baggetta stared at him from across the top of the paper that hid his features. "How long have you known Ms. Harris and how well do you know her?"

Thomas noted his voice was moderate, without inflection, giving no clues how he should answer. His mouth went dry. "I've known her awhile. We've gotten very close in a very short time."

"Can you tell me if she knows any of these students?" he persisted. Baggetta read a list of seven or so names. Thomas responded positively to two names he recognized from her classes. His inquisitor focused on a certain student. "Did you ever see her with a student named Marc Albritton?"

The one that committed suicide, he remembered. Thomas replied no, and felt the skin on his neck crawl. Chief Baggetta's intentions were becoming abundantly clear. He frowned when asking the next question.

"One of my men found her outside the women's dorm before dawn last week. Did she mention this to you?" The pressure mounted.

Thomas tried to swallow. A drink of water would have been out of the question. "She, uh, tends to—," he started. "She's restless many nights. I don't know what she was doing out—" He caught himself starting to say, … out all night.

Baggetta sat forward, immediately alerted. "This is a serious matter for her and the rest of the student body."

Thomas sensed the Chief's tone change from impersonal to personal; his questions came in a rapid-fire staccato.

"Where is Mary Harris now?"

"I don't know."

"When do you expect to see her again?"

"When she comes back."

"When did you last see her?"

"The Friday she left."

"Where?"

Thomas paused. "I drove her to a place four miles from campus, and left her on the road." The truth hurt. Baggetta could easily find out he had driven her off campus. Chief Baggetta's eyes widened appreciably. Thomas tried to get his bearings while Baggetta mused over the last juicy tidbit. *Mary*, he swore silently, *how could you do this to me*?

"I had hoped that the students of today had better sense," Baggetta snorted, then asked, "What makes you think she's planning to or even able to return?"

A weakness starting in the pit of his stomach spread both ways. Nausea.

"She may have been killed, or have hitchhiked to Canada by now," Baggetta said somberly. Then he asked bluntly, "Why had Mary disappeared?"

Thomas knew he was caught; dare he confess the true scope of her unusual behavior? He spoke painfully, hesitantly, with unrecognized sorrow. "I'm the last person capable of explaining what Mary does. We're going through a rough time. She's still seeing other men. If she doesn't come to her senses soon, we can forget it. I wish I could help you." He sighed, then added, "I want to see her come back more than anyone."

"Thomas, you are the closest thing to an actual relation I've been able to find. I've not been able to confirm most of her background. When she returns, we will all sit down and have a talk." Baggetta rubbed his chin with his forefinger. Thomas tried to look shocked. "You knew?" Baggetta asked.

Shaking on the inside, Thomas asked him what he planned to do. He said he would place a memo in her file, describing her inappropriate student behavior and would recommend to the school board that she be suspended until she could provide a complete background and convince him she planned to adhere to all campus rules and regulations permanently.

He asked if this would affect his student standing.

"Frankly, son, you were duped. I'll let you off this time with a warning. Your record has been very good so far. I'd hate to see it blemished because of one thoughtless act." Baggetta scribbled a note on what looked like her file.

"I have to call the police, too, and report her missing. Stay available. They may want you to take them to the place where you left her." Baggetta dismissed him.

Thomas stood, wiped his hands on his pants, and shook Baggetta's hand. The sound and feel of the office door latching shut filled him with relief. He gained momentum as he neared the exit. The patrolman spoke to him as he went by. The words were muffled and meaningless sounds. He pushed outward, free at last.

The lounge chair was hard where the bony parts of his body crushed the cushion to the wooden frame. It was an old worn chair in Baggetta's living room. It supported him and that was all he cared for. Albritton felt the high wraparound support. His arms were as lifeless weights and he slumped; something he rarely did. The warming sunlight that poured through partially open curtains illuminated the contoured furnishings and revealed the glory of a fresh new day.

Albritton felt the rows of stitching along the armrests where the off-white upholstered fabric was joined. To get up and lay down would have required more effort that he wanted to exert. His lower back and neck muscles ached in protest as he shifted positions. Marc was now laid to rest beside his mother. The skin around Albritton's ribcage tightened as he heaved deeply. Baggetta urged him to continue a normal life, but what could ever be normal in a world without his family?

Where was righteousness, he wondered, charging out of the heavens to punish the guilty? He asked himself if he had done enough to find out why his son had died. He clenched his fist and tapped weakly on the solid armrest. He had to put Marc's tragedy behind him, and find the will to live. Cold fingers reached for the gold-framed picture cradled in his lap and he turned it over. He touched the family portrait taken years before of his beloved Teresa and Marc. The likenesses comforted him.

Chief Baggetta arrived home later than his usual hour, but with a great burden lifted. An extra two hours were spent helping the Trenton police wrap their useless decoy operation, ending the active investigation of the slasher on campus. The killer had disappeared, mysteriously. The coed eventually regained enough of her composure to give the police a hazy description of a man. Baggetta's features turned to stone as he flipped through a jingling key ring.

Murder was an ugly, ugly crime. It was difficult to understand how any person could willingly and deliberately take the life of another human being, except in war. Baggetta entered his living room in darkness; his nightstick banged noisily. When he turned on a lamp, he found Albritton asleep in a lounge chair. Exhausted. Baggetta knelt beside his guest. He had rallied for a short time, he remembered, but fell apart after the services. The beautiful requiem was little comfort.

Baggetta considered getting a quilt from a closet, but rejected the idea. Daniel would scoff at him. His friend needed rest; what he needed more was peace. No physician or friend could give him that. Baggetta studied him carefully. His clothes were unkempt and wrinkled. He then noticed the gold-framed picture turned down in his lap. Baggetta lifted it gently. A family portrait of Theresa and Marc. "Wake up, Daniel," he prompted.

Albritton opened his eyes immediately. They were a sharp blue. "I must have dozed off." He slurred his words, then glanced around the bulk of his host to check the time on a large blue luminescent clock. He set the picture on the lamp table.

"Are you hungry?" Baggetta asked.

Albritton moaned as he sat up and shook his head in a broken rhythm.

"You have to eat something, to keep up your strength."

Albritton agreed and followed Baggetta into the

white kitchen. A bright fluorescent light bounced off the gleaming counter. Baggetta busied himself removing pans, utensils, and seasoning from a shelf. He heated leftover beef stew.

"Vincent," Albritton said, "did you talk to the boyfriend today?"

"I talked to him," Baggetta said. "No one has heard from her all week and the kid's very worried about his girlfriend. He said he never saw Marc and her together, and I believe him." Baggetta removed a wooden spoon from the stew and tasted it, then stirred. "Thomas told me something I didn't expect. The night she disappeared, as you say, he drove her to a place four miles from campus and left her."

Albritton put down the two flat bowls he was carrying. "Why?"

Baggetta shrugged. "He didn't know. I reported her missing to the police, even though he says she's coming back." He caught himself adding salt to their stew. Daniel did not like salt. He split the stew into the two bowls.

"How can she be coming back?" Albritton said while pouring coffee on the counter, and some in the cups. "She's cleaned her belongings out of her room, you said."

"Thomas believes she will return. I think he has

to believe this. He usually meets her between classes in the afternoon, but what she does from his after-noon class to the time his evening practice is over is a mystery."

"You believe me then," Albritton said enthusias-tically.

"All we really have," Baggetta said soothingly, "are remote possibilities and still no evidence. What link is there between your son and her?"

"She's a whore and she lied about knowing him," he spat.

Baggetta frowned; his dinner companion was get-ting worked up. "I've recommended suspension for Mary Harris until she can act like a responsible stu-dent. I hope that pleases you."

"I don't care," Albritton seethed. "I don't care what it takes to get to the truth about Marc!" He turned away from Baggetta.

"Daniel." He propped his elbows on the table as he tried to reason with his friend. "I hesitate to remind you what the police think happened to him. One. By your testimony Marc was involved with a woman who you claimed to be Ms. Harris, and she turned him down. Two. Marc was extremely upset. Three. He was found alone with your gun and only his fingerprints on it." Albritton's eyes began to moisten at the edges. "That is where the evidence points, and that is what the police believe."

Albritton stiffened as he spoke. "She killed my son."

Baggetta shook his arm to break the spell. "Daniel, do you realize what you're saying?"

"I know," he wheezed pitifully, "what the police and everyone else says about my son. There were no witnesses and it was my gun. They are saying he was a junkie, or mentally disturbed." He tightened his fist. "I told the police myself that he had been depressed. Over someone," he added.

"Many things are hard to accept, but we have to for our own sakes, then go on with life." Baggetta softened. "If you loved him, then let the police find the culprit."

"How, Vincent," Albritton replied lowly, "when they believe his death was suicide, not murder?"

Baggetta had no reply.

Thomas saw a beautiful, wheat-covered field, where he and Mary meandered through the countryside in the bright sunlight. The young woman in front of him grinned mischievously as she led him to a shaded area. A large wicker picnic basket and thermos dangled from his arm. Mary carried a blanket, and spread it under a large tree. They sat down. Alone with her; how he wanted her. She was barefoot, so was he. The earth was a soft cushion, a pillow without rocks or thorns or pain. A perfect world.

She was so beautiful! He rested against the tree and she snuggled under his arm. He supported and held her. Her body was firm, though her skin was smooth and soft to touch. She felt real; a dream come to life. He liked the way her hair tumbled over his arm and down to her waist, and he imagined traces of copper and hints of gold in it. She wore a woven, loose-fitting pure white chemise tied with a simple knot and long cotton skirt. The sounds of a stream gurgling nearby and the sweet melody of birds singing were their only accompaniment.

He moved his arm lower to the bare cool skin of her waist. Her chemise parted slightly, and he struggled to remain fixed on her lovely face and eyes. She was smiling, happy, and content; that was all that really mattered. She closed her eyes and rested her head on his shoulder. More than a hint of her breasts were outlined in the fabric. He nudged her gently in the ribs. She moaned softly.

Thomas kissed her. Their picnic basket lay undisturbed on the edge of the blanket. Hunger was a vague memory, and he sincerely doubted he could get her to eat anything. Right now, he wanted to feast on her love. She told him she wanted him and needed him and cherished him. He marveled that she actually wanted him. Thomas lay down and placed his hands behind his head, content. Mary remained sitting, leaning over him and idly writing her name on his open plaid shirt. Buttons parted and slender fingers toyed with his chest.

From his vantage point, he saw clouds begin to gather overhead. Thomas willed them away. Mary was sliding her hand up and down his chest. They truly belonged together and he hoped she felt the same way he did. A very thick cumulus cloud threatened to block the sunlight. A memory of a girl Thomas knew in high school flashed through his mind. That was not love; it never was. He had learned. Slowly, the cloud moved from sight. He reached for Mary, telling her she was the girl of his dreams. It sounded kinda corny, he thought, but she laughed. She was free from secrets and other terrible things. She was his.

She leaned over and kissed him deeply. As their mouths parted, her hot breath came in slow gasps. She began to unloose the knot of her chemise. Thomas clearly heard the swishing sounds of wheat stirring in the breeze and of birds chirping. The woven fabric parted. She leaned over him, hooked her fingers in the straps of her top, and began sliding it off, sliding it off her shoulders. He heard knocking; his world became much dimmer. The pounding grew louder. He reached for her, but she was gone. She was never there.

A heavy pounding and knocking on his door persisted. Thomas found himself in his room alone. He swore under his breath, then snapped, "Why now?" He mumbled that it sounded like a mob outside his door, and angrily bounded out of bed and stumbled half-asleep to open it. Four pairs of hands pulled him out roughly and dragged him down the hallway.

Thomas recoiled in uncertainty. It could not be a razing; he was at the end of his sophomore year. He repressed an urge to laugh at the ridiculous spectacle of being dragged down the stairs in his underwear by his dorm mates. Many angry faces along the hallway greeted him from partially open doors. A few joined in the procession. It ended downstairs at the telephone. The telephone, he wondered, at two in the morning?

A sea of perturbed young men parted and closed behind him. He said hello. A long missed voice answered. "Mary!" Thomas gasped. He momentarily forgot about the hour and his lynch mob. "Where have you been? Are you all right?" he asked in rapid succession.

"I'm fine, everything is fine," she replied. Her voice sounded muffled as if she was calling from a pay phone. "I, uh, finished my little project and couldn't wait to talk to you. This week seemed terribly long to me. How are you?"

"I'm okay," he said. "Just great," he mumbled sardonically while looking over his escorts. "When are you coming home?"

"Tomorrow afternoon at the latest. I tried to finish before the banquet. You haven't asked someone else, have you?"

Thomas vaguely remembered something about an award's banquet, and plans made before Mary disappeared and Chief Baggetta gave him other things to worry about. "I still want us to go."

"Mary," he started, "something happened today you should know. Campus security called me over to answer a lot of questions about you. Chief Baggetta said he was going to recommend suspension until you show him a new application. I think he also called the police to report you missing."

"What else did you tell him about me?" she asked.

"Nothing he wanted to hear." Thomas became

flushed. So much of their relationship had been on display. He glanced at the students around him, placed his hand over the receiver, and whispered to his dorm mates, "Do you mind?" A few of them left. He returned to his girlfriend.

"Thomas, did he ask you about a specific student?"

"Some guy named Marc Albritton; the one that shot himself."

She cut in. "I'm sorry. You got caught in part of a misunderstanding. I didn't know him nearly as well as they think, and I have absolutely no idea how or why he died. I'm sorry you were dragged into this. It's partially why I left."

Thomas felt many things become more clearer.

"What about your suspension?" he asked.

The phone went dead.

"Hello, Mary, are you still there?" he prompted.

"Yes," she said dejectedly. "Did he give you any details about why I was suspended?"

Thomas hated to talk about this. "It's a disciplinary action, mostly to bring you in line. And why was he checking into your application?"

She sighed. "I believe a friend of his put him up to it." She perked up. "What time do you want to go to the banquet?"

He held the phone expectantly, wishing he could see her. "When are you coming home?" He heard a scrape, like she had put the receiver down, then picked it up again. She sounded apologetic when she spoke.

"I'll stay in the city tonight. Can you pick me up at the rail station at six tomorrow evening? I'll be dressed and ready."

"Where are you going to sleep tonight?" Thomas insisted.

"In a few hours, it'll be morning. I have to be going. Don't worry. I've taken care of myself for this long."

"Is there a chance I could find out what all this is about?" he asked quickly. She was going to hang up on him and disappear from his life again.

"Yes, Thomas," her voice sounded subdued, "it's time you knew the truth. If you want, I'll even show you where I've been staying this week. But, please, let your questions wait until after the banquet."

Thomas agreed, having waited this long. She also asked him not to discuss her return until she had time to think about what to tell Chief Baggetta. They exchanged goodbyes and Thomas hung up. It was scary to think he would actually find out what had been going on all this time. It was sobering. She once said he would learn the truth when he was ready. Was he ready? he pondered. He did not feel any different as he trudged very quietly to his room.

Majken hung up the telephone and moved away from the lighted enclosure to the shadows. A stiff, early morning wind whipped tendrils of steam rising from a vent in the street. She stood alone, carrying only her shoulder bag. The other vampyr was gone; sent away after their last meal at midnight. John would travel by night and sleep by day until he was far away.

Trenton would be a haze, an unpleasant memory to be avoided permanently.

From where they parted, she had walked and hitchhiked back to Trenton. Majken clutched her bag tighter and headed deeper into the city, driven by her quest for a victim. Her unfortunate association with John and the week's deprivation had sharply increased her blood need.

The thought of telling Thomas about herself frightened her. The majority of her belongings remained at the mansion. She wondered if she decided before she left to bring him there? Majken ran down a list of suitable checkpoints in her mind; she had time to feed, yet. But this was nowhere as convenient as being in her dorm. She would have to move carefully to reestablish herself on campus. As Majken searched, she planned on how to tell Thomas. A chill penetrated her beige overcoat as she realized she needed him, and was unable to say why.

Thomas restlessly paced from the rail station lobby to the receiving area outside as he waited for the first sign of Mary. He came inside to compare his watch to the large wall clock suspended over the departure area. Officially, he was early. Tonight's festivities were to start at seven. Waiting made him uncomfortable, and lately, he had been uncomfortable a lot.

While standing next to a row of vending machines, he idly hooked a finger into his collar to loosen his tie. The starch of his newly pressed shirt scraped his neck. As a school athlete, his presence was highly desirable, and a formality he wished he could avoid. At any rate, it was a chance to see the new banquet hall.

His roommate had returned from home this morning, and was actually looking forward to going. Thomas smiled, knowing that Phillip's mind was actually on his date, Ann Russell. Mary did not know her. Inevitably, Phillip asked about Mary. Thomas discretely avoided telling him about leaving her on the roadside, her weeklong absence, and about his talk with the security chief. He felt it was all best forgotten, which did not leave much to say.

Thomas stared at the lobby entrance harder, as if his concentration would make Mary enter sooner. Why would she choose a place like this to meet? Perhaps he had agreed too quickly. She did have a way of getting what she wanted. Phillip had suggested that she was using him; that painful thought crossed his mind more than once. Tonight, she promised the truth. He knew this could be their last chance to make it.

A soft voice spoke his name. He wheeled about and caught his breath. Majken smiled, letting her hands brush the sleeves of his coat. Thomas gently took her hands. He had never seen her like this! She wore a long gown with ruffles at the top, drawn at the waist with a slender band, and the skirt swept over her hips to the floor. A white laced shawl covered her bare shoulders, and a black choker was fastened around her neck with an oval clasp. Her hair was finely brushed and arranged to the left, held by a red ribbon. Her smile broadened with his.

"You're beautiful," he said breathlessly.

He embraced her and she held him lightly. They

kissed in greeting, warmly and leisurely. When they parted, Thomas held her at arm's length. Words were inadequate to express how he felt as she looked at him with liquid violet eyes. Thomas escorted her to his car.

"I missed you very much," she said as he opened her door, "and I promised to come back." Majken slid gracefully into the seat. Thomas allowed her to pull the skirt of her gown inside, then closed her door and came to the driver's side.

He looked at her, silently, waiting. He wanted badly to ask where she had been and what she was doing.

To his unspoken questions, she replied, "It is time you knew." She murmured softly, allowing her gaze to drop. "But, let's have this evening to enjoy together first. My problem is not easily explained. I need the right ... place."

Thomas clutched the steering wheel; he should have known! An expression of pain mixed with a glimpse of hopefulness in her eyes kept him from beating the steering wheel in frustration. Having waited months ... a few more hours ... he sensed the sincerity in her request and nodded. Thomas started his car. The downtown banquet hall was fifteen minutes away.

The parking deck was full of expensive cars. Thomas showed his student ID and received a time-stamped ticket. He circled the deck; his too quiet girlfriend asked him to drive to the very top. He circled and pulled out from the harsh fluorescent lights inside to the cooler night sky. He pulled into a scarcely populated corner and parked.

He checked his watch in the dimming light.

Mary opened her door and walked to the edge of the deck overlooking the street below. The banquet hall was a three story brick building framed with swathes of blue and gold banners. He joined her and peered over the railing with her. She smiled at him, but her eyes were far away. The tepid breeze from the city streets stirred tendrils of her chestnut hair. She was so beautiful.

The expression on her face was hard to fathom.

Thomas pulled her close as he placed his arm around her.

"It's almost night," she said.

Thomas looked out. "We have a few minutes. Want to relax here for a while?" She responded by curling under his arm in such a way as to arouse his protective instincts. As they settled and Thomas held her, he noticed that she felt different. Tense maybe. He told himself it was the newness of the situation, multiplied by not seeing her all week. Had she changed, or was it him? Tonight, in her own time, he would find out what she was really like. He held her only a few moments, then announced, "It's time to go." She pulled away, again relaxed.

They descended the parking deck to the ground floor and crossed arm in arm to a newly paved walkway that led to the banquet room entrance. Four floodlights lit the exterior rough hewn brick. Majken asked what the interior was like.

"This is the first off-campus building," he explained. "It's designed for entertaining with a large dining room and a second floor theater-style auditorium for speakers. I'm told the banquet room can be partitioned into meeting rooms and it has a kitchen." Thomas and his date found themselves in the banquet room, where the catering staff was putting last minute touches on the linen-draped tables. Piped music served as a backdrop to multiple conversations.

The room was large and elegantly decorated, with richly stained paneling, a floor polished to a deep luster, and electric candlelight along the walls. Many couples lounged in couches placed on the sides. Several had gathered around a table of refreshments, snacks, and appetizers for those that wanted to fortify themselves before the proceedings began. Majken commented on the subdued lighting.

Phillip and Ann crossed the room to join them. He gave Thomas a friendly slap on the arm. "Hello, you made it."

Thomas smiled generously. "Of course."   He grinned as Phillip looked over Majken; and he, Ann. "Mary," he said, "this is Ann Russell, a good friend of Phillip's." Majken shook her hand.

Phillip broke in. "Would you girls like anything?" He pointed to a table laden with cups of punch and fruit juice. Ann was thirsty. Majken went along. Phillip hooked Thomas and dragged him away. Out of hearing range, he whispered to Thomas, "What did she tell you?"

"What do you mean?" Thomas asked.

Phillip munched on a cream cookie. "You forgot to tell me about a few things this morning. I asked around. She's in trouble, and if you don't watch yourself, she'll drag you down too."

Thomas glanced at the two girls who were chatting like old friends. "I thought we weren't going to bring this up. She's here, isn't she!" He picked up a cup of punch for him and fruit juice for her.

"Don't get mad; I want you to work things out, but I can't stand it when she gives you the runaround and you put up with it."

Phillip retrieved two cups of punch and followed Thomas. He pleaded, "Watch yourself."

Dr. Albritton came to the award's banquet at the firm insistence of his friend, a totally sublime effort on Vincent's part to thrust him back into the mainstream of campus life. Albritton was grateful he had received help when he needed it the most. Soon it would be time to go home. Everyday, he became stronger and more able to cope. Remembering the good times helped. Later, he would actively entertain the idea of returning to teaching, but would work up to a full schedule gradually.

His duties on the award staff completed, he looked forward to the various speakers and the presentations scheduled to start in five minutes. He made his way to the banquet hall for some refreshment. Albritton reeled when he saw her. His features went pale and contorted; his right hand crushed a programme tighter and tighter.

Majken found herself drawn closer to Thomas, reluctantly. Seeing him again helped to overcome a blanket of apathy that had engulfed her during her forced absence. Her clearest threat on campus arose from Marc's father with his grief and suspicions directed at her. She considered it best to resume a normal life and allow his rampant speculations to end quietly. Fortunately, the slasher was gone forever, and the hysteria and paranoia would leave, too. Her suspension was a different matter. Chief Baggetta had to be attacked directly. She planned to resubmit the same records she had prepared originally, with extra supportive documentation she had just happened to find, like "her" medical records at age twelve.

Phillip's date, Ann, was a vivacious and inquisitive girl. She was blonde, deeply tanned, and wore a royal blue gown. Ann stood squarely across from Majken, keeping the conversation polite; first admiring her chiffon gown, now faded, then commenting on the fine, embroidered stitching along her waist. It struck her how unusually observant Ann was. She had to be careful. Earlier, she had felt the subtle internal signals that warned of her impending blood need. Besides improvising a suitable excuse to leave the banquet, she feared she would require blood much sooner than she had planned.

She caught a glimpse of Thomas and Phillip across the room. Ultimately, Thomas would be the deciding factor of whether she returned to campus life. She needed him, wanted him, and wanted to stay. Majken realized he had fallen for Mary Harris and she had allowed certain things to slip by, revealing more of her true nature gradually, subconsciously. Now, she was willing to take the risk that he would want her enough to become a donor. Odds were, he would not understand.

Thomas returned to Majken's side and gave her a small cup of fruit juice and waited anxiously until she took the first sip. Actually, he noticed, she wet her lips and the juice did not go into her mouth. He wanted to hold her, but a palpable force separated them like a thick mist. Phillip and Ann were busily engaged in munching and drinking. Thomas watched Majken. She just stood there with the small cup balanced in the palm of her hand. He had never really noticed this before. He chatted with Phillip a few minutes, absently, noting that she was actually looking for a place to set the cup down. When Phillip and Ann excused themselves to join the students milling reluctantly toward the auditorium, Thomas was alone with her.

He took her cup from her and laid it with his own on a nearby table.

"Mary," he said. She faced him. The mist between them swirled higher and higher.

He noted the sadness along the corners of her eyes. She was alert and scanning the entire room. When he reached to pull her close, she melted into him. He felt her shudder, then the sensation was gone. "What's the matter?" he asked.

"Just hold me," she whispered. She tucked her head on his chest and tightened her lips in determination. He asked her again what was wrong. "Thomas," she began slowly, "I must leave before the banquet, and I want you to come with me."

Thomas shook his head. "Why?" His limbs felt cold, as if he were standing on the edge of his own freshly dug grave. Majken held him and seemed to look around herself before speaking. She whispered so low he was forced to place his head next to hers to even hear. "I must survive on a special diet. I cannot take regular food like you."

He frowned, greatly disturbed.

She held his face gently with her fingertips. "I'll explain, but not here," she emphasized.

Thomas told her they had to at least stay for the ceremonies.

Phillip wasted little time in corralling Ann to a safe distance from Thomas and Mary, well out of earshot range, to have a talk. Ann jerked her arm free.

Phillip apologized. "Find out anything?" he asked.

Ann stared across the room. "Nothing," she said. "It would help if I knew what you were looking for."

Phillip told her anything suspicious. Ann asked why.

"I'm worried about him," he replied. "She plays him for a fool and he goes right along with her." Phillip had already told her the rumors.

Ann gestured toward Thomas. "He's a big boy now. They're not children."

"He's crazy about her and not thinking straight," Phillip argued.

Ann lowered her voice when another couple passed close by. "Look at them," she implored. Phillip glanced over his shoulder. "Anyone can see they're in love with one another. What gives us the right to butt in?"

Phillip acquiesced with a shrug. "Actually, I was worried more about you than him." Ann laughed nervously. "She's not right in some way. Promise me you'll be extra careful when you're around her."

That moment, Thomas tapped him on the back. "Let's find a seat," Thomas said. Phillip and Ann confronted him.

"Where's Mary?" Ann asked.

"Powder room," Thomas replied. "I'm going to save her a seat."

Phillip and Ann exchanged a knowing look, then Ann excused herself also. Thomas chatted with Phillip while standing in line. "Mary wants to leave before the banquet."

"What for?" he exclaimed. "The banquet's the whole reason for coming. That's why they place it after the award's ceremonies, so we'll stay."

Thomas waved him down. "I know, I know." The pair made their way past the double doors into the corridor. Thomas waited. "Something else she said, I'd better not repeat," he mumbled.

"What?" Phillip prompted. The girls were taking a long time, he thought.

"She said she had been staying in this old house this week, somewhere, and she's thinking about buying it. I asked her where she'd get that kind of money. She asked, 'How expensive could it be?'"

Phillip had a sudden attack of heartburn. Thomas was being very foolhardy, not even knowing where this place was.

Thomas concluded. "I know you're worried, but I think she'll be honest with me now, tonight after the banquet. You understand, I have to try."

Phillip's resolve crumbled under his roommate's earnest gaze. Thomas had wanted her for so long. The two young men entered the auditorium. Phillip tapped his friend's arm lightly, for luck, before they separated in the crowded theater. Phillip claimed a pair of adjacent seats near the aisle; Thomas found seats three rows back near the center.

Phillip glanced over his shoulder at Thomas. He whispered thoughtfully, "I hope you know what you're doing, buddy."

Majken steadied herself next to a banquet table as the pressure to feed mounted another assault. Thomas had let her go reluctantly. She was only beginning to explain and hated to lose this night, this chance. Time was not on her side. She had to feed before losing control and in no way could she risk taking Thomas to the mansion in her condition. Majken searched from the lounge to the rear service entrance: all deserted. The ceremony was ready to begin.

She entered the ladies room and turned on cold water in a basin. She concentrated, tense. The running water sounded very loud against the basin. She heard approaching footsteps; her hand slid into her purse and held a scoring knife. It was Ann. Majken dropped the knife as Ann walked over.

"You going to make it?" she asked. Her question echoed in the tiled room.

Majken cupped her hands and splashed cold water on her face; her need for blood started to abate. A temporary reprieve. Ann gave her some paper towels to dry her face. Majken examined herself in the mirror. She was presentable, at the moment. "I'd hate to ruin Thomas' evening. We may leave early," she said, as she faced Ann.

"I'm sure you'll make it," Ann said cheerfully.

Majken surveyed the tall, athletic girl who was too close to Thomas to risk it, and instantly decided not to attack. She followed Ann out, directly into Marc's father. The sensations that drove her blood needs started to return.

Albritton stepped away from the opposing wall. Majken hoped to avoid a scene, but could only mutter, "Dr. Albritton?" The older man smiled sadly and offered his hand.

"I want to apologize for my rude behavior, Ms. Harris. I truly hope we can mend our differences." Albritton stepped back a respectable distance. Majken studied him, quite in shock at his change.

"You were under a great deal of stress," Majken replied.

"Please, if you know anything about Marc, I promise—" his voice cracked.

Majken shook her head, sorry for the broken father. Albritton turned away. Majken prompted Ann to move on.

"What was that all about?" Ann asked when they reached the auditorium.

"A misunderstanding," Majken answered with a deep breath.

Majken joined Thomas, passing half a row of students. The dean was speaking. Thomas asked her self-consciously where she had been. That was the last he spoke to her.

Twenty minutes dragged into an eternity. Her side started to throb, the pit of her abdomen started to burn. She trembled in the press of very many human beings. She had to get out! Majken told Thomas she would return in a few minutes and left before he could answer. She again crawled over countless feet, then sprinted from the theater.

Another, waiting, saw her leave and followed her.

The banquet hall was void, filled with rows of lifeless, bloodless tables. Majken was frightened. She stared outside, beyond the glass partition and flood lamps into the night. She squeezed her eyes closed and pressed her fists against the cool plate glass.

Thomas would have to wait, she decided. Dressed as she was, the fastest way seemed to be go to the nearest club, and try to get picked up. She needed a ready victim and would deal with consequences later.

Majken reached for the door, but froze on hearing an angry cry. Albritton! He charged her, and pushed against the door with his frail body. The muscles of her back coiled, her eyes narrowed.

"You're not leaving until you tell me about my son!"

The urge to kill trickled strongly through her brain, she could imagine her fingers ripping his throat apart. She held herself. His death would make it impossible for her to return to the campus, and Thomas. When she tried to speak, her voice caught in her throat. He made her decision for her. She bolted away and reached the other side of the room before the older man could react. Majken dropped her purse and shawl and kicked her shoes under a table, then disappeared out of the rear entrance.

Albritton pursued, his footsteps clicking loudly on the tile floor. The metal door was ajar. He pushed it open cautiously and stepped down. A large garbage disposal unit rested on a thick concrete slab next to the building. The slab ended in another step toward an alley, three feet from the corner of the building. Albritton pushed the door closed while his eyes adjusted to the outside lighting. He went to the corner and peered the length of the deserted alley. A sound came from the shrubbery on the other side of the chain link fence. Movement.

He gripped the wire fence like the bars of a prison cell and strained to see into the darkness. He called. He knew she could not escape. After a period of silence, he heard a louder disturbance in the woods farther down. Albritton rushed to where he perceived the sounds had come, held the top of the fence, and started to climb. He shoved the toe of his shoe into the link at knee level and pushed upward, panting from the effort.

Eerie, faint sounds of applause from the auditorium were far away. He climbed halfway, his wrist shaking to miss the wire barbs, and called.

Majken attacked from behind by holding his arm and impaling his thigh deep onto the pointed wire. The older man screamed; she pulled him backwards.

He must not die, she thought quickly, nearly out of control.

She supported him as he fell, hitting the newly laid pavement and knocking the wind out of him. His head followed the momentum of his body and struck the ground, not hard enough to break his neck.

She hiked the skirt of her gown to her thigh and knelt beside her victim. He was no longer Marc's father, her tormentor. He was unconscious, breathing in small gasps, but alive. She ripped the expensive fabric of his trousers, making the hole wider. Rich blood flowed from the wound; she lowered her mouth and drank. Majken, herself, began to lose touch with her surroundings as the precious fluid filled her, satisfying her need. Her extremities felt numb, her mind ebbed, as her body began to absorb the blood.

Thomas knew he should have listened to his instincts and followed Mary immediately. He stumbled past the students, having waited too long, and chided himself for ignoring her. She had been frightened! This realization jolted him and he prayed to find her. A sorrowful attitude was little help, he thought. He hoped to see her returning as he left the auditorium. His heart sank in the empty hallway.

Phillip and Ann burst out of the swinging doors. "Mary's disappeared," he told them. Thomas read the expression on Phillip's face. It hurt all over again.

He led them to the banquet hall, where Ann spotted something on a table. Ann found her shawl and purse abandoned. Thomas found her shoes kicked under the table. He held her shoes by the strap. This was unusual, even for her.

Thomas suggested they split up. He went to the parking deck to check his car. Untouched as far as he could see. Her side was unlocked. Dejected, he dropped her shoes in the car seat, locked his car, and scanned the street below. He called her.

The night air stood still. He waited, then called again. The woman, who less than an hour ago had sat in his car, was nowhere to be seen. As Thomas searched, he asked himself why he came. "Because I love her," he said. Why did she come? "I don't know." The short distance to the banquet hall stretched. "Oh, Mary."

Thomas found Phillip and Ann standing next to the table where they split up. Phillip had searched the kitchen area; the staff there had seen or heard no one. The storage rooms were locked. Ann went to the washroom. It seemed an obvious place to look. Phillip asked if she might have gone with someone. Thomas emphatically said no.

Phillip nudged Ann on her arm and became a statue. "Tell him what you told me."

"He's your friend," Ann reminded Phillip.

Phillip stared at the polished floor. Thomas asked what. He was considering calling the police. She told him earlier that she had called the police and declared herself alive and not missing. She told them she had gone out of town on business. Phillip pointed to the rest rooms.

"Ann told me that a man, an older, well-dressed man, spoke to Mary as they were coming to the auditorium. His name was Al—," he glanced at Ann, "britton. Yeah, Albritton."

Thomas knew the name.

Phillip continued. "He apologized, he said, for his rude behavior. The old guy was begging her. He didn't threaten her, or anything." He glanced at Ann who nodded in agreement.

Thomas sighed deeply and felt like banging his head on the wall. What an idiot! Marc Albritton's father was here. That's why she left. Phillip and Ann studied the expression on his face.

"What is it?" Phillip demanded.

Suddenly, Thomas understood much more and at the same time, felt a deep compelling need to keep his mouth shut. He said, "Nothing." Many nebulous images were forming, dissolving and reshaping in his head. Was he in love with a murderess? Could she? The question clogged his mind.

"Have we looked everywhere?" he asked.

"There are rooms next to the auditorium stage,

and out back," Ann said. Phillip and Ann chose the rooms; Thomas chose outside.

Thomas paused in the auditorium hallway before traversing the outer corridor alone. A round of applause echoed through the swinging doors, signaling the end of another speaker. One more to go, Thomas calculated. He thought he heard a few whistles, too. The students were getting hungry. He wanted to find her fast.

The service entrance creaked open on new hinges. A gust of air escaped, raising the hair on the back of his head. The silence and stillness of the night was unnerving, like he had stepped into a black, sound-proof envelope. His stomach churned. The area was dimly lit. It took him several minutes to adjust. He called her name.

Majken heard a steady, rhythmic throbbing, the sounds of blood swishing in her ears. A pervasive calm filled her as she felt her skin tingle, open and sensitive to the night. Inside, her meal was absorbed. Consciousness spread to her extremities. Her hands rested on her victim's chest. He was unconscious and of no further concern to her.

His wound was smeared with a thick, dark clot. Dried blood matted his trousers and formed a circle on the black pavement. Majken   could barely remember squeezing the wound closed with her fingers. Her hands were stained and she tasted blood on her face and lips. She fished through his coat pocket to find a remarkably clean, pressed handkerchief, then examined herself.

She shifted her position on the pavement. Her knees were raw, though not scraped, and her toes and feet tingled when the pressure was released. Her gown was crumpled and soiled on the skirt. Instinctively, she had carefully avoided staining her gown. Majken wiped her face and hands. Some blood around her cuticles would remain until she could get to the soft fiber brush in her purse.

Majken checked Albritton. She probed his neck and the back of his head for signs of bleeding or fractures. He breathed slowly, but deeply, with an occasional wheeze. His rib cage seemed intact, though a hairline fracture was entirely possible. He would wake up with a splitting headache and would require, hopefully, a few months of recuperation in the hospital. Majken almost grinned.

The most serious danger came from his lowered body temperature and the impending night chill. It had to appear as an accident. She assured herself that all he should remember is losing his grip, sticking his leg on the wire barb, and hitting the pavement. A distinguished figure like Dr. Albritton would surely be missed at the banquet and found. She hoped he would look like a fool when trying to explain this stunt. Majken stepped over his body and padded softly toward the rear entrance.

She froze on hearing her name called. Thomas, she realized. She met him at the corner, braced her hands against his chest, and pinned him to the building.

"Mary," he gasped. "We've been looking for you. What are you doing out here?"

"I became ill and had to get out." She held the blood stained handkerchief over his head, out of his direct line of sight. Thomas jumped when it brushed his ear.

"Your disappearing act wouldn't have anything to do with Marc Albritton's father being here, would it?" As Thomas pushed on her arms, she stepped back.

Majken answered pensively. "Yes."

Thomas crossed his arms and refused to move until she told him the whole story.

"He came after me," she began. "Dr. Albritton is convinced I know something about his son's death. Last week, he harassed me on campus. Tonight he cornered me in the banquet room, ranting like a madman. I ran out here to lose him. "

"Where is he now?" he asked.

"I don't know," she answered, looking straight at him.

Thomas kicked off the building and paced around her. Her fists were closed and tucked under her arms. Thomas might have assumed she was chilled. "You were late meeting me in the lounge the night he shot himself, I remember." His voice turned cold.

"Marc was exactly like his father. Stubborn. He chased me, saying he loved me and wanted me. I tried to discourage him; I didn't want you involved. That evening, he pounced on me. I told him I never wanted to see him again. That's why I was late. Marc killed himself."

Majken bowed her head, but watched Thomas. He glared at her, pacing like a caged animal, then spat angrily, "How long did you and he sleep together?"

"A few months," she admitted.

"That's almost as long as I've known you!" Thomas exclaimed. "Why?" he implored.

She felt the hurt pour from his eyes again. When she came closer, her arms helplessly at her side, he stepped away. "Thomas, they serve a need," she said quietly.

Thomas spun toward the corner.

The night was cooler, now, and she wished he would understand. She placed her hand on his shoulder and gently pulled him to face her. "I'm sorry that what I am hurt you."

He leaned back, rested his head against the cool metal door, and stared into space.

"What are you?" Majken remained silent. His body was tense and rigid; he pursed his lips bitterly, and said, "We haven't got a chance with you sleeping around."

Majken walked slowly from his end of the slab to the other, placing one foot on the grass. The quiet whisper of the wind stirring the limbs, and even the few cars passing on the streets, reminded her of desolation.

She faced him. "You mean more to me that I can say. I wanted us to have this night, a night of peace and togetherness." She held her arms toward him. "We've come this far."

"Why didn't you tell me Marc Albritton was giving you trouble?"   She came forward and placed her hand gently on his arm. Even by the corner neon light, his eyes were still a warm brown, she noticed. "Things could have been much worse."

Thomas reached and held her, embracing. Her

body relaxed and pressed calmly next to his.

Majken felt alive and whole. Her life seemed more secure now that she accepted the part he played in it. She needed him, but telling him proved to be more difficult. He loved Mary Harris, not her. For now, they were one and the same woman; it was due to end as soon as she told him the whole truth.

"Thomas," she coaxed gently, "we need to leave."

He brushed his fingers through her hair, held her neck and kissed her passionately. "What's the hurry?" he asked, starting to kiss her throat above her choker.

Her senses tuned to a muffled cough and the heavy scrape of an arm falling to the concrete. Albritton, she remembered. She tugged Thomas. "I want to show you where I stayed this week. Please, come with me." He started to follow her; she halted and listened within.

Phillip, followed by Ann, cautiously stepped into the darkness.

"Here you are," Phillip and Ann said in unison. Ann was carrying Majken's shawl and purse. Majken retrieved them and hastily stuffed the blood-stained handkerchief in her purse. "The banquet's starting," Phillip said.

Thomas seemed to look at Majken with uncertainty. "Mary wants us to leave early."

Ann stood next to Majken. "Are you feeling better?"

Cold blue-white fluorescent light was cast through the open metal door. Majken blinked and squinted; she noticed Thomas and Phillip were staring at her. Her hair was clearly disheveled and her gown crumpled and dirty.

"What happened to you?" he asked.

Majken said lamely that she slipped on the grass and fell. She heard another cough, followed by a low rasping sound. Next would come a cry for help. Majken moved boldly between Thomas and Phillip.

"Where are you going?" Phillip asked warily. "Back to campus?"

Majken said brightly, "It's a surprise."

Phillip grabbed Thomas' arm. "Do you realize what you're doing? Don't go with her, buddy," he pleaded, "she's dangerous."

"What kind of bullshit nonsense is that?" Thomas snapped.

"She's involved in that student's death."

"Listen, friend," he said icily, "I would rather believe her over you any day!"

Phillip glared at her; Majken held her peace.

"I hated to be the one to tell you about her in the

first place. If you're determined to go off and get yourself killed, that's your business!" Then, Phillip's voice softened. "Think about what you're about to do."

Majken held her breath while Thomas looked from her, clinging to his arm, to his best friend and roommate, standing ready to jump down her throat.

"We're leaving," Thomas said slowly. Phillip stepped aside and made a sweeping gesture with his arm. Thomas led her around the outside of the building. Majken heard a dull thud as Phillip apparently struck the siding.

Once in his car, he sat petrified behind the wheel. "I'm not sure this is right," he admitted.

Majken curled her feet under the car seat. "We're together tonight. That's all that is important."

Thomas started his car and pulled slowly out of the parking deck, leaving the gala banquet. Majken told him to head north, away from the city and the campus.

Phillip ignored Ann as she paced around him.

"Proud of yourself?" she sneered.

Phillip took the insult in stony silence. If Thomas was determined to get killed, there was nothing he could do to stop him. Nothing. He hit the wall again, harder. He then turned to Ann.

"You haven't been there," he sputtered, "all this time watching her manipulate him. I know he's in love with her." He paused to catch his breath. "That's what makes it worse."

"Well," Ann asked, "what now?"

Phillip smiled slightly. "I guess we eat." They started inside; he stopped, when he heard a sound. "Wait a minute," he whispered as he held her back. They listened; the night was ominously still. He cautiously approached the corner of the building. He eased against the door and held his date's hand tightly.

The alley was even darker than the entrance, but on the ground, he saw a form lying still on the black pavement. An arm moved. He ran to the body, an older man. Ann came up behind him.

"Oh, my God!" he exclaimed.

Chapter Nine

Thomas ignored the echoes of long dead warnings as he drove Majken to the unknown destination. He still wanted her, although tonight's date had been far from romantic. It could be called disastrous, especially the showdown with Phillip. He hoped his friend would forgive him. Leaving with her was the right thing to do. Thomas wished he could explain the change in her since they left the banquet. She seemed to be charged with an energy; an aura he had never seen before. It was like every moment until now was pretend, he thought. Tonight, she made it clear she wanted him, too. That was why he came.

She instructed him on how to find a small winding road cutting away from the two-lane and disappearing into the forest. She told him she was happy because he decided in her favor. They stopped briefly for his dinner, a quick snack compared to the banquet feast. Majken disappeared in the washroom while he ate, then smothered him with kisses as they left the restaurant and pulled on the road. Even the way she curled her body and legs, caressed his arm as he drove, and leaned toward him told him his patience was about to be rewarded.

He listened how she described their destination as a place isolated and majestic in its day. She described how the family might have lived there at the turn of the century. She pictured for him the bedrooms, the once great dining hall, the sitting room, her study, and the one bedroom she was reconditioning. Majken told him of her search through the property titles; she hoped to purchase it for taxes.

The nights were becoming distinctly cooler; a sign of approaching autumn. Majken rolled her window down and asked Thomas to drive slower. A great *déjà vu* feeling swept over him as he watched her scan the dark roadside, much as the night he had abandoned her, or she abandoned him. This time he promised no matter what to keep her in his sight. He pulled off his tie for comfort and tossed it over the seat.

He slowed to a crawl when she pointed to an invisible crease in the grass off the road ahead. His Honda tipped slightly as he left the road and slipped on gravel.

"We found it," Majken said excitedly.

The headlights spread far enough to the side for him to see the opening in the trees. Thomas hesitated. "Look how high the grass is," he pointed out. "Are you sure we can make it?" She reassured him.

His car scraped bottom as he crossed a ditch. The winding road was little more than a fire trail, though maneuverable. Tree branches scratched the windshield through endless blind curves. Majken grinned sheepishly when his car jutted across several large rocks in its path. Then, they cleared the trees. Atop the hillside, the old mansion rested in a clearing. Thomas stopped and gasped audibly.

"It's beautiful," Majken said.

The late evening sky was crystal clear and filled with stars. The waxing moon caught it at a sharp angle off the horizon, creating a haunting, ethereal glow. A presence. She invited him to have a closer look. Thomas edged forward.

The mansion was ancient, and small compared to modern standards. His girlfriend's close sense of association for the mansion imbued it with a certain charm. Thomas parked short of the broken wooden gate that circled the front, and stepped out. The exterior was weathered; most of the windows had rusty grates over them. Majken rushed to his side; he embraced her. He noticed the chill air did not seem to bother her.

Majken hugged Thomas when he placed his coat over her bare shoulders. She led him across the short, dried grass. They looked up as branches of a large gnarled tree scraped the ironwork over several second-story windows. Majken stood on a porch step, making her nearly Thomas' height, and kissed him.

Thomas kissed her warmly in return. She explained that this was her first home in Trenton. The campus was her second. All of that was behind them as they stepped up to the front door.

The entire mansion was basically a rectangle. In the very center of the front was a small porch with crumbling tile plates. The front door was solid oak, and held. In the bright moonlight, the gray weathered door facings appeared white. He watched his girlfriend trace the tooled brass fittings and ornate knocker with her finger. Sadly, there were signs of attempted entry and vandalism. He started to ask how they were going to get inside when Majken opened the old-styled lock. The door swung open.

Thomas followed her and stumbled slightly in the dark vestibule. She took advantage of his helplessness and kissed him without warning, then moved quickly away and asked him to wait in the hall until she could light some lamps. He stood in the open doorway, feeling a cold draft brush against his legs, and examined the peeling wall. It was silly to ask if there was electricity. Soon, he saw a soft warm glow come from a room down the hall to the right. He closed the front door. Another light flickered on. Thomas started forward as his eyes adjusted to the dim light.

He stood transfixed in the doorway when he saw her. The combined effect of the old mansion, the soft lamplight, and her antiquated gown stunned him. He smiled broadly and stepped inside. She looked like she was made for this place.

The sitting room was adequately clean and simply furnished, he noticed. The velour-covered couch had faded to a yellow ochre; a new dark brown comforter was spread over the top. Majken lay Thomas' coat to the side, held her delicate hands open, and bade him enter her world. She waited for him next to a heavy, low table stained a rich mahogany, the color of blood.

"Do you like it?" she asked. Thomas crossed the room.

They sat together on the small couch. Thomas laughed self-consciously. "Not what I expected," he said, bending over to examine the top of the table in detail. "Is this the original furniture?"

"This is my home away from home," she said. "I bought the table and couch at an auction, and had them delivered. The rest, I fixed or picked up."

An appreciative smile spread across Thomas' face. His history major was involved in hands-on research. Majken stopped talking, then slid off the couch past him, and began to stack kindling in the fireplace. Thomas came over to help her.

"This room was once the reading room, a library for the master of the house. In that day, the men would retire to a room such as this and talk over important issues. Women were allowed to participate only on special occasions."

Majken struck several matches and held them to the dried wood. Thomas held a piece of yellowed, crumbling paper over the flame and nursed it. Black streaks of soot coated the upper rim of the mantle and spread along the wall to the ceiling. The chimney was doing a marginal job.

"We came in the main hallway," Majken said as she arranged a larger piece of wood on the fire. "It runs from the front vestibule to the kitchen."

She gestured around them. "This place is too isolated to be practical, but it is peaceful here. We're on a hill surrounded by woodland. To the southwest, you can see the city lights over the trees." Majken moved away from the growing flames and balanced another large split piece of wood on top. Thomas replaced the iron grating in front of the fire. The room filled with warm, yellow light.

"To the west there is a steep drop-off. It's unsafe to wander around at night in this area."

Thomas stretched out on his side of the couch.

"How often do you come here?"

"I've used the mansion only once since I've moved to the campus."

Thomas stroked her hair and neck gently, reliving the intimacy on the slab at the back of the banquet hall. The dried wood crackled in the flames. He felt his breath quicken; he became aware of the small telltale whistling of the wind around the structure. Majken smiled at him and seemed to melt in his hands. It was an utter turnaround, he thought. How open she was, how freely talking, how beautiful. He wanted to tell her right then.

Majken got up and checked the fire, then excused herself for a few minutes. Thomas followed her, but the hallway was darker than he expected. He bumped blindly into the stairwell railing. It protested loudly.

"Don't try to follow me," she cautioned. "Most of the flooring was warped or rotted through. Wait for me in the library. I'll only be a few minutes."

Thomas strained to see her dim outline hovering halfway up the stairs. He assumed she must know her way by memory. He went to the study and attended the fire, rearranging logs with an old twisted iron poker. The study became deathly quiet. The mansion had its own set of mysterious creaks and groans, as any old building. A perpetual breeze over the empty hillside stirred the limbs of the large tree against the roof and windows. Thomas then heard the sounds of a trunk latch opening and the swish of clothes.

The lone window in the room had long ago been boarded up; the wind whistled through the cracks. The study was bare and dusty in that section. He could imagine a desk placed in the sunlight. Pictures, no, portraits, on the ancient walls. Thomas smiled. The mansion was getting to him. He waited to hear her approaching steps. She was already there, barefoot.

Majken hesitated in the doorway, balancing a tray of unopened fruit juice, a plastic decanter and one glass, and a hairbrush in her palm. She stood there for a moment, watching, before placing the tray on the floor next to the couch.

Thomas rejoined Majken on the couch. "What's that?"

"Refreshment for later, if you want it," she replied.

Majken's eyes scanned the room beyond him, then cast a furtive glance at the bottom of the low table. She had prepared too well.

Majken and Thomas faced each other. When she tried to reach for him, he averted his gaze to the fireplace. Majken eased toward him and asked if he still wanted her, knowing the things she had done.

He answered simply, "Yes." He reached for her and traced a ring on her throat where her choker had been. His touch lingered on her skin.

Majken let Thomas caress the nape of her neck. She touched his face lightly with her fingertips. His fingers teased her earlobe and the soft strands of hair tumbling over her shoulders. She pushed her hand toward his thighs. He cupped his hands behind her and pulled her toward him. She pressed her body against his, closer, her breath grew deeper and slower.

They joined in a kiss, embracing. A deep inner pain racked Majken's heart. *Condemned*! She trembled, but held herself still next to him and whispered fervently, "I need you." She kissed him, but felt him grow stiff and unresponsive.

"We ... we had a good practice last time," he stammered. "Did I tell you about it?" Thomas straightened his shirt. "Alex had a torn ligament in his ankle. The doctor had to give him permission to practice with the team." Thomas rattled off several other interesting anecdotes.

Majken was bewildered. He avoided looking directly at her. "Thomas," she said gently, "are you afraid of me?" He froze. She smiled and said jokingly, "I usually don't bite."

He seemed to relax, then leaned over and mumbled under his breath, "... all those other men."

Majken tucked her legs defensively under her body. "I'm afraid, too," she responded softly. She curled herself into a tight ball. "I wanted you to love me."

Thomas touched her gingerly on the hip, pressing his fingers into the smooth fabric of her gown, and told her time for angry words and hurt was past. She knew he had wondered for a long time what it would be like with her.

She sat upright and faced him. "Have you?" she asked.

Thomas nodded hesitantly. "I didn't bring anything."

"I've taken care of that," she reassured him.

He sat next to her and slid his hand along her spine. Her muscles arched. Smiling at him, she pulled her hair aside and asked him to unbutton her gown. He trembled slightly as he pushed each pearl button through; his fingers felt warm on her cool skin.

Thomas supported her in his arms.

Majken felt an unusual numbness spread slowly through her body, much like after feeding. Thomas kissed her passionately. The sensation spread from her hands to her feet. She tried to map her body's internal signals while unbuttoning Thomas' shirt. Thomas was planting small kisses along her neck while sliding her gown lower. She wanted him. Kissing her deeply, his mouth parted against hers—then he screamed.

Thomas swore and jumped to the opposite side of the couch with his hands over his mouth and moaning in pain. Shock and betrayal flashed in his eyes. Majken stared at him, uncertain. She saw a small trickle of blood between his fingers before she tasted his blood in her mouth. He recoiled when she reached for him.

"Thomas, I didn't mean it!" she pleaded.

He grimaced and began probing his mouth with his finger. Majken produced a white cloth. He snatched it disdainfully.

He flinched when he packed it in his mouth.

Majken sprang restlessly to her feet and began to pace nervously. Her anguished expression reflected an extreme reaction to the accident. Thomas was still tending his injury. Majken clenched her fists and crossed her arms tightly over her breasts. She repeated, "I'm sorry," in an endless whisper.

Thomas mumbled something incomprehensible.

Majken bowed her head. She looked at Thomas like she was going to cry. He got up and spat into the fire. The cloth was packed into the side of his cheek, giving him the appearance of a squirrel with a mouthful of nuts.

"Youhvsharpteeph," he tried to say.

She said nothing. She had lost control. For a second time this evening, her unnaturally high blood needs dominated her will. Gradually, Majken realized she could seriously injure or kill him before she knew it. Thomas stood in front of her. She sidestepped around him and went to the couch and wrapped herself in the dark brown comforter. She propped her legs on the heavy table.

Thomas sat next to her. "You'd better go," she said solemnly.

"I'm all right," he said. He opened his mouth and wiggled his tongue for her. "See." The nip on the side had stopped bleeding. "Mary?" he said earnestly.

Majken tightened handfuls of quilted material under her chin. It ripped. She searched his brown eyes. "There is much you do not know about me," she said.

"What are you talking about?" he asked numbly.

Majken squeezed her eyes closed at the first signs of burning. The truth now, she thought, would mean losing him forever. She giggled nervously. "My name is not Mary Harris," she began.

"I don't understand."

"You know," she said, reaching out from the comforter and touching his face, "if you let yourself believe it." Thomas pressed her hand against his face.

"Nothing you say would drive me away from you," he said bravely.

Majken continued her painful confession.

"I took an assumed name when I moved here. The person you know as Mary Harris is a—exists only to give me a place in your world." Majken trembled again from the inside. "Please, leave," she begged, "or I might hurt you."

Thomas tried to touch her, but she shied away. He moved over her and pinned her arms by pushing on the comforter. He made her look at him. "I came here to be with you," he said. "I don't care what you call yourself."

Majken sighed sadly. "It's more than a name. I knew when I got to know you, the truth would come out eventually. I knew I couldn't fool you forever." Her voice strained.

When Thomas tried to kiss her, she bolted forward, nearly knocking him in the floor. In a moment, he righted himself and tried to pull her to a sitting position. Majken resisted.

He stopped trying and just sat next to her.

"I've loved you for a long time," Thomas said with finality. "I'm not letting you go." He cradled her shoulders and pulled gently. She yielded.

Thomas kissed her deeply, as before. The taste of his blood in her mouth had faded. She smiled at him in a heartbreaking kind of smile, and whispered, "Quoth the raven, nevermore."

Hesitantly, Majken extended both arms from the comforter and wrapped them around Thomas' neck, held him, kissed him, then removed his shirt. His hands slid across the back of her gown. She kissed him gently, then standing, spread the comforter over the low heavy table.

The room was filled with the warm sounds of cracking, burning wood and a sweet, smouldering scent of oak and birch. The glowing embers and lamplight filled the room and gave her skin a pearly white appearance. Majken unfastened the tight waist of her gown and pulled the bodice downward; her hands smoothed the faded gown sensuously over her hips. She stepped free of it and draped it over the couch.

Nude to her panties, she helped Thomas out of his shoes and socks. She could see his anticipation and tenseness. A close embrace, a deep kiss, Majken paused to search his eyes. He told her he loved her.

They stood, embracing. Majken slipped her panties off and lay down on the table, propped on elbows, waiting. Thomas numbly let his pants fall to the floor. Majken heard his heart racing. He stopped and told her how beautiful she was. In a final embarrassing gesture, he thrust his shorts off.

Majken held her hands toward him. She had long admired his athletic body. For a brief second, a memory of him struggling on a difficult play, flashed through her mind. His pale skin matched her white skin. Majken gave herself to him.

They made love, slowly at first, then increasing. Majken refused to consider it merely sex. Knowing that she needed him left her open and dangerously exposed. This time, she could not assuage her deep swelling needs. Thomas and Majken shifted side by side, embracing ardently.

Still, Majken thought, she would force herself to do what she must. She could not delay much longer. Their bodies writhed in pleasure. Thomas' skin was warm and moist to touch. Her skin remained suspiciously cool; it was a silent condemning testimony. His lower arm was nestled under her waist, pulling her closer. His upper arm was free to stroke, tease, and caress. His fingertips lingered on the smooth curve of her hips, storing a memory, and cupped the tender flesh of her buttocks and eased her thigh over his.

She drew and expelled a deep, deep breath. Again. She willed herself to relax as Thomas' body trembled, then lay still next to hers. He cradled her face, and kissed her softly, around her lips and cheek, and down her neck. He seemed extremely content and blissful. He teased her, saying that he still loved her.

Whatever else happened, they still had this time. She wanted to tell him that as they lay together. Thomas held her, innocently, as a new burning sensation tore through her. She let him see her face as calm and peaceful and serene. If this were their last night, she wanted him to have some fond memory of her after the pain went away.

She leaned next to his ear and whispered her real name. Majken. He whispered her name. The furrow in his brow reflected his puzzlement, his lack of understanding. Majken wiggled down a foot, then lay on top of him. Her breasts were pressed against his chest, he supported her. Nothing she could say would change the trusting expression on his face.

She was out of time. "Thomas."

She smiled, sadly, then kissed him hard.

He gasped when they parted.

She whispered, "I need you." Thomas grinned. Majken let her hand drift over the side of the table, to the underside, to a knife held with surgical tape. Thomas was tenderly running his fingers up and down her back. "Thomas, I ... I have to—," she mumbled. She shifted to the side and eased his arms toward her, over his head, with her free hand and looped her leg securely around his waist.

She kissed him lightly. "I must take something from you to survive." He looked at her blankly. "There is no other way. Try not to hate me so much," she whispered.

With three lightning fast strokes, she cut his left shoulder, near the shoulder blade and away from vulnerable arteries and veins in his neck. He lay in stunned silence as his blood started to flow from the wound. Majken dropped the knife and held his wrists firmly. She fed, lapping his blood as it began to pool on the surface of his skin. He struggled. She held him fast as her long hair spilled over into his face. She could not bear to see the shocked expression on his face anyway.

Soon, it was over and she released him. She drank no more than if he had given two units of blood at the blood bank. His skin was clammy to touch, he lay still and unmoving. Majken rested on her side. Her mouth was smeared with blood, but it hardly mattered if he saw her now.

She retrieved a second item taped under the table, a wide, absorbent gauze bandage. She folded a thick mat over the area, and wrapped the remainder over his shoulder, across his chest, and under his armpits to secure the dressing.

He was limp as she bundled him in the comforter and lifted him to the couch. Thomas stared at the ceiling, his mouth drawn tightly. He may have been conscious of her, or maybe not. Majken pulled on her panties and sat next to him on the edge of the couch. His lips parted, but his eyes carried the full weight of speaking for him.

Majken ran her fingers through his damp hair, then gathered her gown and left for a few minutes. She reappeared wearing a simple cotton pullover and resumed her position next to him.

Thomas tried to speak. "Why?"

Majken phrased her sentence carefully and spoke it slowly. "I must drink blood to live." His eyes widened. It might have been better, she thought, if they expressed hatred, instead of deep hurt.

"Do you understand?" she asked. "I am a vampyr."

Words gurgled in Thomas' throat, barely coming out. She took his pulse at his neck. He was regaining his sense of where he was; next he would remember what she had done to him. Majken felt a slight coolness in the study. While placing extra logs on the fire and stirring the ashes, her eyes swept over the still form on the couch. It was impossible to guess what he was thinking. She feared she had taken more blood than she had realized.

The small knife, stained with his blood, lay on the hardwood floor. She hefted it in her hand. "It wasn't meant for you," she told Thomas slowly, bitterly. She threw it to a far dark corner of the room. Majken examined his pupils and breathing. Slightly dilated. What could she say to him? She had already done her worst.

His eyes closed unevenly. Unable to bear the sight of her, she assumed. When he closed his eyes, he reminded her in some ways of a little boy that had fallen asleep in his mother's arms. Majken talked.

"I know you hurt, because of me. I know you'll never forget what I've done to you. You see, I have no choice, no room for hope." Her voice faded as she looked beyond the walls, into the darkness. "Forgive me, Thomas," she whispered to the silent walls, "because I would do it again if I had to."

* * *

Thomas stirred slightly, his body extremely weak, as if crushed and beaten. His wounds stung sharply, blistered and raw. Gradually, hazy impressions soaked through his mind. He remembered the banquet, her running away, and his coming here, reluctantly, with her. They had just finished when she cut him.

His entire body ached, and his shoulder must have been cut to ribbons the way it bled. And she drank it. Thomas had heard about certain people that liked to hurt, and be hurt, during sex. He was not one of them. *Oh, God*! he thought. It was more than that. She had actually drunk it.

Subtly, he opened his eyes. She was still there, sitting nearby. *Everyone tried to warn you,* he lamented, *and you only have yourself to blame*! He wondered how he could have let her do it. Why had he not fought? Now he was utterly alone and defenseless with someone who could kill him.

Thomas watched her closely. She placed the canister of fruit juice on the low table, opened it, and poured half a glass. She was talking to him, or had been talking to him. He could not remember. All that registered on his mind was the shock. He coughed.

She had been his friend and companion, once. He

thought he loved her. She asked him to try to sit up and take a sip. When she first spoke, for a brief second, she became the girl he thought he knew. She had the same face and hair and figure. "Mary?" he whispered hoarsely.

The stranger shook her head. "Majken."

"Ma-j-k-en," he tried to say.

Majken slipped off the table and knelt before him on the floor.

Thomas went pale and pushed with his hands in front of him. "Are you going to kill me?"   His lips trembled and he breathed in sharp gasps.

She froze. "I never intended to attack you, Thomas."

"Why did you do it?" His tongue and mouth moved like they were filled with cotton.

"I must have blood to live," she answered simply.

Cold fear made his normally brown eyes appear wide and black. He weakly kicked the comforter loose. "Is this what you've been hiding?"

She hesitated, then said, "I've lived this way for many years."

Thomas broke into a nervous laugh. "Are you trying to tell me you're some kind of vampire?"

Majken nodded solemnly with no hint of amusement or frivolity. "I don't like to call myself that, but, yes, you could say that I am a vampyr."

Thomas blinked several times and stared at her hard. She never turned into a puff of smoke or a bat. She remained frighteningly solid. "How long were you supposed to be this way?"

She reacted to the sarcasm in his voice. "I have too much self-respect to play guess-how-old-I-am games with you!"

He regretted his tactic. He had never seen her angry. He had never seen a lot of things in her before tonight. As long as he could keep her talking, he hoped he would be safe. "I'm sorry," he said quickly, "but all of this is hard to believe."

Majken picked up the glass. "I poured this for you. If you are strong enough to sit up, it would help you regain your strength."

Thomas failed his first attempt, dizzy. The second time he managed to prop himself on one arm, but his dressing stuck and he fell again. Majken put his glass down. "Will you let me help you up?"

He gritted his teeth and succeeded on his third attempt; his head swam. He took the drink and sampled it nervously. Majken smiled. The fruit juice was warm and had the slick, pungent taste of being stored too long. *Beggars can't be choosers*, he thought. He felt better, and when he did not choke and die in the next few minutes, more confident. He tried to sit up, but collapsed against the velour covering.

Majken quickly supported him by his opposite arm and helped him lie flat.

"Why did you come here?" he asked, his words slurred.

"I brought you here to see this once beautiful mansion, and to ask for your help." Majken fell against the couch, facing the wall, and appeared to watch the fire. "I wanted to have time together, then I was going to explain what I really was and all of those things you didn't understand."

Her voice became small and distant. "More of John's ways rubbed off on me, than my ways affected him." Majken bowed her head between her knees.

"John?" Thomas stammered.

Majken frowned. "It's not a pretty story."

Thomas considered what he had heard so far. She spoke easily and rationally, as any sane person. In fact, now that she was talking to him, she seemed most free. Phillip would be thrilled. He was more than apprehensive to hear what her version of not a pretty story would be.

"Face me," Thomas said. Majken sat below him and crossed her legs.

"John is a vampyr, like me. You remember the

news reports of the slasher? John was responsible for all or most of those killings, and if I'm right, more than they would ever find."

Thomas interrupted. "Why most?"

"When incidents like this occur, humans have an unbelievably strong tendency to copy. Several murders might have been committed by his less bloodthirsty brethren, and blamed on him." Majken sighed. "The girl in the parking lot, he did. I saw him briefly that night."

"I'll never forget it," Thomas said.

Majken described the warehouse incident, and what happened when John followed her to the campus.

"What did you do?" Thomas asked, absorbed by her incredible tale.

"Females of our kind can sometimes influence the males of our kind with a form of hypnosis. Nature's way of compensating, I think. It works by pulling away part of their will, but it's temporary."

"What kind of compensations do the males have?" Thomas asked.

Majken tucked her legs close to her. "They are usually stronger, depending on their maturity and blood needs. Fully aroused, John could easily crush your skull."

Thomas grimaced. Her tone was deadly serious. He shifted his position uneasily and asked her to continue. She paused to collect her thoughts.

"The guard was already dead and he had already dragged Rebecca away. I found them too late." Her voice trailed. "Rebecca was badly cut, mauled, and fortunately, unconscious. I tackled him and pinned him down until he went under." Majken grinned. "You would have been proud of me."

Thomas punched the couch. "Why didn't you turn him over to the police?"

"That level of influence isn't possible." Majken straightened her legs and lower back, and tensed them. "We walked for hours. I stored him in a shed and barely made it home before daybreak."

"You'd been walking all night!"

She nodded. "The rest you know. I conditioned him to leave Trenton permanently. That is the last anyone will hear of the slasher." Majken turned to watch a burning log collapse and crumble in ashes.

What she said, Thomas thought, was wrong. It struck him at once. "Where did you send him, Majken?"

Majken picked herself up and silently poured him a second glass, three-fourths full. She left it on the table and strolled to the blackened fireplace. "What he does after he leaves my territory is not my concern."

Thomas jerked his head up, staring at her. "He's a killer!"

She turned to watch the burning embers. "Enough of his temperament affected me, wouldn't you say?" she said icily.

Thomas felt his chest constrict painfully. The events she described, the reasons for her strange behavior, did seem rational in light of what she told him. The woman he thought he knew was far, far away, watching the flames. He reached for his glass.

He sat up and finished the last draught in his glass. The way she looked at him made him nervous. Having no clothes on was part of the problem. He bundled the comforter around his waist, and searched the floor for his strewn clothes.

She gathered them, emptied the remainder of the juice in the decanter, swirled it and poured him a full glass. "Drink this first," she instructed.

When he drained the glass, she threw his clothes on the couch. She watched him dress. "I have a final request," she said. He stopped. "It's very important to me that you believe I never meant to hurt you."

He nodded quickly. "I can leave?" he asked warily. He slipped on his pants and shirt.

"Yes, but I'm afraid I won't be returning to campus under the circumstances." Thomas laced his shoes and stood shakily.

"Are you sure you've recovered enough to drive?" she asked. "It is after midnight."

Thomas made a determined lunge for the door; the world was spinning wildly around his feet. The creature standing in front of him blurred. He reached his hand to balance himself. "Mary?" he gasped.

Majken caught him as he collapsed. As she cradled his head in her lap, she reached to extinguish the lamps, and swayed easily as the last of the coals in the fire burned out. Once the room became dark to human eyes, she listened into the night. The faint crying of a little girl carried on the wind and an unfamiliar, hollow ache gripped her chest. She gently squeezed her eyes closed, trying to restore calm.

She bowed her head and gently whispered, "I promised to come back, Thomas."

John hiked the dark, winding road, driven by a compulsion to reach the next city. Refreshed by the crisp night air and invigorated by his rest, his limbs carried him with powerful strides. He slept by day in the confines of the woods. He was leaving ... his memory failed him.

Suddenly, ahead, he saw numerous police, fire, and ambulance vehicles blocking his path. A major accident had occurred where the highway dipped sharply at the bottom of a hill. John instinctively withdrew, and watched. He smelled alcohol-tainted blood, mingled with twisted metal and shattered glass. The revolving red lights flashed in his eyes.

He vaguely remembered a flash of gold, and a face hazy and blurred in his mind. Slowly, the image came into focus. Then he remembered—she had manipulated his will! His eyes narrowed as the wind whipped around his backpack. He swore she would pay; blood would flow in the streets!

John retraced his steps out of the city.

Chapter Ten

Majken and Thomas slept. Her bedroom was dim and filled with a damp mustiness raised by the morning sun. Thick curtains protected her from the harsh light. The slow, perpetual creaking silence was broken by heavy breathing and occasional movement in bed. Thomas slept peacefully, his body extended and relaxed. Majken lay curled beside him, her arms reaching for him, yet apart.

She awoke quietly. She had stopped him because he was too weak to drive and she wanted time. Majken stretched without disturbing him and carefully withdrew from the bed. She quietly stood in front of him. This morning he would choose. Thomas stirred, holding the cover over his head.

Majken had carried him upstairs. His pants and shirt were arranged at the foot of the bed. The bandage and dressing were gone to give his wound a proper airing. Majken trimmed a lamp for him to see. She felt oddly at peace when he opened his eyes, but wondered if he was still afraid of her.

Thomas rolled over sluggishly and yawned. He rubbed at his eyes filled with sleep, and asked, "What happened?"

"You collapsed," she said softly, "and I brought you up here."

"Last night feels like a bad dream."

She watched him strain to bring her into focus. Fully awake, he sat up and examined her bedroom in great detail. The walls appeared the same dingy yellowish-gray as the room downstairs. The canopy bed was the only usable furniture; the mattress and sheets were new. His gaze ended at the curtains, then shifted to her.

He reached for his injured shoulder. "My arm hurts, and I'm starving, too."

She examined his wounds as he turned. The cuts had faded to a deep scarlet. Scar tissue had begun to form. Majken sat easily on the edge of the bed, keeping her distance. He had to understand her attack was forced by ravages out of control. She touched his knee lightly, through the bed covers. He withdrew it.

Majken spoke gently. "All I told you about myself is regrettably true. I must have blood daily to live. You've seen enough to convince you that what I say is true."

Thomas wrapped his arms around his drawn up knees.

"I will not hurt you again, and you are free to leave. Before I can safely come with you, I must have your vow that you will tell no one."

Thomas jerked hard out of her reach and stammered angrily, "What happened to the Mary I used

to know? If you don't stop talking like this, someone's going to put you away!"

"If you can bear to be with me, I'd like to continue
our public relationship as before. I want you as a donor, once a week possibly, depending on your health.
I need you, Thomas." Her choice of phrases had a
negative effect.

"I thought you felt for me the same way I felt for
you." He shook his head bewildered. "I thought you
really needed someone; that maybe you were afraid
to open up. Fine. I accepted that and gave you all
the time you wanted. Then what? Everyone in my
dorm finds out how promiscuous you are before I do!
I came to you to patch things up. Then, you disappear and Chief Baggetta calls me into his office to
explain where you were and why he couldn't verify
your papers. I told myself you were in trouble, and
needed my help. Phillip told me there is a connection
between you and that student, and I haven't figured
out what really happened between you and his father. If that wasn't enough, you want me to believe
you stayed here for a week with a crazed maniac
killer and that you are a vampire!"

Majken let the dust settle. She laid his clothes
within reach and paced to the far side of the bedroom.

Thomas laughed bleakly as he swung out of bed. "I thought you were in some kind of trouble with the mob." She stared forlornly at the wall as he dressed. "Majken," he finally said. She faced him. "I'm afraid to say things couldn't get any worse. This vampire thing is too much to believe."

She walked carefully to the bed. "Look at your wrists," she said.

Thomas lifted his sleeves to find a circle of bruises on both wrists. She pointed out the band of discoloration formed the same pattern as her grip. Thomas stood with his mouth open. He stumbled to the window and opened the curtain to see. Majken fell on the bed like she was stabbed. She cried out; Thomas snapped them shut and rushed to her side.

"Majken, I'm sorry."

She panted heavily; her delicate skin was shielded by part of the covers. "I wasn't ready," she gasped. She crawled farther on the bed and drew deep breaths as the tension drained out of her. She twisted on her side and looked up at him.

"Do you still desire me, Thomas?"

He paced nervously to the end of the bed. "I ... love you, Mary."

Majken rolled to her feet. "Mary does not exist."

"How did you get into this condition?" he asked.

His question was probing; her eyes cast downward. "I was assaulted, and our blood became—" her voice had become small and fragile as a little girl's.

Thomas pressed her to the baseboard. "What happened between you and Albritton?"

Her expression was vacant, far away, hurting. Majken sighed hopelessly. "He wouldn't let me go and I attacked him."

Thomas stood as if nailed to the floor.

"Dr. Albritton is a very persistent man," she said, clasping her hands in front of her and stepping lightly around Thomas. "His son was a donor I picked up in a bar shortly after I met you. Marc didn't know who I was or where I really lived until he saw me on campus. He became obsessed, and dangerous, because I refused him. That night, he came after me with a gun and forced me to go with him into the woods." She eased onto the bed. "The gun went off."

"Is Dr. Albritton alive?" Thomas asked.

"He should be, unless he has a weak heart."

Majken saw wild fear creep into his face as Thomas started backing out of the room. He held his arms poised, ready, as if he was handling a rabid animal. "I think you've been here too long, and we should go home now. We can go in together," he said hopefully. "I'll stay with you, and we'll just talk."

He bumped into the doorframe.

She followed him, matching his pace. "I wish I could have been what you needed, Thomas. Dr. Albritton will never leave me in peace. It's time for me to leave." Thomas turned down the stairwell. "Where will you go?" He stumbled blindly on a warped step and caught the rail. It creaked loudly.

Majken stopped midway. "I know you loved me, once. Give me until tonight." Majken hated herself. What she was doing was so dangerously close to begging, and she swore never to get in a position to beg for her survival, again.

He disappeared into the study for a moment. She saw him pick up his coat and pause, looking at the room and table. She wondered if he was remembering the delights of her body, or how she bled him when she could wait no longer. She stood when he came out.

"Please, come with me," he urged.

"Goodbye, Thomas. My life is in your hands."

He tossed his coat over his arm and strode for the door. She called him; he waited.

"Before I hurt you, and we were together, were you happy?"

Thomas glared. "Do you always sleep with a guy before you cut him?"

She shook her head. "There are other ways."

Thomas pulled on the heavy brass latch and sunlight filled the hallway for a brief moment.

Majken listened as the familiar whine of his engine faded.

Thomas drove slowly into the abandoned street. The empty banquet hall reflected golden rays of the morning sun. The world in his eyes appeared strangely different this morning. Everything. He parked close to the entrance and jerked on the parking brake. He needed something solid and real. He sat, staring for a few minutes, then climbed out. The banquet hall was deserted.

An uneasy chill swept through him as he strummed the hood of his car. He forced himself to move. Bits of paper napkins littered the carefully trimmed grass. The award's banquet must have been a complete success, he mused sarcastically. Memories popped fresh into his mind. This was where he held his arm around her waist and guided her inside. He tapped on the glass and tested the front entrance. It was locked. He cupped his hands to the glass and tried to see inside.

He stepped away, turned, and headed for the service entrance. He was completely stupid last night, he thought. Seeing where they were, he desperately hoped to find where he went wrong. Deep inside, her story rang true. If only it were not. He hesitated on the edge of the slab where he found dark reddish-brown stains dribbled on the step from the alley into the building. Bloodstains.

Pressure welled in his chest as he followed the stain trail into the alley. He remembered the corner, where Mary, or whateverhernamewas, pushed him against the building. The fresh asphalt was black and unlined. Each faltering step tested his resolve to see this through. Finding bloodstains would mean she cut him, or worse. If she actually believed she was a vampire, she might have bitten him. How naïve he was. He knelt over a dark stain near the midpoint.

"What did you do to him?" poured from his anguished heart.

Now weaker, he collapsed to his hands and knees next to the nearly invisible stains. Thomas imagined the alley at night and saw it as extremely dark and treacherous. The stains sickened him. He stared into the rich foliage. "Fool!" he whispered to the gently swaying leaves.

Thomas ran to his car. How many times does something like this happen? he lamented. Visions of her floated by as he drove mindlessly, without direc-

tion. Weekend traffic was building steadily. Abruptly, he swung off the road and parked next to a telephone booth. There was something he had to know.

He fumbled in his pocket for change, and finding none, he swore and stomped to the convenience
store. He walked out thoughtfully. He studied the
directory for hospital listings, starting with those
closest to the banquet hall.

On the fourth try, he tried St. Francis Medical
Center. A busy receptionist answered, "May I help
you?"

Thomas gripped the receiver. "I want to know the
condition of a patient. His name is Dr. Albritton."

"What is his first name?"

"I don't know," he admitted. "He was brought in
last night, I'm sure."

"Is he a physician on staff?" she asked. He heard
a thick book being searched.

"No," Thomas corrected, "he's a college professor."
He waited, wishing he had bought that soft drink.

The receptionist spoke. "We have a Daniel Albritton, admitted last night through Emergency."

"That's him! How is he?" Pin needles pricked up
his arm.

She hesitated, suspiciously. "What is your name?"

Thomas stammered, "I'll call back later!" and

nearly slammed the receiver on his fingers. He waited until his vision cleared before driving away.

Chief Baggetta knocked lightly on the private hospital room door before entering. "Daniel?" he called.
He checked the new number given him by the nurse.
A curtain was drawn around a single bed. Albritton lay, apparently asleep, with his upper thigh and
head bandaged. The room's stillness and antiseptic
scent was disquieting, so unlike the raging man he
helped admit very early this morning.

He gently prodded his friend. "Daniel."

His eyes blinked open, and he lifted his hand.
Baggetta grasped it, then unfolded the newspaper
under his arm and took Albritton's reading glasses
out of his pocket.

"I hate to disturb your rest. Phillip Barton was in
my office early this morning, frankly having a worry
fit about his roommate. Thomas left with her just
before you were found."

Albritton's eyes narrowed. "Thomas Kline, the
boyfriend you said knew nothing of her activities."

"I believe she caused you to fall, but Phillip was
adamant about Thomas' knowledge of her." Baggetta paced restlessly to the window. "He may be dead
this morning."

An orderly came in and took the untouched breakfast tray.

Baggetta waited until the man left, then faced Albritton. "I'm disappointed in you, Daniel, for confronting her by yourself."

His friend gripped the gauzy bed sheet. "My son is dead! I tried to question her about Marc, and she attacked me. You were so helpful earlier, I couldn't resist." He twisted bitterly.

"That may be true," Baggetta said calmly, "but the ambulance crew told me you were delirious. The ER physician said you had only a concussion, and very luckily for a man your age, nothing broken. I want to believe you didn't dream she attacked you."

Albritton stared beyond Baggetta, into the morning sky. "What do we do now?" he asked quietly.

"I've instructed security to detain Mary Harris for questioning when she returns. We wait. The closest connection we have is through her boyfriend." Albritton grimaced. "It is your decision whether to call the police. You never actually saw her. But at least Mr. Barton is willing to swear she was in the immediate vicinity after your fall."

"Will the police reopen the investigation into Marc's death?"

Baggetta towered over his friend's bedside. "His

actions were too erratic; they still believe he was imbalanced." Albritton trembled with grief. "Rest, and get well," he urged, "you have a home to return to."

Albritton shook his head. "I've decided to go to my home to be close to Marc and Teresa."

Cooler afternoon breezes drifted and swam lazily into the open window, circulating through the dorm, as Thomas balanced in the frame. White cracked paint was sprinkled on the floor. He had to force it open with a screwdriver. Life was wonderful, he thought, as he watched a couple stroll by. Life was slow. Most of the student body and faculty were off campus, attending the many after-award's banquet parties as was traditional. He propped his chin on his other knee. The muscles of his lower back hurt from staying in a hunched position for so long.

Thomas felt as if his body had been drained of energy. He frowned at the analogy. He drew a deep sigh, unable to watch the idyllic couple. His thigh prickled as circulation returned. Too late to help her, he thought. He was alone. The ache was barely manageable as long as he kept his eyes open to keep from seeing her face. He massaged his right thigh as he trudged to his room. The door was still wide open. His bed was still crumpled where he threw himself in exhaustion hours ago.

Physically, he suspected he might live. Emotionally, he was certain he would die. Thomas dropped on his bed, pushing aside the old magazine he had tried reading to take his mind off his troubles. With his mouth set tightly, he crumpled it angrily and threw it over his roommate's bed. It smacked on the far wall and slid to the floor. Blind. Stupid. Slowly, the tension dissipated.

He wailed aloud, "Why, Majken, why?"

Thomas turned with a start. Phillip stood silently in the doorway. He was staring at Thomas as if he had seen a ghost. Phillip moved with deliberate slowness, pulled a chair from the desk and sat, leaning across the back of it.

"What are you doing here?" he asked.

"What?" Thomas did a double take.

"I thought you were never coming back, alive," Phillip said dryly. He tilted the chair and let it fall. He seemed deceivingly calm.

Thomas wanted to run, but was paralyzed from the neck down.

"Maj—Mary and I, we, dammit Phillip, I had to try!"

Phillip let his chair drop with a heavy clump and frowned. "Sure, you had to try. In fact, I couldn't stop you to save your life."

Their friendship was on the brink, Thomas thought morosely.

Phillip stood and paced to his side of the room, bracing his arm on the wall. "What happened? Where did you go?"

Thomas sat up, his mouth dry. "We went to a mansion," he said light-headedly.

Phillip gawked.

"It's hard to explain. I was nervous, going to this decrepit old place, but she loved it. Actually loved it. She was happy there." His face drew with re-membered pain. "Everything went fine, until we got inside."

Phillip looked speechless.

"We were going to spend the evening together, and we did. I knew something was wrong by the way she acted. She changed so fast!" He held his fist to his open mouth for a second. His eyes were glazed, unsee-ing, as in that moment. "I knew she had a problem, whatever it was, and I wanted to help her and show her I really cared for her. She's, uh, confused. She said strange things about herself, and," he laughed nervously, "she almost had me believing it."

"What did she do?" Phillip asked.

Thomas covered his face with his hands. "I loved

her, Phillip, I really did. Now ... I hate her!" *Betrayer*! he thought. He felt his eyes moisten and his skin became warm and flushed. He spoke with exaggerated slowness. "I can't tell you," he murmured.

"You talk like her now!" Phillip exclaimed. "Listen, Thomas. After you left with her, we found an injured man in the alley. Guess who hurt him?"

Thomas felt a stabbing pain. "She told me this morning," he said casually. He refused to meet his roommate's intense gaze. Phillip asked him about going to the police. He choked. "She didn't know what she was doing, I think. She said Albritton came after her, pressuring her. She did it in self-defense."

"I knew it! I knew it," Phillip muttered.

Thomas recoiled as a desperate realization surged through his numb mind and heart—that he was covering for a dangerous, sick young woman. A young woman he still loved, he admitted sadly. Thomas jumped up. "I've got to do something." A hand pressed on his shoulder.

"You have to take this to the police," Phillip said.

A thought tried to form in his mind; a comment tried to form on his lips and failed. "I'll go," he said finally. Phillip offered to go with him. No, this he must do on his own, for her. He commented to Phillip. "I went by the campus psychiatric office on the way here. It's closed. I guess students don't need help on weekends."

His roommate offered a wane smile. "You're helping her."

Thomas willed himself forward. He knew Baggetta would help her. Leaning in the hallway, he turned and locked his eyes into Phillip's, and for a second, saw the same fire he had seen in Majken's eyes.

He returned a smile. "Thank you, Phillip," he said, then left.

Dr. Albritton stood uneasily in front of his home, balancing with the walking stick his doctor insisted he use. The sun had dipped to an angle barely below the roof of the two-story colonial home. He stood in the shadow. Albritton hesitated, then poked at the fence gate with his stick and crossed a threshold.

His pulse beat harder. Marc, he thought. His son still lived in this house. He ambled slowly, painfully, towards the porch steps. Their home remained unchanged. His home, now. Merely a place to live. A wave of sadness swept through him as he reached for the smooth wooden banister. Albritton smiled at the sweet memory of the first time Teresa and Marc entered this house.

He had just accepted a professorship position, but

kept this house as a surprise, a house Teresa liked. He was clever. He remembered driving his wife and son, younger in those days, all around the city. Marc hopped livelily from one side to the next as they shopped for a home.

He parked, and asked her if she liked this one.

Albritton paused, looking at the street, deep within a memory. He smiled at Teresa as she led Marc by the hand across the street. He teased her, prolonging the moment, asking her if they did get this house, how much it would take to redecorate it. A smile played on her lips as she realized this was to be their home. A younger Marc bound joyfully up the narrow path, his small voice carrying in the breeze, "Our house, our house, our house!"

The wide front porch was empty. Albritton halted on the edge to find his key. Then he opened the door. A tingling warmth of a former love spread around him. His gaze circled the porch a final time before he stepped inside, leaving his walking stick outside. He locked the door and limped toward his study, but decided he first wanted to go to his son's bedroom. He climbed up one step at a time.

A tightness clogged his throat. His son's room was cluttered with cardboard boxes half-filled with clothes. Albritton scanned Marc's belongings. He stooped to pick up a newspaper, dated the day after, and stared at the smiling picture. The brief notice held no details of the tragedy. A flash of anger rose and subsided quickly. Albritton pushed a box off the bed and smoothed the newspaper flat.

Time to heal, he thought. Baggetta had warned him about leaving the hospital too early, about coming home so soon, about many things. His tour completed, Albritton turned out the light and went to his study. His beloved son! He wished in his soul for another chance, wished the pallor of disgrace away. He opened the curtains behind his desk and slid into his comfortable swivel chair. The late afternoon light melted into memories. If God would give him another chance, he promised to accept more and criticize far less.

Thomas' heart sank lower as he neared the campus security building. He was scared, especially for her. There was no way to predict how Chief Baggetta would take this, or how much force the police would use. Certainly, Chief Baggetta would let him speak on her behalf, about her years of loneliness as an orphan and her struggles into young adulthood. Thomas prayed they would take her gently. He paused on the final step as he tried to recall exactly what she had said.

Her image floated over the stairwell, blurred in a haze of shock and rage. He shoved the pain out of his mind. There were other, more pleasant memories to dwell on: her soft skin and hair, holding her in his arms, their urgency. He hoped to get by with a minimum of intimate detail. A transformer hummed ominously from behind, as before.

Thomas grasped the unfeeling metal door. The soreness in his wrist was another reminder. At the last, she had apologized, then asked about his happiness. He threw off the foreboding presence and laughed at the absurdity of what he was about to proclaim to the world.

Inside the headquarters was ridiculously quiet, like the rest of the campus. When he was here before, the building was frantic with activity, after the patrolman had been killed and the coed attacked. A stale queasiness twisted his midsection. Was it possible his girlfriend killed Dr. Albritton's son and the patrolman, mauled her dorm sister in a sick blood frenzy, and attacked Dr. Albritton at the banquet?

A young uniformed officer greeted him, pushing aside the paper work and a section of his sack dinner spread over the desk. They seemed to be alone. "Can I help you?"

"I need to see Chief Baggetta," Thomas announced.

Gilbroski continued to peel his apple, pushing a sharp blade through the core and splitting it in two. "Chief Baggetta was called away on an emergency. Can I take a message."

Thomas frowned sarcastically. Great! "When will he be back?"

Gilbroski scanned the empty desks, then quartered his apple and popped a section in his mouth. "I wish he were here now. It gives me the nerves when I'm the only one here."

Thomas felt exposed just standing there; he sat down.

"I shouldn't tell anyone this, but we've got big problems in the city, and I'm afraid it's going to blow this way." He shoved the point of his knife in a section and twisted.

Thomas asked, "What kind of trouble?"

Gilbroski cut another section of apple. "It started again this morning, just before daybreak. The police found two hookers in a cheap hotel ripped apart. The sleazo manager remembered enough of the killer bulletins to call the police. It's been going on all day; they think they've got him cornered and he gets away. He's got to be insane to kill like that."

Thomas nearly fell in the floor. His mind reeled. The slasher had returned. She had told him the truth. The slasher had come back for her.

Gilbroski stabbed at the core and flipped it into the trash. "Chief Baggetta may not come back for hours, and I'm stuck here."

Thomas slumped forward and dove for the exit.

Gilbroski sprang up. "Hey!"

Thomas was gone before he could stop him; an all consuming conviction burned in his brain. Majken had to still be there.

Streaks of red, pink, and mauve radiated from the west, spreading over the woodlands and distant city. Thomas reached the mansion late. He slowed to a crawl to pass over a rut. The weathered mansion seemed devoid of life; the way it had appeared the first time he saw it. He was not alone then. Thomas searched the upper windows for a sign of a lamp glow, then pressed on the car horn and waited. No response.

His knuckles were white as he gripped the steering wheel until his fingers hurt. The old mansion was more than an old mansion. Even in its decaying state, it was attractive to her. Whether she was, or was not, what she claimed to be was unimportant compared to the rising terror in the city. If she stopped him once, she could stop him again, he hoped. Coming here made him feel like an utter fool.

Dry, crusty grass stubble crunched under each step. The large, twisted oak spread menacing fingers over the entrance. Thomas laughed at himself for trying to sneak inside after having already announced his presence. The front door was slightly ajar. Come into my parlor, Thomas thought.

He called, peering hard into the dark hallway. He turned and scanned the reddened horizon before going inside. "Majken, this is Thomas," he shouted. He groped along the peeling wall and started to hum nervously as he reached her study. Faint twilight spilled into the hallway from the wide open front door. "Majken?" he croaked dryly. He looked into the study.

It was dark. He could barely see the outline of the couch and table. The table where they had made love, and afterward, where she drank his blood. His stomach twisted into a knot. The sitting room had been stripped of all but the barest essentials.

Thomas briefly considered climbing into darkness and searching her upstairs bedroom. The light in the hallway was twice as dim as when he first stumbled inside. He called upstairs, "Majken, we have a problem." He listened carefully, tilting his head like he had seen her do on campus during a long ago nightly stroll.

Birds flew and cried in the distant trees. For an instant, he felt a low moan from the ancient structure itself. Thomas gulped. He sidestepped nervously to the nearest exit. He watched the night birds he heard. They were free; he was bound. His last alternative was to go to the police with what he knew.

Thomas practiced in his mind, standing before a police desk sergeant explaining that his girlfriend knew the slasher personally. How would he say it? "She said his name was John, and he's a vampire." *No*, he thought, *she left me to hold the bag.* The policeman scowled.

A soft voice startled him. "Why did you come here?"

Thomas wheeled. A silhouette waited at the far end of the hall. "Majken?" he said tentatively. The dark shape moved forward. Thomas wiped his mouth with his sleeve. "The slasher is in the city."

"How do you know it is John?" came a disembodied reply.

"The police found two girls in a cheap motel, ripped apart, and the man got away. That was early this morning while I was here. There were more, all over the city." He strained to see her in the twilight.

"Where did you hear about the murders?"

Thomas crouched at hearing a heavy dragging sound. He relaxed when she told him she was getting a lamp for him. Faintly, he saw her push the heavy trunk under the stairwell.

"I went to see Chief Baggetta, about you. The other officer told me about the girls. It happened early this morning while I was here with you." Thomas paused to swallow the fear in his throat. "What you said about him, how dangerous he is …." He let his request hang.

A velvety yellow glow surrounded Majken as she trimmed the lamp. She held the lamp at waist level and stepped closer. "Baggetta would not have known how to help me, Thomas," she replied.

Her facial expression remained impassive as she considered his question. "If my hold over John has somehow been broken, he would certainly want me out of his way. I will need your help," she said.

He moved toward her cautiously. "Please, Majken."

They stood, motionless, separated by scarcely ten feet. Her voice was sadder. "We will never have what we had before you learned the truth. Our," she paused, "relationship will be forever different."

She was forever a puzzle, Thomas thought.

"What did you do after you left this morning?" she asked.

"I went to the banquet hall and found the stains. You must've really done something. Dr. Albritton was admitted to St. Francis last night." He asked, bewildered, "Why did you do it?"

"He gave me no choice." Majken motioned for him to sit down.

He followed her at a distance into the study. She pulled a dingy cloth off the couch and sat on the far end.

Thomas sat reluctantly, greatly relieved when she left the cover on the table. Too clearly he relived what she had done to him the night before. She was still beautiful to him. He shifted before his interest became noticeable. He told her what Phillip had said about her. She laughed and said he was right. It was Mary's laugh. Who was she now?

Outside, a stranger waited, patiently listening. Kneeling, he removed a triangular blade from a sheath and tucked it safely in his belt. He moved stealthily toward the open front door. He would wait until she started to feed, when she would be the most defenseless.

* * *

Majken ignored the deep sense of hollowness being close to him and yet distant created. She resisted the internal signals that cried for his blood. She squelched the desire to touch him, even by accident, or even to warm to his presence. He had only come because of the worry that the new Trenton murderer might be John; a highly remote possibility. She chided herself to let him go. "Will you take me to the city?"

Thomas asked, "What are you going to do about the slasher?"

"I no longer have a home territory to protect."

"You have to stop him," Thomas protested.

Majken smiled faintly, sadly. *We are worlds, Thomas, centuries apart*, she thought. "I have learned when it is time to leave a territory and start fresh. If it is hard for you to accept what I am, or what I must do to survive, then let me live only as you remember Mary Harris."

Thomas shook his head and mumbled, "It's time for me to leave. I didn't plan to stay this long."

John pressed to the interior wall, allowing a blind rage to block his memory of her conditioning. In this room, her former influence would be strongest. The boy was her weakness. His first intentions, to kill them, subsided. They were leaving. He shut his eyes and forcefully expelled his breath through clenched teeth to relieve the tension. He stepped easily into the room. She had heard him and already glided to her feet, but to no avail. Now was the time for payment.

"John!" Majken gasped. Thomas stood, frozen in awe, between them.

The other vampyr smiled cruelly, triumphantly. "It was beyond your right to interfere with me, Majken. It would be within mine to kill you both."

Majken kept her eyes firmly locked on his, searching. When she moved right, he moved left to keep Thomas between them. His eyes were black. "What do you want?" she asked quietly.

He pulled his knife into view. John avoided her direct gaze to resist her influence. "First, I shall have this one," he taunted.

She quickly glanced at Thomas. *Remain still*, she pleaded. The other vampyr moved closer to Thomas, whose face showed lines of fear. Majken tensed, helpless.

"When I again make my place in the city, you will bring humans to me as I require."

Enforced servitude, Majken thought glumly. She struggled to pass his defenses. *Remember*, she urged.

Thomas' judgment snapped with fear and he tried to run. John easily smashed him in the face with his knife hand. He fell to the couch, unconscious and bleeding from the mouth, and toppled it. Majken fell to her knees beside his body.

John poised the blade over his throat, seduced by his lust to kill and greatly weakened. He stopped at her command.

Majken held their lives by a slender thread. "Outside," she commanded gently. He stood, automatically replacing his knife in his belt. His eyes remained sharp and clear. The body on the floor threatened to break her concentration. She coaxed John into the hallway.

The illusion faded instantly. Returned to his senses, he reached for her. She ducked, holding his arm and twisting it behind his back. As he started to pull free, she jerked his arm up savagely and shoved him hard into the crumbling wall. Stunned, she pushed him outside. He stumbled, then righted himself. Majken grabbed his backpack sitting in the doorway and threw it. The projectile caught John in the chest as he was rising. It knocked him into the yard.

Majken quickly sealed the front door, breathing heavily, then leaned against it to listen. The heavy oak door muted his scream of rage. He swore vengeance.

Then silence.

Majken calmed herself by degrees, and tried to sense his presence through the closed door. She listened throughout the mansion. Deserted. When she was convinced the other vampyr had actually gone, she went to the study. Thomas lay as he fell.

She knelt beside him and placed her hands on his chest to feel his heartbeat and breathing. He moaned and rolled his head to the side. She cradled it. "Thomas," she whispered. He stirred, but kept his eyes closed. Fresh blood flowed from his lower lip.

Thomas pressed his palm to his temple and leaned his head against the couch. Majken was bandaging new razor-thin cuts on his upper arm, where she said she had acquired her latest meal while he was semiconscious. He now believed her. She was a vampyr. Between the two of them, he hardly stood a chance.

"Your lip will be better tomorrow." Majken placed her bandages in her shoulder bag. The glow of three lamps filled the tiny room with unusual brightness. She smiled painfully. "I'm sorry. If I had trusted your instincts, John would not have ambushed us."

"Do you think he's gone?"

"For tonight." She added, "Tomorrow we go after him."

Thomas felt a new ache. "It's going to drive Phillip crazy for me to disappear twice in a row."

Majken touched him lightly on the arm. "We must go into the city tomorrow, if only for me to find a new donor. Two nights feedings are the limit."

He traced a line across her cheek. "How are you going to stop him?"

She stared blankly ahead. Her hands were folded in her lap. "Majken?" She did not respond. As she leaned toward him, he supported her. "Did he hurt you?" he asked frantically.

She smiled reassuringly. "It is normal for me to go under after feeding. Don't worry, Thomas. He shouldn't return here tonight." She closed her eyes and fell limp against him.

Thomas held her. He reached to extinguish two of the lamps to save oil, and cradled her in his lap. It was going to be another long, hungry night.

In the heart of the campus, Daniel Albritton awoke from his stupor as darkness enveloped the landscape. He brushed his hands lightly over his smooth polished desk, trying to focus his mind. Depression would reduce his life to a weary blur of memories. Baggetta had warned him this might happen. His final admonition was about her. Albritton frowned;

Vincent had not lost a son to that whore!

The loss of his wife and son, he must learn to bear. His work had given him solace before. He should try to return to the classroom, he thought. Albritton reached for his memo folder, but found a sealed letter to him. From Marc! He tore into the envelope, hands shaking, and read the note. She was responsible! She did kill his boy! Grief spilled from unknown depths. He held the tearstained note to his chest and sobbed.

Chapter Eleven

Thomas woke in darkness, alone. He reached to where his head hurt. The mansion, this room, his memory drifted like a fog. He breathed deeply. The cobwebs started to clear. John had struck him. He opened his jaw and worked the tender muscles, then his stomach growled. The room was inky black. His hand explored the couch. Where Majken had gone, he did not know or care.

The comforter was spread over him like a tent to protect him from the night chill. Thomas settled toward the middle of the couch by bending his stiff knees and arching his back. The faded brown velvet nestled snuggly around his head, caressing his fear. Yes, fear, he admitted. Thinking of her lapping the blood that pooled from fresh cuts on his arm made his stomach retch. At least it was empty.

He tried, but found it impossible to see her as Mary. The image refused to stay put. Instead, he saw her face awash with golden light as she lay on top of him, the moment before she—his eyes! She always looked deeply into his eyes!

We have a problem, he told her. It amazed him how easily he made a connection between John, as she described him, and the person that killed the two girls in the city. Or did he grasp at the first flimsy excuse to return to her? Thomas shuddered.

Questions she was loathe to answer plagued him. How did she get this way? Will she ever get over it? Has she killed before? Thomas' heart involuntarily skipped a beat. He rolled into the comforter. It was too gruesome and too close to think about it now. Maybe she was a part-time monster. He shook the silly idea from his head. It started to throb again.

An unsettling fear gripped him. She might have abandoned him to face the slasher alone. His chest constricted. He knew too much for John to forget him. Then he heard the front door being unlocked and opened. There were soft footsteps in the corridor. He felt an invisible presence hover nearby. She would have killed him by now if that was her wish, he thought. He croaked a whisper, "Majken?"

"Thomas," she replied. Majken held an oil lamp and lit it, but trimmed it very low. She knelt and spread her long skirt over her thighs. "I searched the entire mansion and grounds. John is in the city by now, I imagine."

Relief exploded from Thomas in a sigh. He held his watch next to the dim lamp, trying to read the time. "Three A.M.?" he said.

Majken touched his knee briefly. Her skin was as cool as the night. Thomas jumped. "Everything's packed in your car," she said. Thomas started. "Your car looks fine. John left in too big of a hurry to damage it."

When Thomas stooped over to lace his shoes, his face came close to hers. "I'm new at this," he said. "What do we do?" He watched her lovely features pull into a tight mask.

"We follow John." She eased away from him, and crossed her arms. "John is no longer under my influence. He's too strong for me to deal with directly, and now, he'll try to kill both of us." She paused, her words suspended in midair, then spoke assertively. "I have a weapon, a stabbing weapon that can inject a compound that might kill him. It is unpredictable and extremely dangerous—to both of us."

Thomas rolled to his feet. "Why are you trying now?"

Majken stood up. "He took something important from me," she said softly.

Thomas extinguished the lamp. The late night, or early morning, sky sparkled through the open door. He shivered and followed her. She retrieved her shoulder bag piled at the entrance and carefully locked the mansion tight. Thomas' car started reluctantly. As they pulled away, he noticed her watching the mansion. A hidden part of her seemed to stay behind.

* * *

The city streets were noisy in the immediate vicinity of a late-night lounge at closing time as the manager escorted the few remaining members out. John entered the fenced parking lot by stealth when only one vehicle remained. The last patron, a well-dressed young businessman by his appearance, protested loudly at the door. He had been celebrating his rise to assistant manager at a car stereo shop; cutting short the party now was blasphemy, he shouted. His date tugged on his arm and whispered in his ear. They wobbled to the parking area in the rear. John lay down next to the van and waited.

"Louise," the man said, "you're drunk." The woman laughed lightly. He fumbled in her purse for the keys to the van as they rounded the corner.

"I'll drive," he said as he escorted her to the passenger's side; he opened her door, rounded the front of the van, then he stumbled. The woman laughed hysterically.

The young man muttered angrily. Frivolity and anger drained out of him when he found a body lying facedown on cold pavement. John felt him motioning wildly for his date, who was still giggling. Louise crawled over and opened his door. A sharp intake of breath signaled her surprise. "Kyle?" she asked.

The small light from the van spread over the prone body. Kyle commented on the man's old denim jacket. A silvery object glinted in the man's outstretched hand; an empty whiskey bottle. Kyle swore and prodded the body with the toe of his shoe.

"Call an ambulance," Louise said fearfully.

Kyle ignored her. "Goddamn drunk," he muttered. He kicked the body hard in the ribs. "Move!" he ordered. John remained corpse-like.

"Is he dead?" the woman asked.

Kyle knelt over him, closer, and saw breathing. "He's probably asleep."   He bent down to turn the drunk over.

John struck with startling speed; his solid fist crushed the young man's nose and face. The woman screamed and frantically kicked, then huddled to the rear of the van, a whimpering cry locked in her throat. John instantly pursued, easily lifting the unconscious man by his collar and pulling him inside. The woman's struggle was mercifully brief. John sated himself on the young man, saving the woman for later.

With his first goals of satisfying his blood needs, as well as acquiring transportation and shelter accomplished, John retrieved his backpack hidden in an empty garbage can and listened for signs of human interest. He picked up the keys that had fallen from his victim's fingertips, started the van, and eased carefully onto the street.

Certain she would come after him, he would be ready, waiting at the one place he knew they would come.

Majken tried to relax as Thomas drove on a main expressway entering the city. She watched the neighboring cars pass as he changed lanes and slowed down to exit. He commented on the number of cars. She described a host of local people going to or from work, with a few she called the wanderers and the perpetually restless, then finally the trucks. The nighttime was shared.

Much of the time, she mused in silence. Many lights sparkled across the dark, sleeping cityscape. She knew he was out there, waiting. Disturbing thoughts of what John might do churned within her mind and body, making it harder to rest or concentrate. She had learned that his actual blood needs were not as great as he had supposed. He chose to kill in a casual regard for human life. Nothing had prepared her for his seething hatred.

"When do we eat?" Thomas asked, breaking her chain of thought. Majken stared blankly at him.

He gulped. "Sorry."

He drove toward the inner city, all the time searching for a restaurant that stayed open all night. She asked him to pretend and drive like it was the middle of the day, with plenty of cars around. The police tended to stop vehicles that circled aimlessly, or moved too slowly at night. She heard his stomach complain.

She worried about Thomas. He seemed to be adjusting to the task before them. He seemed to understand what they were facing and what they had to do. But how did he feel about her now that fate had thrust them back together? He would be a constant target and her only source of help. He had already refused to leave with her.

Abruptly, Thomas pulled into a parking lot where he saw a grocery store open. Before she could protest, he jumped out of the car, and counting his money in his wallet, disappeared inside the store. Majken watched the slow changes in the sky that heralded the morning. Thomas returned twenty minutes later with a bag full of cold cuts, bread, snacks, and juice. She smiled broadly as he got in, munching happily on sliced ham.

"We have very little time before daybreak."

Thomas replied, "I know." He made himself com-

fortable, jamming several snacks between the front
seats and storing the rest of his groceries behind his
seat.   He opened a small carton of chocolate milk
and took the first gulp.

Majken watched a pedestrian carefully as she
spoke. "John could be anywhere. He's here, waiting to see what we try." The man she was watching
crossed the street and headed away from them.

"How did you find him the last time?"

"Remember, he followed me to the campus."

"Would he go there again?" His voice wavered.

Majken looked away. "He might."

Thomas pulled onto the street. Early morning
traffic would begin to pick up in less than a half-
hour. Majken wanted to be off the street before then.
She commented, "Searching the city by day will be
futile. Only when John wants to be found will he
make his presence known." She directed him to a
specific area of the city, and noticed his brow crease
in deep thought. They were travelling toward the
campus.

"Where was that warehouse?" Thomas asked.

Majken pointed to an adjacent avenue in the direction of the approaching dawn. He pressed her
for the exact address. "He wouldn't go there," she
warned.

He stopped at a red light. "How do you know?"

She sighed wearily and refused to answer.

Eventually, they found an apartment to serve as their base of operations in the city, an apartment that met her requirements of twenty-four hour access and seclusion. She insisted on handling the details of their room, and soon emerged with two keys. He parked in a secluded corner. John knew his car by sight and might be touring the city looking for it.

Majken carried only her shoulder bag to the room. She allowed Thomas to open the room with his key. She walked in first, dropping on the bed away from the window. Thomas set his groceries and her suitcase on a table, then collapsed on the second bed. Majken arranged her hairbrush and several toiletries from her bag on the counter and tossed a cotton pullover on her bed. She wanted a shower and needed rest.

Thomas sat on his bed looking deeply concerned. "It's hard to believe this is really happening," he said. "If John goes to the campus looking for you, what can we do then? Most of the students and faculty will be there for classes tomorrow."

"We have to hope John comes to the campus."

Thomas' jaw dropped. "What?"

"I must find and stop him quickly, or not at all. He

tends to rely on brute force, and may not be thinking clearly. At least I can confront him at a place I know best."

"How many of my friends will he kill before you stop him?" he said bitterly. He grew extremely agitated, and more useless.

Majken remained calm. "John wants me," she reminded him. She needed Thomas in one piece. "He may believe I'll try to hypnotize him, as before. He will not expect poison, but I have to inject it in a main artery in his neck or chest to be effective."

"Chief Baggetta is waiting to put you away."

Majken smiled slightly. "With any luck, I'll be on and off the campus before he knows I was there." She sighed. "At least, Dr. Albritton is out of our way. Be flexible, Thomas." She turned down her bed covers and left to take a shower. The sound and feel of the water soothed her. The first rays of sunlight reached the horizon as she came out. She dropped her old clothes on the carpeted floor and crawled into bed.

Within a few minutes, she was asleep.

New sunlight filtered through the window Daniel Albritton was facing. The brightness stunned him, making his eyes hurt and chased away the dull haze that surrounded him. He rubbed his hands over his beard. His last thoughts were of Marc. Albritton glanced at the crumpled paper in his right hand; his son's last will and testament.

Albritton was torn because it was difficult to remember Marc before that whore changed him. The promise he had made in Baggetta's home to accept his son's death was far away. A small cry escaped from his lips. It was a small concession to a crushing sense of betrayal. The note, Marc's note, gave him his final opportunity to show his love for his son— the chance he missed while his son lived.

His old body lay wearily and exhausted in his chair; he willed his right arm, clutching the note, to raise, his left leg to push and turn the chair. The swivel creaked. He held it an inch off the desk and released it. He watched it float to the surface.

Marc's note failed to mention her by name; the student known as Mary Harris did not exist. It described when and where they met. Shock mercifully numbed him. The note described in intimate detail how she withdrew blood and drank it after she seduced him. Whore! Shock lessened the blow of how she pursued him and deliberately hurt him. Marc, he thought gently. Albritton found it impossible to believe his son could have still loved that creature.

The last paragraph was cautionary. Marc said he

wanted to reason with her peacefully; to make her leave him alone. He had borrowed his father's gun for self-protection. There it stopped. No goodbye or signed with love or even his name. His son's note ended abruptly, cruelly, as did his life. If only he had known these things when his son was in the intensive care unit. She took his life. Marc was hurting when he wrote this, Albritton realized. He tried not to see the bloodstain on his shirt or the thick crust of blood in his sneakers. Did his son throw them away? He never found them. His son penned this note while sitting at this desk. Albritton was in class at the time, but Marc could have easily come to him, to talk, for help. He stifled a cry of horror. The thought of any person abusing his son, let alone killing him in cold blood, cut deeply.

Albritton's pain-racked mind sought the answer, searched deeply for inspiration. How could he live normally as long as his son's murderess roamed free? He pledged to settle this matter for Marc's sake. The last few weeks in his friend's home faded from view. He concentrated on finding her. He wanted her to pay for her crime.

Slowly, Albritton picked up the telephone and dialed the police. One digit. The next number. His son's murderer roamed free. The receiver clicked in his ear. The police believed his son's death was suicide! The investigators had to believe him. The final digit clicked, it rang once. Albritton hung up.

The word *justice* rang in his mind. She could escape the police or even Vincent. She could disguise herself and disappear as quietly as she had come. He would follow her, find her, and chase her to his son's grave! He wanted the privilege of obtaining her confession for the police. He wanted her himself.

Albritton pulled himself together, forced down a quick breakfast, showered and dressed in his suit, then came to his study to contemplate. It was fully day, a bright clear Sunday. An idea was planted in his mind. The police had sealed his gun and Marc's personal effects in an evidence bag. Albritton walked to his cabinet. He barely remembered throwing the bag in there. He unlocked the cabinet and reached inside. The gun vibrated like a living thing.

He held the bag securely. The evidence bag was labeled, Property of the Trenton Police Department, and was sealed at the top with orange tape. He rubbed his hands over the plastic. The forensics people had cleaned his son's blood off when they examined the gun. Marc's fingerprints were the only ones, they claimed.

Marc's wallet, his house keys, and a miniature

penknife were also in the bag. Albritton went to his son's bedroom, holding the bag close to his heart with one hand and steadying his ascent with the other. He hesitated a second before entering, then entered and sat on his son's bed. He glanced around the empty room. "I miss you son."

He cradled the gun in his lap, as he once held his infant son. His jaw tightened grimly, and with a vengeance his fingers ripped open the tape seal. He slowly pulled the murder weapon out with his right hand.

The small knobs on the handle made his grip sure. He examined its shiny finish and judged its weight in his palm. Without ceremony, he slipped his son's wallet in his coat pocket, over his heart.

"I promise Marc, she won't get away."

Thomas reclined fully on his bed, reading the morning paper and watching Majken pin her hair up. He turned to look at the full morning sunlight slipping through the closed curtain. She was dressed to travel in a blouse and jeans. It would be warm by day and cool by night.

"I'm surprised you're up so soon," he said.

She glanced at him. "I will rest before night."

Thomas stared at the jar she was holding. She dabbed the cream on her face and neck and rubbed it in. She held the jar up. "This is a highly concentrated sunscreen to protect me from the sun." Majken replaced the lid and made a face. "My supply is low."

"Where do you get it?" Thomas flipped a page.

"Mail-order supply." Majken closed the latches on her suitcase and carried it to the door. She sat next to Thomas as he turned to the front page.

"It's worse that I thought. Four unknown deaths are attributed to an unknown male Caucasian police officials describe in the mid-thirties. The subject was reported to be wearing a dark brown leather jacket, brown pants, and heavy work shoes." Thomas stared ahead. "I don't remember a brown leather jacket."

"John picks up different clothes from his victims. That description is useless. He may turn up wearing a business suit and tie and have his hair lightened."

Thomas frowned sarcastically at the composite drawing. "This doesn't look a thing like him."

"John has been surviving this way for a very long time. Before the sun gets high, I want to reach my cache and prepare the stab device."

Thomas questioned her. She explained that a cache was a hidden storage area where she kept supplies she might need. Thomas pointed to the jar on the counter. "Does he use that?"

"No, he is more sun tolerant than I am, but he is

mostly active at night." She slipped off the bed and put the jar away. She began packing her other supplies.

"I don't understand," Thomas said hurriedly. She explained further.

"We are alike in our daily needs for fresh blood; we differ like the human populations. Many of us exist as loners. We establish and defend territories for our own safety. Imagine the problem if several vampyrs tried to feed on a given population. That is why I first tried to persuade him to leave.

"John does not lapse into a comatose state like I do; he sleeps lightly, during the day mostly." She added, "I have not seen many whose lust to kill exceeds their need for blood, like John."

"Do vampyrs usually ... kill many people?"

She hesitated. Her reply sounded carefully phrased. "It is rare to find a true vampyr that has not been forced to kill in defense or out of necessity."

Thomas grimaced involuntarily.

"I have lived on as little as seven or eight ounces, and have needed as much as thirty ounces per day. My blood needs vary according to my activity, environment, and physical state."

She rattled these tidbits casually, Thomas thought, as if she was trying to harden him for the real thing.

"We tend to use different tactics to get our supply. I try to keep regular donors." She spoke thoughtfully, reflecting. Majken leaned against the counter.

"When I am feeding, I tend to draw within myself. For a short time, I am not as acutely aware of my surroundings as I would wish. Since I need rest soon afterward, I try to feed at night. My mark is usually in deep sleep or unconscious. John goes too far; his victims are on the verge of death."

Majken broke away and clenched her arms tightly. Thomas sensed her bitterness, her nervousness, her loss. She turned to face the counter. She needed him. "Majken," he said lowly, "I was happy."

She faced him, and unclenched by degrees, then finally appeared to relax.

Thomas asked, "How did he become a vampyr?"

"He was very secretive and highly resilient. I do not know what made him vampyric, but once, only once during our sessions, he mentioned a woman. I could not find out if she was human or vampyr or what happened to her. He despises humans for an illogical reason."

Thomas was speechless.

Majken put on her sunglasses. "We should go," she said, gathering her shoulder bag. Thomas followed her out.

* * *

Dr. Albritton checked to see if his coat was securely buttoned, then hit the glass pane with his open palm. What could these girls be doing on a Sunday? He considered the woman's dorm as his first logical step to tracking down the elusive Ms. Harris. He muttered as he knocked again.

The latch clicked. A wary coed opened the door slightly and asked what he wanted. "I am here to talk to Mary Harris." He enunciated her name carefully, to make sure the girl understood. The coed turned uncertainly to someone behind her, then shook her head. "It is important," he said, "I've misplaced her exam." The first coed spoke to the second, an acceptable reaction.

He listened as the second girl bounced up the stairs, possibly to check her room. Albritton tried to enter, but the young woman held the door firmly with her foot. She told him no strange men were to be allowed in. He held his temper. "You don't have to fear me," he said, "I'm a member of the faculty."

Albritton tensed as he heard a pair of footsteps approach. The element of surprise would be lost in the first few seconds. The door opened wide, a coed with black hair greeted him.

"I'm Mary's roommate. Can I help you?"

He asked politely. "I have to speak with Mary on an important matter. Do you know where I might find her?"

She brushed her hair out of her face and squinted in the bright sunlight. "She's been gone for nearly two weeks. I don't know where she is."

"I have to find her!" Albritton anxiously pushed himself toward the entrance. The girl frowned at him.

"She's gone," she said flatly. "She took her suitcase and most of her things are gone." Albritton asked her determinedly where she went. He watched the coed study him suspiciously, then her face brightened with recognition.

"You're Marc Albritton's father!"

Albritton steeled himself in the doorway, the flicker of irritation he felt was a mere hint of the anger buried far beneath the surface. He was unable to deny it.

"Why are you causing her so much trouble?" She seemed shocked to hear herself defend her former roommate.

Albritton appraised the girl carefully.

The way she was wringing her hands and leaning on the door for support told him she was upset and frightened.

He replied coldly, "I want her!" The girl stood, trembling silently. Albritton raged, "If you're hiding her from me—" He choked when the vile, unspeakable things that creature did to his beloved son entered his mind.

The girl held to the curtain and numbly shook her head.

Albritton stomped away.

Majken handled the compact cylindrical device with extreme care. Thomas watched, spellbound, as she laid the components on a newspaper. The main body resembled a stubby, oversized hypodermic. It fit Thomas' palm, but was oversized to hers. In place of a needle, the front aperture accepted a sharpened piece of tubing an inch long and a quarter-inch in width. Merely stabbing John in a vital area would not be enough. Majken removed a glass jar from her bag. Inside was the poison. Scarcely breathing, Majken opened the jar and removed a foil wrapped, smaller container that appeared to fit inside the device. She opened the ends of the foil with forceps, then pulled the remainder with her fingers.

The clear plastic container was sealed with a rubber septum on one end, and was filled with a finely packed, off-white powder. Majken pushed the smaller cylinder into the larger, then placed a plunger over it and twisted. She hissed sharply as the septum broke and flakes of powder splattered inside the container. The final assembly involved coiling a spring over the plunger, sealing the end and engaging a tension wire from the plunger to the trigger mechanism in the head. She placed the entire device in a paper bag, point downward, and twisted it shut. She leaned back slowly and breathed deeply. They were ready.

Albritton smiled indifferently at the cup of steaming black coffee offered by Chief Baggetta, and ignored the open package of snack cakes. This Sunday, the headquarters buzzed with activity.

Baggetta's gun and holster was wrapped neatly on his desk. He rarely wore it. Albritton closed the door to his friend's office.

Baggetta explained the anxiety. "It's started again. Trenton police found what they believe to be the slasher's latest victim; a male in his mid-twenties dumped in the railyard in the path of a train. His neck and wrists were cut, like the others. If the servicing crew hadn't spotted the body, we wouldn't have had much left to identify."

Albritton leaned forward on his walking cane. He saw obvious stress pooled around his friend's eyes, deep creases permanently etched in his face. Baggetta eased tiredly in his chair.

"What worries me is that this man has gone underground and he could surface anywhere. We've tried with limited success to enforce a complete blackout on the media. I did manage to convince the Trenton chief that sending twenty squad cars here will not help the terrorized student population. We're closer to catching this maniac. How, Daniel, can a man kill like that?"

"The workings of the criminal mind are beyond me, Vincent." He quietly sipped his coffee. The trail had grown cold. The last several hours he had spent driving and searching were frustrating. Albritton smiled warmly at his compatriot.

"How are you holding up?" Baggetta finally asked him.

He rubbed his injured leg gently. "As well as I expected," he said meekly. "My first night was spent remembering my family, the years we had together. Next semester, I hope to return to my classes." His face tightened. "I need your help, Vincent. I've given that night much thought. I want to talk to the boyfriend, Thomas Kline, in your office so my questions don't get out of hand. As far as I know, he was the last person to see Mary Harris after the banquet."

Baggetta smiled. He took a long, relaxing sip, then picked up a snack cake, dunked it and ate it. "Thomas should be on campus this evening. We'll have a talk with him together."

"Thank you, Vincent." Albritton searched his friend's intense eyes, a man that would defend justice to the death. But not this time, Vincent, not this time.

Students milled everywhere. Unsuspecting. Frightened. Vulnerable. Thomas scanned the sea of faces in the cafeteria; he swam as a tiny speck in an ocean. His spirit groaned. Why could they not stay away a few more days, until Majken had a chance to root out the killer she strongly suspected would come here.

Anyone could die. His friends, his fellow classmates, and even the faculty. He checked his watch. It was nearly an hour until sunset.

That was when the fun was scheduled to start. Majken's plan was to use herself as a decoy, a plan he objected to strongly. She said she could handle campus security. But could she handle campus security and John? She hoped to avoid getting another student hurt or killed. He had asked her how she planned to get away, and she had not replied.

They both worried about his part. How callous could he be? Hers was the greatest risk. Get something to eat, rest, she said, because we may be up all night. He was to be her lookout, her safety. He was to call the police if John—if he—if Majken died. The long cafeteria line snaked endlessly.

It was his enviable task to learn as much as possible without being obvious. Several students gawked at him for his strange questions. Have you seen any strangers recently, anyone that did not belong? Most everyone talked about the award's banquet and how much fun it would be to hit the books tomorrow. Maddening. Finally, the line moved to the point where Thomas could pick up a tray. The rows of delectable sweets tempted him; the patient cafeteria staff waited for his order. He was in another world.

Thomas lugged his tray to a table where one student was digging into a hamburger and fries, with lemon pie for dessert. He suddenly felt nauseated; he had learned that a new food was blood, and remembered two night's feedings on one person was her limit. She had disappeared into her dorm. He was afraid one of those poor girls would receive the same treatment he had.

His fellow diner asked him what had happened to his lip. Thomas felt the swollen, bluish lip as he chewed his food. The boy suggested a fight; Thomas nodded lamely. The memory chilled him. He finished his meal quickly. Majken planned to meet him in the grove at their bench. Heaven help if another couple is there, he thought.

Before dusk, she had stressed, because John liked to kill at dusk. His supper knotted in his stomach. A wave of nostalgia compelled him to remember each detail of the cafeteria and the times he and Mary had come here. It may be his last time—a glimpse of burning eyes petrified him. In a fraction of a second, the shadowy figure melted into the crowd.

He rose steadily, holding his tray as a shield, moved, stumbled with leadened feet; his eyes were drawn and paralyzed with fear. John was there! He was gone now, and maybe was never there. Maybe he had lost his mind. Thomas left the cafeteria with a hearty group of students. Basic survival told him not to travel alone.

The sun was dying slowly; the brightness was fading in the treetops. He looked all around himself. There was no sign of what he thought he saw, but Majken had to know. He might be here now. Distracted, Thomas bumped into a campus patrolman and a smaller, wiry, silver-haired man.

* * *

Majken rested on her bed in darkness, waiting for Lisa to enter. The gentle, soft familiar contours of her bed begged her to stay. This was once her home; leaving tore a jagged scar. She could easily become too attached to do what must be done. Her thoughts turned dark.

The only items she brought with her were the stab weapon, safely wrapped and hidden in the first drawer, and a puncture set tucked in her back pocket. While waiting, she checked her former room carefully, under the mattress and deep in the folds of her closet. Satisfied, she passed the time by listening to the muted sounds from the hallway of happy, playful voices and subdued movement, scuffling feet. Her ears sharpened. She tensed.

Lisa entered the room and snapped on a light. "Mary! What are you doing here?" She almost dropped her towel in surprise. Majken sensed her joy was masked by numbing shock and fear.

"Hello, Lisa." Majken settled into a familiar pattern. "Have things settled down around here?" She slid to a sitting position between their beds.

Lisa looked puzzled. Her hands flitted nervously as she made her way to the closet. "Are you going to stay?" She awkwardly pulled on a quilted robe, then folded the towel around her damp hair while watching Majken out of the corner of her eye.

Majken took casual interest to avoid scaring her more and smiled. "You know me," she said lightly, "never stay in one place too long." Her heart became heavy, but she continued to smile. Lisa paced to her bed and sat, her long legs extended and crossed at the ankles.

"Is it any of my business where you've been?" she said sharply.

"I'm sorry I had to leave in a big hurry." Majken was briefly silent. "I didn't have time to tell you or Thomas where I was. I talked it all out with him after the award's banquet. He knows what's been going on and what I've been doing and why."

Lisa was taken aback. "Why should it matter if you have anyone to take up for you while you're missing, and you don't bother to tell those people where you've gone? You're a bit late," she said sourly.

"I'm scared, Lisa," she said softly. "We have a serious problem and I may need your help." She paused thoughtfully. This might work. "A man is after me, one of the professors. I've been cleared by the police, and he still believes I had something to do with his son's accident."

"Dr. Albritton," Lisa offered. "I saw him when they brought him inside, in the middle of the appetizer." Majken bowed her head and stifled a smile.

"Thomas and I left because we needed to talk."

Lisa accepted that. "Where were you all week?"

"I was taken into protective custody by the police." Lisa's eyes widened in disbelief. Majken glanced furtively over her shoulder and whispered. "The night of the murder, here, I was outside, and I saw him."

Lisa shoved her fist into her open mouth, a muffled scream rose from her throat.

Majken put her fingers to her lips. "Shhh," she begged, "not even Chief Baggetta knows. Only a few loyal Trenton detectives know. They believe," she lowered her voice more, "that the slasher is on the police force. That's why they haven't been able to catch him!"

Lisa panted breathlessly. "What are you going to do?" Majken gripped her roommate's hands, gently, and sat beside her. She solemnly produced a folded envelope and crumpled it in her fingers for several seconds before giving it to Lisa.

"Take this," she asked. The envelope was addressed to a newspaper. Majken's hands trembled. "This gives the names of the police detectives I'm working with, a description of the slasher, and everything I know. If something goes wrong ...," Her voice trailed off.

She took it lightly, like it might burn her fingers, then flipped it over and over, staring.

"Don't tell a soul," Majken pleaded. "I have to be a decoy tonight, and possibly for the next few nights." Lisa cringed. "They told me not to tell anyone, but I couldn't keep it from my best roommate!" Lisa started to cry. Majken hugged her.

"You understand, don't you, why I'll be sneaking in and out for the next few days. It may be over tonight," she said with extreme calm. "Just keep that under your bed, and don't open it. It's supposed to be anonymous." Lisa was holding the letter up to the light. She did not know it was only blank pages. "If things go wrong and I get killed, wait twenty-four hours and mail it. You must wait twenty-four hours, understand?" Lisa nodded. "Oh, yes," Majken added, "put a stamp on it."

Lisa wiped her eyes. "Is that all you want me to do?"

Majken held to Lisa. "By holding that letter, you've helped me more than you know. There is something else you can do, only if you want to."

"Anything."

Majken sat close to her, sheltering her. "The psychologist told me this guy kills to get blood, he's a blood fetish freak. It's like a pyromaniac can only get it on by watching a fire." Her voice was tinged with fear. "They said if he gets to me before my backup can stop him, he'll tear me open. The doctor gave me a way to slow him down. I'm going to carry fresh blood in a special bag and bust it in his face. I guarantee it'll slow him down."

Lisa looked uncertain. Majken produced the wrapped stab device, then unbuttoned her sleeve and showed Lisa the puncture marks on her arm. "The doctor gave me this to use, but I've given blood all week. Can I draw some from you? It won't hurt very much. I think tonight, I'll need all of mine." Lisa chewed her lip.

"What do I do?" she asked hesitantly.

"Lie on your stomach and relax. The doctor taught me to take it from the leg, so it wouldn't hurt." Lisa stretched out and lay her head in her folded arms. Majken placed the stab device at the foot of the bed and made a pretense of unwrapping it. She opened her leather case, reassuring Lisa as she prepared: alcohol, Betadine swabs, puncture needle, tube, pressure dressing, bandages, and surgical tape. She exposed the left leg. "You'll feel a tiny stick," she said, preparing the site.

Lisa squirmed. "I can't see a thing."

"It takes less than five minutes. Relax, and be

very still. You'll want to rest and will feel sleepy. That's normal. I'm going to lay down for a time, too." Her toes curled when the needle penetrated her lower leg.

Majken fed carefully, quickly, silently directly from the site.

Thomas cowered beneath the bright light aimed directly in his face. The deep resonant voice of Chief Baggetta came from his left. "Thomas," he said evenly, "you could get into big trouble. I want you to tell us what we want to know." A shrill, tenored voice came from his right, demanding, and a bony hand pulled on his arm.

"Where is Mary Harris now?" Albritton demanded sharply.

Thomas squinted in the light, holding his hand to his forehead. "I don't know."

"When did you last see her?" he snapped.

Thomas reflected. "Saturday morning."

"You're lying!" Albritton accused.

"Daniel!" Baggetta growled a warning. He spoke to Thomas calmly. "Son, you told me you hadn't heard from her all week, yet you took her to the banquet. When did you hear from her?"

Thomas cleared his throat, a gesture, and turned

toward the more sane voice. He started to sweat around his forehead and neck. "She called me Friday morning. Whatever business she was doing was finished, and she said she was ready to come home." *Those were her words*, he added silently.

Albritton pushed in. "Where did you last see her?"

"On a street corner!" Thomas answered without thinking.

Baggetta modulated. "Why didn't you tell us she contacted you?"

Thomas flinched. "I didn't think about it." Semi-truthful. He felt a spasm jerk in the small of his back. He pushed his hand behind the curled hard chair and rubbed the spot. They questioned him at a desk in the open area, visible to everyone.

Thomas turned when he heard a metallic creak. Two patrolmen entered. One of them, he recognized. He quickly propped his arm on the chair as a shield. Gilbroski and the second patrolman went to the dispatcher's console to exchange battery packs in their walkie-talkies.

Albritton hammered a new question. "Why did she leave before the banquet? It's as good as an admission of guilt."

Baggetta listened attentively.

"She, ah, we wanted to be together." He felt his face become flushed. "We wanted to be together."

Gilbroski stopped by his chair. "You were in here yesterday." Thomas shrank to an inch high as Gilbroski explained to a startled Chief Baggetta, who was an extremely curious man. He excused his junior officer with a warning to stay alert.

"What did you want to talk to me about, son?"

Baggetta's smooth, fatherly approach contrasted greatly to Dr. Albritton's bulldozer approach; it made Thomas think of the carrot and the stick. He stammered, "I ... thought you, uh, came to tell you Mary planned to clear up everything when she came back this week."

"Did you know that she attacked me in the alley?" Albritton flared.

Thomas ground his teeth. "If she were here, she would say you were chasing her." Albritton looked like he was starting to come unhinged. Baggetta cast a warning look.

"Where did you and she go after the award's ceremonies?" Baggetta asked with great restraint.

"We sat in my car and talked," Thomas said. His palms sweated on the wooden chair. He closed his eyes for a moment's respite, then stole a glance outside. It was getting very late; Majken had to know

John was already here.

"Your roommate told me she took you to a mansion." He chuckled politely.

"A motel," Thomas countered. "Phillip heard wrong. We went to a motel." He held his knees to keep them from trembling out of control.

"How did she explain her presence in the alley?" Albritton asked.

Thomas drew a deep breath.

Gilbroski hated patrol duty. It was a major facet of his job, but he still hated it. Someday, he swore, he would finish the business degree he started. Someday, soon. What was worse, was being hooked to a rookie. Why was he so lucky to get these assignments? Breaking in a new patrolman was not so bad—it was just that the death of Mr. Charles left a gap the size of a diesel truck. Having someone new might not be so bad, he reasoned. At least he would not be on bottom anymore.

He started to issue an order when an out-of-place vehicle caught his attention; a van was parked where it was not supposed to be. He gestured to his partner and headed toward the van. Caution screamed through his jangled nerves. In the last few weeks, too many things that had started out routine ended fatal. The large bubble window, tinted brown, was covered. He looked through the front while his partner checked the rear. The curtains were drawn.

Gilbroski had an itch, an insufferable nervous feeling. The other patrolman checked the front doors, locked, then casually flipped out a ticket pad and started to scribble the license number. Gilbroski unclipped his radio and called control to check the vehicle for stolen. There was no student parking sticker. Minutes later, he heard the van had not been reported stolen and it was registered to a Ms. Louise Cisco of Trenton. It still felt wrong.

He hesitated, then tried the side door.

It opened. A young woman's mangled body lay inside.

The sickly sight of blood sent nausea, vertigo rushing through him and he choked the burning mass in his throat as he turned to his partner.

"Keep spectators away!" he barked. Gilbroski ran as he called for help.

Urgent!

Get me the police, an ambulance, the coroner. Run! A small crowd of students began to gather at the van. He would never forget her open, staring, glassy eyes. The alarm was raised. He hurried to bring help.

* * *

Thomas refused to answer any more questions hurled by his inquisitors. They had goaded him into admitting that he and Mary had slept together. He firmly told them any further discussion on the matter would have to wait until an attorney was present. Albritton asked if she ever cut him. It was a startling question he did not ponder. He said no, thankful for his long sleeved jersey.

They could not hold him all night!

A cry of alarm rose from the dispatcher. Baggetta went to the console and began dialing furiously, leaving Thomas alone with Albritton. He turned off the light in his face. Albritton tried to stare him down. Thomas stood angrily; his blood started to boil. He had had enough! Suddenly, a winded patrolman flew into the headquarters. They found the body of a woman in a van, he wheezed. Baggetta grabbed his cap and followed.

Thomas glared at Albritton a final time, then savagely kicked the gate and strode for the door. Albritton called, but Thomas ignored him.

The sun was setting; the sky reddened in the west. John liked to kill at dusk, he remembered with a chill. A siren started to wail in the distance. There were seconds of indecision. Students were jogging toward the source of the alarm. He looked over his shoulder, alone, then ran toward the grove. An iron hand suddenly gripped his throat from behind.

John twisted his arm and held him fast. Thomas flinched when John pressed his face close to his. His pale features were twisted in a mask of hatred. "Keep silent, Thomas," he sneered. "And she thought I was after her." He dragged Thomas in the direction of his car.

Dusk. Majken stretched as feeling returned to her extremities. She rose, knelt between the beds silently, and gently brushed her hand through her roommate's soft black curls. Lisa was asleep. Thomas would be waiting, she thought, jolting her to move. She gathered the weapon under her arm. She heard sirens.

Her fingers tightened on the doorframe as an impression of heavy dread coursed through her. She was too late! Majken paused to glance at Lisa, then stepped into the hallway. One girl saw her leaving; a matter of small consequence. She walked outside and down the concrete steps with restraint to avoid calling attention to herself. The unsteady buzz of a neon lamp signaled the deepening twilight, and the beginning of night.

She followed a grassy path to the sirens. An ambulance reached the parking lot where many students gathered. She needed Thomas' help. Tan security uniforms kept her from going closer. Majken scanned the area surrounding the lot. Suddenly, she spotted a car, his car, leaving. It was Thomas, and he was not alone.

Majken swore helplessly. An emptiness swelled in her chest; she had failed him. She blindly circled the building to better see which direction they went. His car disappeared, heading south. Then a deep click rang in her ears. She wheeled to find an angry, bitter father pointing a gun at her head.

"You killed my son!" Dr. Albritton raged with clenched teeth. "You betrayed and killed him!" He forced Majken against the building, poised just out of reach. Her head bumped the solid brick. Stupid, stupid! Albritton motioned her toward his waiting car. "We are going to talk to Marc," he muttered.

"Dr. Albritton," she said with exaggerated calm. "I will forget this if you stop now." He prodded her to a red Thunderbird and jerked open the passenger's side.

"Drive," he ordered.

Majken felt weak, breathless. "I can't," she whispered.

Albritton threw his keys on the pavement in front of her, and cautiously stepped back. "You will!" he said coldly, scowling. Majken quickly looked around for possible help before her shaking fingers picked up the ring of metal strips.

She got in from the passenger's side and slid under the wheel. He followed discretely while never moving the gun from her heart. The array of gadgets made her light-headed. She fumbled with the keys. "Which one?" He told her the blue key with the square head. Color-coded. Damn! She held it between thumb and forefinger like she had seen Thomas do. The strain tightened in her throat, raising her voice. "Where does it go in?" she asked nervously. "I've never done this," she whispered.

Albritton started to reach across, but withdrew warily. "Of course you've driven before," he said flatly. He pointed to the proper receptor.

She tried the key, turned it over, it fit properly.

Her eyes tried to stay in focus. It was difficult to breathe slowly, calmly, and rest her shattered nerves. She held her breath as she twisted the key. The engine started; she twisted the metal strip again and produced a grinding noise. "Stop that!" Albritton snapped.

Majken panted as she searched for the other pedal

and the lever from the floorboard. Albritton ordered her to drive, impatiently. She pressed her left foot on the single pedal and gripped the only lever by the steering wheel. Something clicked. She moved her foot and the car edged forward. They moved spasmodically as she turned the wheel into the deserted street. Luckily, there was no oncoming traffic.

She forced her eyes open and steered the massive, terrifying machine, vibrating with a life of its own. She reached an intersection. A stop signal, she remembered. She applied the brake evenly and felt better. Majken reached for the lever again. He ordered her to leave it alone. "Where are we going?" she finally asked.

Albritton sat motionless, pressed to the opposite side of the seat.

The gun seemed like a separate entity determined to take her life.

"If you try anything, or hit anything, I'm sure I can get at least four or five rounds into you before you get me." His eyes were a cold, piercing blue. "We are going to talk to Marc." He directed her to the east.

Majken drove reluctantly, surprised at how desperate she must be. If she could lose Albritton, this was what she needed to follow Thomas. Now, she wished she had accepted his driving lesson. Albritton directed her to side roads, away from traffic, and urged her to drive faster. The sky was turning from red to a deep blue. Conversation was pointless. Several other motorists glared at her. Then, Albritton began to toy with the wrapped bag in the seat, the stab weapon.

Her pulse quickened.

When he started to open it, her nerves screamed; she could not take much more of this!

A truck stalled abruptly in front of her. She jabbed at the brakes.

Albritton was thrown forward with his gun hand pointed up. In a split second, Majken knocked the gun in the backseat and shoved him hard against the door, then grabbed her weapon, and sprang out of his car.

Find another way to Thomas! flashed through her mind as she ran to escape.

She glanced back and saw Albritton scramble to the driver's side, gun his car across a lane cutting off traffic, and come after her.

Majken darted into an alley for cover. *Run*! She cradled the device, and sprinted. A roaring engine and red searing metal licked at her heels. The front fender hit her a glancing blow, knocking her into a rough brick wall. The weapon fell out of her reach and she struck the pavement with numbing force.

Darkness swirled before her eyes.

Albritton examined the fallen girl with vile hatred. He wanted the whore to pay for his son's life, but not before her judgment. He quickly opened the passenger's door and half-lifted and half-dragged her unconscious body to his car. Her body folded limply in the seat. Intent on reaching his destination before full nightfall, he raced forward. The heavy vehicle smashed the stab weapon, leaving a crystalline white powder to scatter desolately in the wind.

Chapter Twelve

Flickers of light and sensation, the millions of attempts to reach consciousness had failed. The sea was endless. Majken remembered being in water with Thomas. Floating. Drifting. Touching. Would she ever see him again? An eternity passed. Motion ceased. She collapsed on cold grass next to gravel, and felt herself being dragged. She fell on her face, then rolled over. The sky was ashen gray. Late twilight.

Awareness began at the feet of a man standing over her, gradually spreading upwards. She recognized the gun. Reality. Her mind cleared. Majken sat up carefully. Her left thigh smarted where his car had struck her. She rotated her hips to ease the throbbing pain.

"You caused me great anguish, Mary Harris." Albritton scowled harshly at his prisoner. His hand trembled as he removed a wrinkled piece of paper from his coat pocket. He held it out and dropped it within her reach. His ice-blue eyes were riddled with anger. "Marc wrote that about you," he said with greatly restrained contempt.

Majken looked at the crumpled note, and turned to read Marc's name on the monument, freshly engraved next to his mother's name. The gravesite was exposed raw earth, without flowers, as if he could not let his son go. The rust-colored earth was moist.

She asked nervously, "What are you going to do with me?"

"You whore!" he said vehemently. "Why did you destroy my son?"

"I did not destroy your son." She tried to rise to a kneeling position—she could jump farther than he might imagine. He waved her down with the gun. She tensed.

"You tortured him and drank his blood!" Anger poured from an open wound.

Majken remained silent.

His voice broke as his face twisted in pain. "Why did you kill him?" he pleaded.

She closed her eyes to block her memory. "He came after me with that gun. When he tried to shoot me, the gun fired accidentally." She quickly scanned the cemetery and saw green rolling hills with rows of slate. This section was bordered with shrubs. The sky was getting imperceptibly darker.

Albritton moaned. Finally, he said coldly, "My son would be alive if it weren't for you. Everyone believes he was sick because of you." The gun hammer clicked to a firing position.

"Do you plan to kill me?" she asked tersely.

He stared mutely at the gun in his hand.

"What are you going to do with my body?"

She urged him to think. His eyes drifted to the heavens. Majken placed her palms flat on the ground, ready to spring in either direction. His cheeks glistened with tears, pale in the sunset. Suddenly, he screamed to the heavens, "Why should she live and my son die?"

Majken listened to the swaying of trees and drew a deep breath. He searched desperately for his lost son. "Marc talked about you when we were together," she said softly. The gun trembled slightly. She wished he would hold still.

"What did ... my son say?"

She hesitated for an instant. Partially the truth, she thought. "I listened to him when he was really hurting. He wanted to get close to you, but he didn't know how." Albritton stared blankly at his son's grave. Then she told the lie. "Marc said he truly loved you."

Grief and loss ripped him apart. His gun hand lowered completely; his body went slack over the grave. "Marc," he wheezed between sobs. The gun dropped from his limp grasp onto the grass. Majken reached for it and pulled it gently away with her fingertips, then stood and held the weapon.

It was fully night. Stars shimmered overhead, watching. She clenched her fist and considered driving it into his bowed skull. In a surge of disgust, she threw his gun far into the woods, picked up Marc's testament, and stepped away from the gravesite. He was finished. Majken approached his car with dread, cursing it as her only possible transportation.

She swallowed the hoarse dryness in her throat as she opened the door. The keys were still in the ignition. Briefly, she glanced at the huddled old man. The night air grew steadily cooler. "I'm sure he loved you," she whispered quietly. She carefully started his car and drove out of the cemetery.

An hour later, she found Thomas' car abandoned.

Majken listened to the deadly sharp silence. A low moaning was carried on the wind as she approached his sideways crashed vehicle. She recognized it instantly. Wide black skid marks bit into the gravel and soil where the tires had left the road. The way the marks swerved worried her. She hoped Thomas did not try to fight John.

She glanced up and down the highway before committing herself to inspect his car. Traffic was scarce. Driving through the inner city to reach him had been a harrowing experience, as well as a long one. She looked through the driver's window for blood inside, then walked around the car. His car was simply stuck in the ditch. Her hunch was right—John was taking Thomas to the mansion.

Majken searched the high grass for signs of a struggle or a concealed body. She found a simple torn path from his car to the road. He probably wrecked it when John was distracted, she thought. Or knowing Thomas, he may have swerved to miss an animal that had darted into the road. She smiled sadly. For several minutes, she stared in the direction John had taken him.

The mansion beckoned, shrouded in the phosphorescent light of a full moon that rested above the roofline. Majken parked at the edge of the clearing, hid the keys under the seat, and got out quietly. She examined the ancient structure from a distance. She wondered if Thomas were there, and how she would get him out alive. She started uphill, tensing and relaxing, tensing and relaxing.

Majken reached the wooden gate, and sighed painfully on finding the front door smashed open. It lay lopsided against the door frame. She removed her shoes to make a silent entry. The inner hallway appeared deserted.

She padded lightly on her toes; her body relaxed and limber. John had sworn vengeance. She hoped he could be bargained with.

Her pulse quickened as she approached her study and found the door firmly closed. She listened within; the impression returned void.

Majken grimaced and steeled herself in case she should find Thomas' skewered body. She pushed the door with her foot, looking up and down the hallway. Her lips tightened to a line with the slight creak. The door swung open. Her heart beat fully against her chest as she eased into the doorway. She struggled to slow it.

The couch and table were outlined black against black. The iron grate had been ripped away from the fireplace and dumped in a corner. Logs had been pulled out of a neat pile and strewn over the floor. A slight afterglow lingered on the smouldering, charred black wood. A crisp scent of mildew and smoke filled the room. Her night-adapted eyes swept the study a final time. It was empty.

Silently, Majken crossed the hallway and searched the former dining hall.

The floor was warped and rotten and she did not enter. She looked through the crater-sized opening in the ceiling. Rain had rotted the wood until the weight of the candelabra caused the collapse many years before. She turned away, sickened by the slimy mold clinging to the exposed joists.

Experience with John should have given her insight. She chided herself and stubbornly refused to believe that Thomas was dead. Majken searched the remaining downstairs without success. Her trunk was undisturbed. She wondered what she would do in his place. An idea struck her—she would observe from the roof. Majken turned and walked softly up the stairs, gauging each step carefully.

She hesitated at the entrance to her bedroom.

Moonlight illuminated an area five or six feet around a silvery part in the curtains. Majken gasped, appalled, and stumbled forward. Her canopy bed had been ripped to shreds. The grim violation assaulted her deeply, making her angry. She stood next to the bed, squeezing the bedpost. An unnaturally deep sound rumbled from a darkened corner. John stepped into view holding a sharpened wooden stake.

"I thought I would be traditional on how you die." John smiled cruelly.

Majken faced him. "What have you done with Thomas?" she asked coolly.

"My dear, I've killed him." An angry sneer replaced his smile.

Majken closed her eyes for a split second as blackness swirled, her mind screamed and a void opened. She fought to maintain a calm posture and hide the crushing effects from him. He moved to block her escape. Majken trembled uncontrollably.

John rushed her, holding the pointed stake like a knife, ready to penetrate her chest or left side. Majken leaned backward and gathered folds of torn shreds. She covered his face and sidestepped as the weapon grazed her arm, then aimed a double-fisted blow at his rib cage, hoping to drive a floating rib and lacerate internal organs. He reached for her. She sprinted for the doorway.

He caught her in the corridor and shoved her hard into the opposite wall.

Stunned, she pulled on his arm and turned around. He pushed her head; a jarring blow, and she almost faded from consciousness. John held her shoulders and pushed again. Her knees buckled. He pushed— she wrenched free and tripped him with his own momentum. He tumbled on the rotten floor, and the edge of the crater gave away. He landed with a splintering crack.

Majken cradled her head on her trembling knees, trying to fill her lungs and clear her senses. She crawled and stumbled into her bedroom, grabbed the stake meant for her, and ran down the stairs.

He was already gone.

Majken panted and collapsed against the wall to

rest. Her body ached and deep breathing hurt. She felt weak inside, still shaky. She gently pressed her fingers into the knotted muscle at the base of her neck, massaging, kneading until the pain subsided. It would be tempting to lay there. The void threatened to engulf her. She fought, digging her fingers into the floor.

Gradually, she lifted herself. The only thing that remained was to find his body. Her mind singled out the cellar, where she had kept him locked. Majken walked in a daze until she stepped in black, greasy tar on the grass. Fresh coal tar, she grimaced, then became instantly alert. He obviously planned to burn her in the mansion.

She found the cellar sealed tight and used the point of the stake to pry the jammed wood. It yielded. She knelt and brushed her hand over the dry dusty earth. A terrible decaying stench of animal remains reached her. She slammed the cellar shut and spun away. Emptiness, a foreboding desolation, swept over her. She held the wooden stake tightly between her breasts and screamed his name into the wind. "Thomas!"

Only the stiff nightly breeze responded.

Her blood burned hot in her skull. Kill him! She found him waiting at the top of the stairs with a thick curved blade extending from his right hand. She bolted forward, attacking. He disappeared in the hallway. Majken knelt and placed her hand on the dusty hardwood floor, sensing. Her eyes narrowed on the room beyond her bedroom.

She moved forward, listening, feeling. She held the shaft in her right hand, and placed her left over the blunt end, ready to drive it through him. John deserved to die for—the air whistled and she fell to the floor. The machete met air where her head had been and imbedded into the wall.

She stabbed around the corner; the point met resistance.

John held his leg below the knee and limped to the window. He grunted and the ancient ironwork broke free. The tile facings splintered as it fell to the floor. He jumped to the waist-high ledge and climbed out.

Majken tugged on the machete with both hands. A section of the wall pulled loose. She scraped it over the doorframe to clear the debris, then went cautiously to the window. She pressed herself to the wall and looked for his shadow. Her fingers curled on the handle of the large knife. Majken jumped easily to the ledge and swung to the roof.

She balanced on the crumbling tile and climbed. She reached the top and straddled the apex, sweeping the gables and the edge of the roof for anyplace to hide. She extended her search to the surrounding landscape. A shadowy figure ambled across the clearing, to the west, to the cliffs.

Majken picked her way down the incline, through the window and corridors, when he disappeared in the woods. She reached the path where he disappeared and smiled. She would indeed follow, but not in the way he might suspect. The woods were filled with large elm that had been growing unmolested for a century. Majken first cut a strip from her blouse and tied the machete to her waist. Then she ran and caught the tree, pulling herself to the first limb. She climbed higher, limb to limb, tree to tree.

A scene on the edge of the cliff petrified her. Her heart leaped across the space. Thomas was alive! She climbed for a closer look, swaying in the branches. John was brutally, repeatedly pushing him on the sharp stones that lined the clearing. The blood that stained Thomas' arms and legs and face appeared as jagged black streaks in the bright moonlight. John pulled him up and dashed him again.

Majken carefully, gently stepped to a connecting limb, now closer. She gritted her teeth as she pulled herself around a trunk and stepped on the opposing limb. High over the clearing, too high, she began to climb down and hoped he would not look up. She was fully visible in the moonlight. Each scratchy hand-hold released tiny particles, floating downward. John dragged Thomas to his feet and shoved him toward the tree trunk. He stumbled and fell loosely, as a rag doll. John would have his vengeance, Majken thought.

Majken propped on a low-hanging limb and un-loosed the machete. John laughed as he drew his knife for the kill. Majken held her breath as she placed her full weight on the limb—the decayed limb broke! The weapon slipped from her grasp as she fell in the clearing and tangled in a bush.

John picked himself up and scooped the machete, and charged Thomas.

Majken held the branch, kicked free of the bush, and placed herself between John and his intend-ed victim. *Not again*, rang inside her mind as she braced for the first blow.

The blade sliced the cool, crisp air and landed on the dried wood and bounced across her upper arm. It bled. She jumped back to reposition. The blade caught and sliced her abdomen; thick dark blood oozed through her blouse.

Majken fell against Thomas. She felt his heart beating. He was alive. John would kill them both. She drew cold air into her rasping, parched lungs.

The limb was too heavy, too slow. She curled instinctively.

John took his stance, aiming for her torso. Majken kicked his knee savagely. He fell, outstretched, toward the cliff. Majken angled the unwieldy branch as a lever, pushing John to the edge. The machete tumbled over as he held to the limb. Majken shoved harder; John fell off of the bare rock facing.

Majken dropped to her knees, exhausted and straining to breathe.

She crawled to Thomas, very slowly, and gingerly touched the lacerations on his face. He was supported in the tree roots with his face turned away.

"Thomas," she said, scarcely even a whisper.

It was over, she wanted to say. He stirred and looked in her eyes, then lifted his arm toward her shoulder. His weight pulled her.

They listened to the muted rush of the wind as it poured over the exposed rock cliff. Thomas closed and opened his eyes for several minutes, looking at her, then grinned weakly. "Did I say thank you, yet?"

Majken rolled off her injured hip and placed her hand gently on his chest, probing. The most profuse cuts were on his palms and forearms where he had caught himself on the rocks. His right cheek and the tip of his shoulder were scraped.

He shivered heavily from the cold.

"Can you move?" She gently coaxed him to lean forward, and brushed her hair out of her face as she steadied his arm.

Thomas winced as he dabbed gritty palms on his pants. "I think so." He dug his elbows into the tree and pushed.

Majken propped herself against the tree, half-standing, and helped him to his feet. He swayed and held to her. Majken lifted his arm around her neck and supported him through the twisting path to the mansion while staunching the flow of blood from the wide gash in her abdomen.

Several hundred feet below, John clung furiously to a porous outcropping; the muscles of his arms and legs bunched under the enormous strain of climbing the near vertical wall. His right leg dangled in space. He kicked upward to reach a crevice, and held. Powerful fingertips probed for the next wafer-thin ripple in the rock.

The night sky had become completely dark as the moon settled behind cumulus clouds. Many layers of trees blocked the sparse moonlight, and a chilling dampness hung in the air. Small twigs snapped underfoot; young green foliage reached and held to their legs. Majken and Thomas wandered tortuously down the invisible wooded trail until they reached the open field.

Majken stared at the deserted mansion. A cold heavy lump knotted between her breasts.

It was empty, desolate.

A perpetual breeze sprayed her hair in her eyes. She moved when Thomas moved, instinctively seeking shelter. She held her arm around Thomas' rib cage; his warmth helped her. Once, he stumbled, tearing her injuries further.

She walked with him to the front entrance, then guided him to the couch in the study. She trimmed the remaining lamp for him. Her dark violet eyes softened and turned warm in the golden light. She collapsed beside him. Her strength was depleted.

Thomas gathered the dingy cloth as a blanket, pulling it over her. She felt him pull away; he was staring at her. Now, in the light, the crimson stains soaking her blouse and her bloodstained arm pressed to her waist was visible.

He touched her hand on the couch, words tumbled slowly out of his mouth. "How can I help you?"

Majken shook her head and gently tugged his hand in response. She lay quietly, and looked curiously at Thomas. Feelings, pent up and restless, tortured her soul. Images. She had fallen through this void once before. She sighed and breathed more naturally. She relaxed gradually. Her body would recover, given time.

"How did you manage to find us?" Thomas asked.

Majken paused a moment. "I saw him take you. It was a chance he might bring you here and keep you alive until he dealt with me."

"I'm sorry I let him get me. He jumped me between campus security and your dorm." He seemed extremely dejected. Majken smiled and tapped his arm.

"I drove Albritton's car here," she said proudly. Thomas acted startled, then grinned.

She needed rest, more rest. Majken ran her fingers lightly over the cuts on her arm. The purplish clots appeared as large sutures binding her pale torn flesh together. Pink scar tissue had already begun to form. Majken gently, gently probed the soft tissue of her abdomen. The burning sensations lessened.

She felt a need to cry, but was unable to. In a small voice, she asked Thomas, "Do you still hate me?"

He hesitated thoughtfully, appearing to weigh his response. She watched his eyes, the way that he looked at her, his face. "I don't know." Thomas shivered and yawned, his eyelids drooped sleepily.

Majken prodded him in the ribs. "Don't sleep until we get you to the hospital."

He protested. "What about—"

Majken cut him off mid-sentence, shoved him quickly to the floor, and rose to her feet. The other vampyr stormed into the room and came at her, his eyes blazing with fury. She stepped forward, but John hit her solidly in the waist, making a splattering mushy sound.

She fell clutching her waist. The floor was soaked with her blood.

Thomas raised up in time to see John reaching for her neck and begin choking her. He crawled to his knees and threw the closest item, the lamp. John swung and diverted the projectile. It spewed oil on the floor and shattered against the far wall, then exploded in flames.

Majken's hand loosened from John's and fell limply at her side. The other vampyr pressed downward. She made a choking gasp.

Thomas felt the twisted iron poker; he grabbed it and charged. The flame spread on the oil and ignited the sleeve of John's coat. He heaved, pressing, choking as the fire spread to his back. Thomas struck him; he fended off the blow with his burning arm.

Thomas hit his back, then aimed for his chest.

John rolled off Majken, swatting at the fire. The room was filled with dense, grimy smoke.

Thomas groped for Majken's body and turned to see John fully ablaze in the doorway.

A horrid shriek was wrenched from John's tortured face. He ran out of the mansion, burning and waving frantically, disappearing through the rear of the dry building. Tongues of flame spread; the smoke grew more dense.

Thomas covered his nose and mouth with his hand to mask the smell of burning, charred flesh. He scrambled to his knees, reaching. His hand bumped her leg. He crawled to her side and coughed out her name. His eyes burned and he coughed again as he pulled her to a sitting position.

Majken heaved and a wad of viscous blood cleared her throat. She held her bruised throat in her hand. She looked dazed, weak and started to collapse again when Thomas jerked on her arm.

He crawled with her in the direction he believed was the doorway, dragging her over the floor. His eyes were burned shut by the heat and smoke; he waved his arm in front of him and bumped the doorway. He felt Majken cough, and take a rasping breath. He curled his raw injured fingers around the opening and pulled himself toward the hallway.

Thomas struggled with her deadweight. He shouted for her to move; the sound came out as a choking
whisper. He groped along the wall pulling on her
arm. She stumbled with him. They gathered speed.

Thomas tumbled with her through a cloud of billowing, dense black smoke with a blast of heat at his
back. She rolled over him. He fell at a crazy angle
on the coarse grass stubble. He shuddered and drew
fresh, pure air, cleansing out the smoke he inhaled.
Majken recovered next to him.

Heat from the fire began to sear their legs.

The mansion crackled, wood splitting and collaps-
ing, in flames.

They crawled, stumbled, fell to safety. Thomas
pulled open the driver's side and shoved Majken to
the passenger side. She curled in the seat and floorboard, and daintily lifted the keys. Thomas fumbled
with them, started the car, and lurched forward.

Majken cried weakly. He carefully turned around,
crossing ruts and hills, until he reached the trail to
the road. He glanced back briefly. The ancient mansion was fully engulfed with smoke rising from the
upstairs windows and the sound of splintering, burning wood echoed in the distance. He eased over the
final rut slowly and pulled onto the deserted road.

He sped for the city and the hospital.

Gradually, Majken raised in her seat. Thomas raced; houses whizzed by in the opposite direction. She cautioned him to slow down to avoid attracting the police. He noticed her feeling for a handle and there was none. Thomas opened her window for her electronically with the touch of a finger. She grimaced in disgust, but leaned her head into the fresh, streaming cold air.

Thomas hurried for the only hospital he could think of—Mercer Hospital. Several blocks away, Majken asked him to slow down. One block away, she ordered him to stop. He reluctantly pulled over in the center of the block next to a wrought iron fence.

Majken leaned her head back and drew a deep breath. "I can't come with you, Thomas. You'll have to walk to the emergency room from here." She pointed feebly across the street. "Alone."

"You're hurt!" he stammered. "Where do you think you're going?"

She reached for the steering wheel and pulled herself to the driver's side. Thomas opened his door and slid out to keep her from sitting in his lap. She closed the door. He leaned through the open window, and kissed her. The sky was becoming brighter; a faint pinkish layer spread to the east.

"I have to leave," she said, "before the sun catches me unprotected."

Her wistful gaze traveled from his concerned face to the thick bloodstains on his arms and hands. She froze instantly and trembled. "Hurry inside. You may be all right."

He leaned on the car. "What's wrong?" he asked.

Her eyes seemed lost for a moment. Majken reached for his hand. "Go, and don't concern yourself with me. I have a cache nearby. I'll come to see you in a few days." She withdrew and put the car into gear. It crept forward.

Thomas stumbled over the curb and sidewalk, blood staining the grass as he stepped to the dark brick wall. He leaned against the hospital and watched her drive a short distance, then abruptly stop and lean forward, probably in pain. He whispered her name and started walking with his hands along the wall.

She pulled herself up, alone, and drove out of sight around the corner.

Thomas stumbled to the emergency room.

Epilogue

Thomas stroked the smooth polished surface of his hospital room window as he looked outward at the night sky and the many sparkling city lights below. He sat immobile and listened, briefly, to a pair of wearily fading footsteps in the hallway. His doctors were very skeptical of his story about falling out of his car on the highway.

Two nights had passed, and he knew Majken had left the city. It must not end this way. *It must not!* Thomas thought.

He had to find her.

In a thick misty woods, John lay immersed to his face in a swirling stream, cooling his fire-scarred body. His fist clenched tightly as he remembered finding their footprints in the soft earth; she lived! He gazed upward at the protective blanket of leaves, and beyond, to velvety blackness, and prepared.

John swore he would find Majken someday.